One Belief Away

One Belief Away

CN Winters

Baycrest Books
One-In-Ten Imprint
Monroe, Michigan

Copyright 2003 by Baycrest Books.
Copyright registration number: TXu-1-048-934
ISBN: 0-9728450-0-3
Library of Congress Control Number: 2003104384
All rights reserved. No part of this publication may be reproduced or transmitted in any form or by any means, included but not limited to electronic or mechanical without permission in writing from Baycrest Books, the owner. Any similarities to persons living or deceased are purely coincidental.

Cover art by Shannon Lynch.
Public Domain photo for cover art attained from the U.S. National Archives.

Visit us on the world wide web at http://www.baycrestbooks.com

Dedication

This work is dedicated to my late maternal grandmother who taught me to view people based on their interiors not their exteriors. She was, and continues to be, the best 'bard' I ever heard. A special dedication also goes out to Shelly, my best friend of over 25 years – the anchor that keeps me grounded when I need it and the ladder that helps me reach my dreams.

Acknowledgements

Thanks to Kate Orlando and Susan Carr for their tired eyes from repeated edits. To Norma, Tina, Laura, Heather, Kate and Mary - for all the feedback on my work over the years. And to Nann Dunne for offering her "two-cents" which was worth far, far more.

To Bridget Petrella for giving 110% when I needed it most. To a sea of on-line friends and their support of my writing over the years and especially to the late Tonya Muir who unselfishly offered advice even though the world was on her shoulders at the time.

A special thanks goes out to my parents for the love, guidance and courage they continue to give me. And last, but not least, thanks to my supportive husband and daughter for believing in my abilities, making my days brighter and for making me smile when I need it most.

Chapter 1

Carol Johnson stood tall in formation. With her gun on her right hip and her nightstick on her left, she felt nearly invincible. This impression of strength, however, did nothing to dissipate the insufferable heat. Although it was late September, it felt more like July at the Upstate New York college campus. Her upper lip grew heavy with perspiration.

She'd heard all the stories and seen all the newsreels of the last few years - Detroit, Watts, Chicago, Kent State and Vietnam. The country was still at war - abroad and at home. And for what? None of it made sense. It was 1972 and nothing had changed since the summer of love in '67, her high school graduation year. If anything, it felt like conditions had gotten worse. The war in Asia seemed to escalate to no end. The political and musical icons of the era were dying off. And the highest government office in the greatest country of the free world was under suspicion. No. Things were not getting better. Some days it felt as if Armageddon had finally arrived.

Carol enlisted with the police force to pay the bills. Simply put, being single without a man in her life, she'd needed work to make ends meet. The first job she took after graduation was as a secretary for the courthouse. It was far too tedious for her. She craved activity and since the only real movement involved was typing and making coffee for the magistrate, Carol realized she wanted more out of life.

At first, being a cop was just a job, too - something to earn an income and it had seemed as good as any, appealing to her stoic demeanor and solitary preferences. She had the strength and the stamina to walk a beat so the decision hadn't been a terribly difficult one. Besides, it had been the family business. Her father, who was a cop, had been proud of her decision, although reluctantly at first. He knew what the job entailed but he also knew of his daughter's abilities so Carol attacked it with a certain amount of relish.

The longer she was on the force, the more pride she felt. It went from a job to a career - from just a paycheck to a reason to get up in the morning. Each day was a challenge she could face and win, each battle deserving of her attention and finesse. She was a guardian of order in an age of upheaval.

Carol, always the peacemaker, hated to see the senseless eruption of violence. She wanted to find the middle ground for everyone involved. That's not to say she didn't understand the need for retaliation or a heavy hand. She'd been trained to use the strong-arm method when there was a time and a place for it. So it seemed only a natural conclusion that the tall woman would be standing here this day with sweat trickling between her shoulder blades, plastering jet-black bangs to her forehead.

After five years on the force, she wore her badge and her nametag proudly as she stood in formation overseeing a 'peaceful' demonstration that looked about to get ugly, perhaps even deadly. Carol had learned long ago how to inspect her surroundings without appearing to be watching. Cool blue eyes slid stealthily across the crowd of people in the field beyond. They were a rag tag bunch dressed in long, flowing dresses or bell-bottomed pants. Their long hair was free and blowing in the minimal breeze of the morning. Chanting and marching, the group advanced toward the administration building's steps where she stood.

The sun beat down uncharacteristically hot for the late fall but in a way, the officer was grateful. That meant the demonstrators were hot and sweaty, too, and that was just fine by her as misery does truly love company. Though their training classes suggested otherwise. In an uncomfortable situation, be it heat, rain or snow, things were more likely to get out of hand since tempers were high. An angry protest could become an angry mob at any moment and if that happened, she had to be prepared.

"Goddamn Hippies."

One Belief Away

The voice of her partner, Randell, hissed in her ear, breaking into her wandering thoughts. It took the tall woman a full second to reel back in her traveling mind. He continued to speak as she took the time to survey her surroundings using her peripheral vision while watching the group advance.

"They should just let us open fire. Might increase the intelligence of the American gene pool," he smirked, keeping his eyes forward. Even without turning to him she could easily envision his narrow pinched face. His deep brown eyes would be glaring at the people around him, the distaste for this bunch evident in every feature. She'd seen that look from him before on several occasions and still despised it. Besides, she wasn't much older than the students out in the field.

He had told her once that she wasn't "one of those potheads" but she didn't quite feel like one of the boys, either. In many ways, Carol felt trapped between two worlds. She understood the protestors' points. She believed in their right to demonstrate. After all, that's what the country was founded upon – the right to speak freely without persecution. However, she also believed in authority – the right to be orderly without violating someone else's rights in the process of exercising your own.

Carol grinned at her partner without really doing more than slightly tilting her head. It was as a show of faith; brotherhood. It was not an agreement with his ideals. Unfortunately, her companions on the force always seemed to be itching to turn a rally violent, to control these kids and their beliefs and ideals with sheer force. Many of them had children who were doing the same things and protesting their parent's work, the job that put food on the table. Carol couldn't imagine going home to that kind of criticism or being raised in a home where your voice wasn't heard. Sometimes being single and alone had its advantages.

Her partner didn't speak again, his wit already dried up for the day . . . perhaps the week. As the demonstrators came closer and closer, her comrades began to look around sizing up what was about to happen, checking their location. Perhaps they were checking out the man next to them, wondering if he would turn tail or stay for the battle that lay ahead. Even Carol found herself searching left and right, looking for anything that might be a hazard if a fight broke out. How many steps did the entrance have? How many rows of officers were behind her? Did everyone have his or her nightstick out? Silently and as quickly as possible her mind computed everything she might need in a matter of seconds.

"Eyes front!" the commander ordered his squad in a loud gravelly voice, his own nerves strung taut. Like his force, he'd heard all the stories, read the news articles, saw the newscasts. And he'd be damned if he was going to be caught up in one of those disasters. His paranoia forced him to rule with an iron fist and his troops responded to his snapped words. The police had enough bad press as it was; his team sure as hell wasn't going to add to it.

Carol complied readily, knowing she'd been wrong to break anyway. She even mildly cursed herself for her stupidity; she was better trained than to be sidetracked by a group of shouting people.

The dean stood on the steps alongside the officers with a bullhorn. "This building is closed!" he shouted. "You are ordered to leave these grounds immediately or face prosecution for trespassing."

Seconds passed, though it felt almost like a lifetime with the minimal breeze and the glaring sun. The group advanced, not heeding the warning. When they were within 20 feet, the group stopped their organized chant and gave a powerful yell.

They ran up toward the steps, hoping to get inside to form a sit-down strike Carol assumed. Leading the pack and heading straight toward her was a young blonde. Determined didn't even begin to describe the look she wore. Reflexively, Carol's hand tightened on her nightstick. Her legs subconsciously parted a bit more as she waited for impact.

The woman was petite, only reaching Carol's collarbone but well built. She had the gusto of a New York Jets linebacker although she lacked the physical size. Carol learned early on that looks could be deceiving. A determined perp, no matter how small, can fight with the strength of 10 men if he or she really wanted to. And female or not, this protester in front of her could pose just as much of a threat as anyone.

A loud shot rang out shattering the air around them and before Carol's mind comprehended what was happening, she advanced to meet the mob. For a split second she wondered if it was just herself who had moved. But looking around her, she noticed the formation had charged and the protesters scattered.

Colorful anti-war signs became weapons for some of the protesters. Others chose fists. With the police force in full riot gear it did little to harm them but a few protesters were old pros. They went for the legs, the only part not protected by the body armor. Before the blonde could get any ideas of doing the same, Carol instinctively grabbed the golden haired girl in front of her, wrapped talon like fingers around slender upper arms before turning her and forcing her to the ground.

Carol watched as feet and legs raced around them. To avoid getting trampled in the chaos, she rose up and placed a knee on the girl's lower back, pulling her arms behind her. Carol was easily able to subdue the young woman by holding the thin wrists together in one large hand leaving her free to reach for her cuffs with the other. She quickly patted her down to be sure she was clean. Her ice blue eyes caught the sight of a fallen sign that read "Make Love not War". With the battle going on around them Carol couldn't help but notice the irony of it all.

"You okay?" Randell called as he watched the tall woman begin handcuffing her perp.

Carol gave a quick nod, feeling in control with the subdued young woman. "Help the others!" she instructed, giving the man beside her permission to leave her without backup.

With a return nod that went undetected by Carol, he charged into battle, nightstick at the ready. Randell wasn't a fighting man like some on the force. He just wanted to put in his 25 years and go home. He was well on his way, but with the streets getting more and more explosive, Carol could feel his reluctance at times. But this was not one of them. He charged headlong into the melee. The sooner the crowd was controlled the safer it would be for everyone – himself included. Randell didn't look for a fight but he wasn't a coward who would run from one either. As annoying as she may have found some of his views, the man was a consummate professional and she appreciated having that on her side.

Continuing, Carol finished cuffing the young woman and read her the Miranda rights in a sure, strong voice. The procedure she had been taught recently was becoming more and more familiar although it felt like more bureaucratic red tape. She said the words so often now that they slipped easily from her lips as she snapped the metal rings into place.

"Why am I being arrested?" the young woman asked, growing irritated but moving minimally.

She apparently wasn't dumb enough to resist arrest and risk personal injury and that made Carol wonder how many times the girl had been through this already. She acted like a true 'professional'. The blonde tried to look over her shoulder at the woman on her back but her own hair fell in her face, impeding her view. In truth, she hadn't really looked at her before. In fact, she didn't care. Carol was just another cop.

"Trespassing for starters. You and your friends were asked politely to leave," Carol said after pulling the girl to her feet, surprising both of them with her ability to literally pick the slight form off the ground and plant her back on unsteady legs. Lighter than she looks, Carol mused. It's hard to tell under that flowing shirt.

The girl didn't fight Carol but she was no great help, either. They moved slowly toward the cruiser with her shuffling her sandaled feet, looking around at the foray the demonstration had become. Carol let it go, knowing they'd get to the car soon enough anyway and not eager to force a confrontation with the smaller woman. The officer saw her commander out of the corner of her eye and moved toward him, changing their direction slightly.

He was flustered and yelling, face red with stress and rage, eyes searching the melee before him to ensure nothing was getting out of hand.

"Permission to take the perpetrator to the station, sir?" Carol asked formally, stopping in front of him and dragging the girl forward for him to see.

"Permission granted, Johnson. Nice job," he grinned at her quickly before scowling at the young woman. He looked her up and down briskly, trying to intimidate her with narrowed eyes and a stern face but realized he was being unsuccessful. Her ho-hum attitude toward his attempt only enraged him more. He waved the two of them off and went back to surveying the scene beyond.

Carol opened the door and the young woman clambered inside without resisting, settling into the back seat as if it were familiar. She bounced slightly on the padded bench and even managed a grin of enjoyment, completely unconcerned with her situation. Carol climbed into the driver's seat and shook her head in amusement, somewhat intrigued by the young woman's upbeat attitude. The officer had barely made it down the block when the girl's soft voice drifted through the mesh partition dividing the front and back seats.

"How old are you?"

One Belief Away

Carol looked into the rearview mirror and raised a slim dark eyebrow, unsure of the question.

"What?" she responded, not certain of the girl's motives. It wasn't the typical chitchat between an arresting officer and perp.

"I asked how old you are? I'd say about 23. It seems odd someone as young as yourself would already sell out to the establishment." The young woman spoke easily, meeting blue eyes with mist green in the rearview mirror before turning her head again to watch the passing scenery.

"I don't care what you think," Carol replied coldly, her icy blue eyes in the rearview mirror emphasizing her point.

"No one in the establishment does," the girl sighed, her voice sounding oddly defeated and conflicting starkly with her previously brash demeanor. "So why should you?"

As Carol came to a red light she turned to face the girl. "You know . . . you do have the right to remain silent."

The young woman chuckled heartily, re-establishing her prior confidence. "I'm waiving that right," she smiled wickedly, green eyes dancing. "So tell me . . . what does it take for a lady to become a cop? Were you raised Republican? Did you see too many episodes of the Mod Squad . . . What gives?"

"Are you looking to join the force?" Carol replied sarcastically, continuing their journey. "Cuz I can get you some brochures that you might find helpful."

"No," the girl grinned slyly, enjoying the teasing banter. "I'm looking to change the world. What do you do in your spare time?"

Silence fell in the car for the duration of the trip as the officer elected to not answer that question, knowing it was rhetorical anyway. The words of Carol's partner came back to her as she looked in the rearview mirror at the woman in the earth toned granny shirt and long tangled locks. "Goddamn hippies." But she still couldn't think it in the same hostile manner he'd spoken it.

Chapter 2

Carol brought the young woman to fingerprinting and when the desk sergeant asked for her name the girl refused.

"Names are irrelevant. My friends call me Skylon and that's all that matters."

Carol and the sergeant exchanged a look of frustration. Carol pressed the issue.

"What's your real name? Ya know, the one your parents gave you?"

"Barbara," the girl replied as the sergeant began to write it down. "Barbara Eden," the girl grinned wickedly.

Carol stepped closer, towering over the girl, hoping perhaps to intimidate her. "I'm gonna ask one more time or I'm taking you to lock up . . . And I want the truth . . . what's your name?"

Though hardly intimidated by the tall woman before her, the young woman had to admit to herself there was a certain fire in the officer that made her skin tingle. Unlike a few of her other friends, she had never been intimate with a woman. She'd never found a woman who attracted her sexually, but the longer she looked into those blazing eyes the more she wanted to see. She liked to play with fire. After all, it was her undeniable need to buck the status quo that had gotten her here to start with. What could be more defiant than being interested in the 'enemy'?

"Okay! Okay!" she said, looking away and playing with her bead necklace. "My name is Jane . . . Jane Fonda," she giggled.

"That's it!" Carol howled in frustration. She pulled her away from the desk and tugged her toward the holding cell. "I'm sure you've got priors so make yourself at home. You'll be here for awhile." She turned the woman roughly and unlocked the cuffs.

"What about my phone call?" she taunted. "I'd hate to see you charged with violating my human rights."

"I'll tell you what," Carol began with a sinister grin. "As soon as I have a phone line free, it's all yours. Until then, you'll have to wait."

"Just how long?" she asked with an equally powerful expression. "I'm a busy woman."

"Oh, I'm sure you are," Carol answered sarcastically. "But this could take hours. Maybe even days."

"You can't keep me here for days. I know my rights." She was quickly growing angry with this little game that had been amusing only moments before.

Carol sensed it, her smirk turning into a full-fledged smile. "Don't blame me," the officer shrugged. "You wanted to play around . . . besides, I'm sure one of your long-haired boyfriends will be here to bail you out soon."

The woman reared back and spat. Carol leaned away before impact and grabbed the young woman by the front of her shirt, balling up the material in her fist.

"You better learn some manners quick. Or I'll teach 'em. And we both know there's not a single soul in this stationhouse who'll say a word about the lesson."

For the first time since the meeting, the young woman looked scared. She knew it was true, too. No one in that precinct would come forward to say that this officer had beaten the hell out of her. The woman's fear left her tongue limp. She simply waited for Carol's next move. She had to admit she felt relieved when Carol pushed her inside the cell and closed the cage, creating a barrier between them. Wordlessly, Carol walked away and the woman watched the officer's cocky strides.

"Goddamn Pig," she muttered under her breath, throwing herself onto a wooden bench.

"Her name is O'Fallon. Erin O'Fallon," the records officer told Carol.

Carol smirked. "Oh really?" she asked.

"Oh yes!" he replied just as conspiratorially. "Would you like her rap sheet?"

Carol snatched it from his hand with a wink and began to make her way to the cage, reading as she walked.

"Erin O'Fallon," Carol smiled in victory as she approached. "Let's see . . . priors include marijuana possession and flag burning. It appears we have a phone line free. Would you like to make that call now?" Carol finished, fluttering her eyelids triumphantly.

"You should have that tic looked into," Erin replied defiantly, pointing at Carol's eyes. "It could be something serious."

"Come on, funny girl," Carol said, opening the cell. Once Erin was free and the cell locked, Carol took her over to a phone and waved casually at it. "Call daddy or whoever it is that usually bails you out."

"Humph."

Carol gave her some privacy and wandered across the small room to the coffeepot but she kept an eye on the girl. She didn't think the woman was a violent threat but having her slip away wouldn't look too good. Carol had a hard enough time proving herself. She didn't need some waif of a perp making her life more difficult.

As Carol watched the young woman, it was obvious to her the blonde was bright. How she got hooked up with these other losers at the demonstration was beyond Carol. She tried to imagine a home life or a strict upbringing that would lead to this. The girl had so much promise - she was passionate and quick-witted with a gentle demeanor and definite self-confidence. And there was something else about her . . . some kind of spark. Carol noticed it from the first moment but witnessed it again when they'd first entered the squad room.

It seemed like every head turned when she entered a room. The girl wasn't drop-dead gorgeous. But she was far from homely either. She was . . . what was the word . . . cute . . . attractive. She was charismatic. Carol knew the attention this 'Erin', 'Skylon', whoever - garnered was a result of the aura the girl projected outward. She was a woman of natural leadership and perhaps someday, she would be a force to be reckoned with because of her attributes.

Erin's slender fingers worked the rotary, dialing the number of someone who would come for her. The officer couldn't help but wonder who that someone might be. Probably some longhaired, guitar carrying, Jim Morrison-wannabe. A pang of jealousy rushed over Carol at the thought as well as a greater sense of confusion. She wasn't attracted to this young woman, was she? She knew that love was given very freely between many people of her generation - regardless of gender at times - but certainly not this girl . . . or was she? *No,* she decided. *She's not. So stop thinking about it. Besides, a radical like that would never hook up with a cop. After all, she did try to spit on you. That's a beautiful start to a storybook romance.* But if the girl *was* willing then perhaps . . .

Erin hung up, turned pale green eyes to the officer and, thankfully, stopped Carol's train of thought. Erin tilted her head slightly at what may have been a blush crawling up the olive skinned features before Carol returned to her side.

"All set?"

"Yes," Erin replied shortly.

Carol wasn't sure, but she felt a bit saddened by the fact Erin would be leaving. So she did the only thing she could think of standing here at the station outside of holding. "Would you like some coffee?" the officer asked.

"Is this some sort of peace offering - cop style? Or are you going to poison me?"

Carol found herself smiling. "No. Unlike you, I have manners. I got a cup for myself and thought you'd like one. But whether you want it or not, it's up to you."

Erin didn't know what to make of the cop before her. One moment she was threatening her with bodily harm and the next she was offering her a drink. *Well, you did have it coming* Erin told herself. She also had to admit this woman was beginning to have an effect on her. She pushed back the admiration to keep what dignity she had left. She didn't need any of her friends walking in to find her 'socializing' with the establishment.

But being one to buck the system, even the system within her own sect, Erin found the idea exciting. What would her friends say if she confessed her attraction to the raven-haired woman? Or even a friendship for that matter. It seemed to her that Carol was trying to be civil. She still hadn't answered Carol's question and soon found herself facing a cup of coffee with no idea of how it got there.

"Cream and sugar?" Carol asked, sliding the cup closer and pulling a chair noisily over so she could also sit at the small phone table.

"No thanks," Erin said, returning her attention to the uniformed woman across from her. "No donuts?" she asked sarcastically.

"That's a myth you know. Not all cops eat donuts."

Carol's warm grin stripped Erin of any acidic comeback. An uncomfortable silence washed over the small space between them. Erin sipped her coffee slowly, not taking her eyes off Carol. Those blue eyes watched her and seemed to burn her skin just like the drink scalded her tongue. There was too much power in that sapphire gaze. Her self-confidence faltered but she wasn't about to let it show or look away. But it did show if only for a second.

Carol sensed the uneasiness that claimed the young woman. She watched Erin fidget nervously with the cup although her gaze remained intact. This wasn't the same brash girl she dragged across campus and put into a squad car. This wasn't the young woman who'd teased the sergeant and made in-processing difficult. This girl seemed older, calmer and quieter yet also . . . awkward? It was hard to pinpoint the change in demeanor. But Carol knew she had definitely thrown Erin off kilter with her offer of coffee.

Carol wasn't sure what had brought this facet of Erin to the surface but she found it almost endearing. Almost. But Carol was never one to hold a grudge for long. She understood her place and she knew Erin's as well. They were on different teams. But in Carol's mind that was no reason for her to not be civil with the woman. She realized she needed to say something - anything - to break the growing, agonizing silence. However, Erin beat her to it.

"Why are you staring at me?"

"I could ask you the same question."

"Yeah, but like I said earlier, I doubt you care. Just another mindless uniform sent out for soulless missions."

Carol chuckled and shook her head. *You gave it a shot Johnson.* "Look, I can put you back in the pen if you'd like or you can sit here and enjoy a cup of coffee. Again, it's your choice."

Erin's cocky demeanor returned in full swing. "You really get off on the authority gig, don't you? Pushing people around, telling them what to do, it's probably in your blood. Bet your daddy was a cop too, huh?"

Carol leaned over the desk, coming within inches of Erin's face. "And lemme guess - you grew up in some nice suburb some place where you had it all. Your daddy worked in the *establishment* to make sure his little girl had the best of everything. And what do you do to repay him? You wreak havoc on society. You detest him for making the choices that got you where you are today."

"Is that so?"

"Yeah and instead of being grateful for the things you've been given you . . . *spit* . . . on it. You detest mainstream America but mainstream America is what keeps a roof over your head, isn't it? They pay your tuition. They pay for your food, your clothes - bet you even have a nice sports car tucked away for graduation."

"Oh yeah. I can smell it. Second generation bacon."

"I can smell it, too. Old money. Spoiled rich kid who kills her time trying to save the world when all she really cares about is looking good in front of her toked up friends."

"You don't have a clue about my life."

"Well enlighten me then."

"You wouldn't understand."

"You're right about that - I don't understand. You could have been killed today. Do you realize your ideals make you not only a hypocrite but incredibly dumb?"

"Look pig - you think you know me but you don't. For the record, Daddy doesn't pay my way. Long, personal story that I don't need to share."

Carol smirked. "Looks like I hit a nerve."

"You're lucky I don't hit you."

"Hippy with an attitude. I thought you were into love and peace and burning flags while burning incense?"

"Love and peace mean little when you get pushed around enough. The time comes when you gotta push back."

"I'm not pushing. I'm just asking . . . "

"Asking what?" Erin cut her short, waiting for the smart comment she was sure would follow Carol's question. Carol's eyes held a sincerity that surprised her.

"Why do you do it? Why put yourself at risk?"

Erin smiled grimly. "Lots of Americans die on a daily basis - here and abroad. If I have to give my life for a greater purpose, then so be it."

"A greater purpose?" Carol asked, raising a dark eyebrow to dance with her disheveled bangs. It sounded a little too grandiose to her. "What do you mean?"

Erin didn't have a chance to respond though she appeared ready to launch into a well-rehearsed spiel. The desk sergeant walked over with a woman, interrupting them.

"Minos!" Carol's slight companion exclaimed, rising to meet the stranger. She sounded thrilled to see this other woman and that tone in her voice caused Carol's stomach to clench for some unknown reason.

The desk sergeant turned to Carol. "I just spoke with the Captain. The campus is dropping the charges against Miss O'Fallon and several others."

"What do you mean?" Carol asked.

"Means my friend is free and clear to go, right sergeant?" Minos interrupted.

Carol paused to get a good look at Erin's friend and apparent savior. Minos was a tall woman, almost as tall as Carol and approximate in age, give or take a couple years. She had flowing brown hair kept in a long braid behind her back. Her dress was similar to Erin's in style but paisley in pattern. She returned the officer's searching gaze with light hazel eyes, which revealed no emotion.

"That's right," the sergeant agreed with disappointment though Carol barely heard him. She was growing increasingly less concerned with the outcome of this case. Soon Erin would make her departure with this woman.

The officer finally remembered to question the captain's decision. "What about-"

Carol didn't finish as the sergeant interrupted. "The shot you heard was some kid with a cherry bomb. He thought it would be fun to see what would happen if he set it off. He's damn lucky he didn't get anyone killed."

"And as usual the police overreacted," the stranger chimed in.

The desk sergeant ignored the comment and continued. "The department has decided to press charges against only those who assaulted officers. And since Miss O'Fallon didn't assault you . . . Captain said she's free to go."

"Well, Officer Johnson," Erin turned to the tall woman, wanting to tease her and boast but finding herself unable to when she met those sapphire eyes. She found herself not really wanting to leave with Minos and briefly considered her options. *I could assault her now and I'd get thrown in the slammer.* "Looks like I've gotten my walking papers . . . It's been real. It's been fun. But not real fun," she grinned weakly, hoping Minos would accept that as boastful since it was the best she could muster. "Minos?" she added to her friend, motioning to the door.

Apparently it was good enough because Minos took Erin by the arm and the two walked away before Carol could reply. *She left,* Carol thought. *Just like that. She left.*

"Are you okay?" the sergeant asked. "You don't look so good."

Carol had collapsed in the chair next to her. She tried to shake off her feelings of abandonment, startled by the clarity of her emotions. "Yes, I'm fine."

"Are you sure?"

"Yeah. I'm just . . . disappointed." *No kidding.*

The desk sergeant grinned. "Well, don't worry too much about it, kid. There will be bigger perps to catch, believe me," he said, laying a large hand on her shoulder in a show of support. Then he turned and walked away, leaving Carol alone with her thoughts and two partial cups of coffee.

Chapter 3

Halloween was just a few days away. Minos and Erin entered the coffee shop, chuckling as they slipped past the heavy metal and glass door, which featured a paper pumpkin decoration. The two young women were wrapped up in their conversation, discussing the entertaining plight of another comrade during the demonstration a few weeks back. Minos, or as Erin called her when she was upset with the woman, stressing the hippie name of Meee-Nooos, studied the chalkboard outlining the available selection.

Listening absently to Minos' voice, Erin's attention wandered through the coffee shop until something caught her eye. Her stomach flipped and she felt her face warm in a blush but she pushed it aside and shrugged into her bravado like a well-worn coat.

"Look at what we have here," Erin announced. "A cop in a doughnut shop . . . and here I thought it was just a tired cliché."

Carol chuckled as she let her gaze wander up and down the small figure several yards away. It was a good shot. She had to admit that.

"I'm here for the coffee," she told the blonde. She'd been standing at the far end of the counter, watching the server fill a box with pastries. She'd seen Erin just a split second before the young woman had noticed her.

"Oh yeah?" Erin nodded. "Then what's in the bag?"

One Belief Away

Carol looked sheepishly at the sack in her hand and gave a little lopsided grin. "Donuts," she admitted.

Erin started to chuckle. "I knew it!"

"They're for my partner," Carol added quickly. She wanted to be firm. She wanted to be tough. But for some reason she could feel a stupid smile on her face from being in the student's presence again.

"Oh, sure. Sure, they are." Erin nodded in agreement but her smirk and her casual stance playfully mocked the officer. "I believe you but the masses wouldn't, you know?"

Carol shook her head with a grin, welcoming this self-assured version of Erin. She'd still like to explore the other side of her some time, she realized with surprise.

"So what brings you out this early?" the officer asked. She discovered she wanted to continue this conversation regardless of topic. "I figured you'd still be worn out from all the orgies going on at that big commune of yours."

It was Erin's turn to chuckle. "Not a bad comeback," she complimented with a nod, raising a honey colored eyebrow. "But you realize that's not what goes on at the house . . . well, at least not on Thursdays, anyway. Orgy night is Saturday." She maintained a straight face for several long beats before cracking the tiniest of grins. Her green eyes sparkled with merriment and made her all the more attractive to Carol's approving gaze.

"Is that so?" the beat cop asked, taking a sip of her coffee, sparing a minor glance at the young blonde's companion before returning to evaluate Erin's wardrobe choice. Today's outfit was much like the one she'd worn during their previous meeting except there were new ribbons braided into sections of her long blonde hair.

"Yeah," Erin smiled. Her next words escaped before she had a chance to pull them back. "Why don't you come visit some time? See what my world is all about?"

She could almost swear she heard crickets chirping as all three women stood silently. She felt Minos' stunned stare aimed in her direction and knew she was going to have to answer some pretty pointed questions. Though she'd surprised herself with the offer, Erin didn't regret it.

Carol was taken aback by the request. The radical wanted her to hang out? She even wondered, for a split second, if the smaller woman had actually asked the question or if her own mind had simply projected what she wanted to hear. The blonde's expectant gaze implied the former. Minos' hazel eyes were luckily unarmed though they certainly appeared dangerous.

"Why?" Carol asked, finally having decided the offer was sincere and not a figment of her imagination.

Erin smiled and felt her earlier discomfort wash away in the blue of Carol's eyes. She pulled out a pen and scribbled on a napkin.

"Here's my address," she said handing it to Carol. "You asked about the greater good and I really didn't get a chance to finish our conversation . . . Consider this your chance to be enlightened."

Both women were interrupted by a stern voice behind them. Minos had apparently grown tired of looking dumbstruck and tossing evil glares between the two women.

"We've got to get going, Skylon, or we're going to be late."

Erin replied without turning to face her, keeping her eyes on Carol. "Go on. I'll be there in a minute," she urged her friend gently. Minos didn't move so Erin turned imploring eyes in her direction. *C'mon, Minos, play along*, she pled silently. *Give me this and I'll tell you everything.*

Reluctantly, Minos nodded and stepped away from the two women, coffee cups in her hands. "I'll be outside. If she arrests you, scream real loud."

Carol had watched the exchange with mild interest but now was easily sucked back into those jade eyes that were fixed on her name badge. "So what do you say, Officer Johnson? By the way, do you have a first name or should I just call you Officer Johnson?"

Erin was playing with her at this point. Or was it flirting? Or was she simply issuing a challenge because she really thought Carol didn't have the courage to meet her on her turf? If so, she was sadly mistaken. The reason for the invitation didn't matter as much as the invitation itself.

"Carol," the officer answered. "My name is Carol."

Erin couldn't understand what possessed her to step even closer to the cop but she did. "That's a beautiful name. It suits you." Again, the wall of apathy had given way, revealing a warm smile and gentle eyes that seemed full of emotions. Carol smiled back softly, wanting to reward the gift. "So what do you say, Carol? Think you're up to seeing what the activist *lifestyle* is all about - well, at least *my* activist lifestyle?"

One Belief Away

Carol swallowed so hard it was audible. It took everything she had to keep eye contact with the young woman. Finally, she cleared her throat. "I'll think about it."

"You do that," Erin smiled.

Without further comment, Carol watched Erin quickly make her departure toward the microbus parked outside. She absently rubbed above her breast pocket before turning back to the counter to pour herself more coffee. Suddenly, her partner's voice boomed from the entrance, making her jump and bringing her back from her musings.

"Is that kid still hassling you? Why don't you run her in?" he asked.

"She's not a problem," Carol assured him, trying to hide her grin. "Just young and idealistic but I'm sure you're too old to remember being that way, Randell," she prodded.

"Ha. Ha. Very funny," he replied with a grimace and a wrinkled nose. Carol realized he had never been like Erin and if so it was decades ago. "Can we get going now?"

"Sure," Carol smiled, making her way past him, coffee and doughnuts in hand. "Cherry filled – your favorite."

"A woman who knows me well. I'm telling you Johnson," he began as they walked out, "if I wasn't happily married..."

"Yeah, yeah...And 20 years younger. I hate to break it to you Randell, but I have higher standards," she grinned warmly before giving him a chuck on the shoulder as they left.

Minos drove down the street in silence for as long as she could bear. The strain of keeping her mouth closed was beginning to show and her blonde companion was diligently waiting for Minos to burst. *You wanna know, you gotta ask, my friend.*

Finally, it was too much.

"What's with the cop?" Minos blurted. The words tumbled past teeth and lips and fell with a tinge of defensiveness between the two women.

"What do you mean?" Erin asked innocently, all playful smile and wide green eyes.

"Don't act dumb with me, Skylon. You know exactly what I mean," Minos insisted, sparing a glance from the road to observe her companion.

Erin reflected a moment, putting her tangled thoughts into a string of words that would properly convey her feelings. "I think she's . . . interesting," was the best she could come up with after several long moments of consideration.

Minos studied Erin's expression before realization set in. Firmly, she shook her head and rolled her hazel eyes. "I don't believe it. You're falling for a cop! And a lady cop at that!"

"Oh come on," Erin found she wanted her friend's support in this. It was all so new to her but the emotions were so intense she didn't feel she could ignore them. "You've told me you've had women in your bed."

"Yeah," Minos agreed. "A little experimentation. But never a woman cop! Hell, she arrested you for cryin' out loud. Have you completely lost your mind?!"

"She is pretty arresting, isn't she?" Skylon grinned wickedly. Minos sat stone-faced, failing to find the humor in the comment. Erin realized this might be much more serious than she anticipated. "For your information I have not lost my mind. Besides, what business is it of yours who I find interesting?"

Minos looked seriously hurt by the short retort and turned wounded eyes from her friend back to the road. Erin quickly made up for it, reaching over to place a warm hand on her arm. "I'm sorry. That was a terrible thing to say. I don't want to fight about this. Besides, at this point she isn't even a friend so I don't think you have anything to worry about."

"A friend?" Minos' voice began to rise. "She's a fucking pig, Skylon. What makes you think you have ANYTHING in common with this woman?"

"Why are you so defensive?" Erin pressed, starting to get just as angry.

"You seriously have to ask that?"

Erin didn't have to ask that. She knew why. Minos was at a peace rally in '69 when some 'pig' decided to use her head for batting practice with his baton. Partial sight loss in one eye and 15 stitches are what it cost her. A small silence filled the space between them until Minos spoke up again.

"If you want a woman I can set you up," Minos offered, glad for the subject change. Erin was her dearest friend and the thought of her free spirit with that rigid cop was more than she was willing to handle.

"I don't want to be set up," Erin replied. "Besides, the last time you set me up was with that Peace Corps volunteer who didn't believe in shaving. God Minos, if I'd wanted hairy I'd date an ape."

Both women began to chuckle before it turned into rolling laughter. Minos calmed down first and looked at Erin as they reached a stoplight. "You really do like her . . . don't you?"

Erin looked out the front windshield as she spoke, unable to meet her friend's searching gaze. "I don't understand it. It's like I'm drawn to her." She shrugged slim shoulders helplessly.

"Like a moth to a flame, huh?" Minos nodded, twisting her lips into a wry expression of defeat. "I don't need to tell you what ends up happening to the moth?"

"You know, for a flower child you really are pessimistic," Erin jibed. Minos preferred this approach to the previous outburst of raised voices and accusing words.

"I'm sorry, I just-."

"Just what? Always hoped you'd be my first woman?" Erin teased, not expecting the reaction she got.

Minos smiled at first but the smile began to fade and she nodded her confession. "Your first time should always be with someone you love and who loves you."

"You know I love you, Minos, but-."

"See, there's that word . . . 'but'. Erin, all I care about is your happiness - even if that person you choose isn't me."

"Even if that person I choose is a cop?" Erin asked softly, tilting her head toward the brunette slightly.

Minos nodded, a weak smile playing on her lips. "God forgive . . . Even if it is a cop."

Erin didn't know what to say but after a few moments she found her voice. "You're my best friend, Minos."

Minos nodded but Erin knew she still had a quiet, defeated air about her. She was going to press the point some more but Minos stopped her.

"No, it's groovy. I understand. I do. You're my best friend, too, Skylon . . . I don't want anything to come between the love we have."

"Neither do I," Erin replied softly. They were only three words but at the moment they meant the world. Minos had been her touchstone, kept her grounded and gave her a reason to go on when many times in Erin's life she could have given up. Coming from an unstable home, Erin found a sense of security with Minos she'd never had before. To say that Erin appreciated it was an understatement and Minos knew how important a part she played in Erin's life. She didn't always understand her young friend but she never once stopped caring for the girl.

"So," Minos sighed. "What am I supposed to do when this cop shows up?"

"I'm not sure. Chances are she won't."

"But what if she does?"

"I haven't thought that far ahead."

"Jeez, Skylon."

"I'm sorry, okay?" Erin started to chuckle. "It's not like she and I are picking out china patterns or anything. The invite just kinda slipped out. But just don't tell anyone all right? You know what the house would say."

"Say? Think about what they'll do. They'll draw and quarter you."

"They might not."

"They will."

Erin looked out the windshield at the world passing around them. She knew Minos was right. The house could very well turn violent against her. Not everyone would do her harm. But she was sure there were a few people in the house that loved a good fight rather than fighting for a good cause. "Don't you find that ironic?" Erin asked aloud as she thought of her roommates.

"What?"

"A group of peace lovers who live for the fight. I mean . . . we spend so much time saying the establishment doesn't understand us. But at the same time we never take the opportunity to understand them. Don't you find that a bit hypocritical?"

"I find it a matter of survival. I've got the scars to prove it. The further I'm away from the establishment the better," Minos answered. Another silence passed between the pair. "Let's just hope she doesn't show up in her uniform on orgy night," Minos added in serious tone.

Minos and Erin looked at each other briefly before filling the bus with laughter.

Chapter 4

A week later, Carol and Randell were in their patrol car when the nervous voice came over from dispatch.

"All units report to Monroe and Main. Repeat. All units proceed to Monroe and Main."

Carol and Randell exchanged a concerned look as Carol turned on the sirens and Randell floored it. Carol's heart pounded and although he might not admit it, she was sure that Randell felt equally shaken. Joyce, who worked the dispatch unit, was always very calm but something in her tone frightened Carol. Joyce was always all business but the voice they both heard could be described better as panicky. They rounded the corner of Elm St. where they could see the campus at the corner of Monroe and Main. It was total pandemonium. People were screaming, police billy clubs were swinging, tear gas was being thrown back and forth and bodies were littering the ground. With a deep sigh Randell pulled the car to a stop. They got out and Carol jogged around to the driver's side to meet her partner.

"I'm getting too damn old for this." He sighed again, pausing to look at the carnage they were about to enter. *Fuck Vietnam*, Randell thought silently. *The war is here, too.* In all of Randell's days he'd never seen anything quite like it. His society was crumbling around him. The Civil War of the 1800's had been called a 'brother against brother' battle. He couldn't imagine the war between the North and the South looking much worse than what he was witnessing. Just over 100 years had passed since the nation warred against itself. Just over 100 years and it seemed not much had changed.

Randell pulled his nightstick and gave one tap to his palm as if testing its sturdiness. "Are you ready?"

"As I'm gonna be," Carol answered.

The pair charged ahead, trying to find a place they could help. From the corner of her eye, Carol saw an officer swing at someone unmoving on the ground. She slowed her steps as Randell raced ahead. When the officer swung again Carol made her way over to investigate. She looked beyond her fellow cop to find a woman nearing unconsciousness on the ground. She looked bloodied and battered. The closer she got the more she realized she knew just who the young woman was – without a doubt it was Erin.

"Come on bitch! Talk back to me again!"

As he raised his nightstick again, Carol stepped between them and used her own nightstick as a shield, preventing another blow.

"I think she gets the point," Carol hissed.

The officer pushed Carol away, his anger now directed toward her. "Get your own collar! After I knock some sense into her I'm taking her to the stationhouse."

Carol's voice went gravely deep. "Hit her again and I'll see they take you to the morgue."

The officer swung but Carol deflected the blow. Nightsticks stood motionless as each officer tried to push the other away.

"I'm warning you," Carol threatened, "be a gentleman and pick on someone your own size. Or are you such a coward that you need to beat unarmed women?"

"How about I beat the bleeding heart cop instead?"

Carol was finished with trying to reason with him. He'd pushed her too far. She watched his eyes widen as his nightstick, and then entire body, was forced backward by the sheer power generated from Carol's anger. "You don't want to do that," Carol replied. She gave him a menacing grin. "You'd never live down the fact that a 'girl' kicked your ass. Now get the hell out of here!"

In the commotion around them, no one noticed the confrontation. She felt him recoil just slightly so she launched him at least four feet away with a final shove. He paused as if considering whether he really wanted the trouble he was asking for. After a few moments and some loud shouting behind him, he turned his attention to other pursuits. She was relieved he didn't start a fight just to 'save face'. Every nerve ending was on fire but she quickly regrouped and turned to face Erin.

The woman was a mess. She knew that Erin could be a smart ass and throw some real zingers but no one deserved the beating this officer gave her. Quickly, she knelt down to check Erin's pulse since she was no longer moving. Both fear and anger coursed through her veins at once. Carol reached to Erin's neck and the young woman opened her eyes briefly. Even in light of the beating she had just taken the young activist grinned, blood covering her teeth, before closing her eyes again.

"Gonna arrest me again, Officer Johnson?"

"No. I'm getting you to the hospital. Just stay with me Erin."

Carol looked around and spotted her partner. "Randell!"

The sound of his name spoken with such urgency by his partner, forced him to turn his head. Giving up on the protester he was engaging, he dashed over to her side and found Carol leaning over Erin. The sight sent a chill through him.

"Jesus Christ," he said softly. "Who did this?"

Carol smiled inwardly at the question. Her partner knew her well. Instead of assuming she had been the one to issue the punishment he asked who dealt the blows. She didn't have time to commend him at the moment, though.

"Does it matter?"

Randell knew it didn't. Cops got overzealous now and then and never had to answer for it. There was an unwritten code on the force: don't hand over your comrades. It may not have been right but it was certainly in place.

"Help me get her to the car," Carol ordered.

Grade and rank didn't matter at this moment. Randell was her superior but he also knew when to take the 'backseat' in their partnership. This was one of those times. So as Carol raced back to get their squad car ready by opening the doors, Randell picked Erin up in his arms as carefully as possible. The young woman whimpered as he moved toward the vehicle. As softly as possible, Randell laid her inside.

After closing the rear door he climbed inside the passenger side.

"If we leave to take her in-" Carol began.

"She's not looking good Carol. If they want to write us up for leaving they can but let's get her to the hospital now."

Carol smiled, grateful she had the partner she did.

Randell watched Carol put the car in drive using lights and sirens as they started down the road. He looked back at the crowd again. *Fuck Vietnam.*

Carol paced, holding a bouquet of daisies. She wasn't sure of the reaction she would get from visiting Erin at the hospital but she wanted to make sure that she was okay. She couldn't quite explain it but part of her felt guilty for what happened. Maybe if she'd gotten there a few seconds earlier or maybe if she'd been patrolling the campus like she and Randell often did, it could have been avoided. In truth, she knew that it was something deeper. She felt guilt by association. Her establishment had beaten free-spirit Erin to within an inch of her life. And for what?

Carol turned and watched the elevators. She realized that perhaps coming here was a mistake. Instead of offering support she might make Erin feel uncomfortable. She decided to leave when the nurse came back.

"I'm sorry to make you wait," she apologized. "Now what was that name again, Officer Johnson?"

"O'Fallon" Carol answered making her way over to the station desk.

The nurse flipped through a few copies of crisp, white paper. As her skimming finger stopped, Carol's stomach fluttered.

"Here she is. Room 509. Down this hall and on the left."

"Thank you," Carol nodded.

She began her journey down the white corridor taking in everything around her. She really disliked hospitals. Maybe it was the white factor – white walls, white sheets, white curtains. Hospitals were like voids without color, without life. Before she realized it she was standing in front of room 509. She considered turning around again but before she could give it serious thought, she charged ahead and stepped inside.

Erin was sitting up, a textbook of some kind on her lap. She turned at the opening door. Carol gave a grin and thrust the flowers forward with an outstretched arm. She was glad that Erin looked much better than when she had left her. The blood was now gone but she had a bandage by her eyebrow above her right eye.

"Thought I'd stop by and see how you're doing," she began.

Erin began to smile herself but stopped and clutched her temple instead.

"Sorry. It hurts my jaw when I smile. Come have a seat."

Even though Erin invited her inside Carol felt like an intruder. As a result, she found herself speaking quicker than normal.

"I didn't want to take up much of your time - you looked pretty bad yesterday. I just thought I'd bring these by and check on how you were doing."

Erin could sense Carol's uneasiness and cocked her head in examination. *Must have taken a lot for her to come here*, she surmised. Instead of debating it, she played it casual and took the offered flowers. She inhaled the aroma before placing them next to her bedside. "These are beautiful. Thank you."

Carol simply nodded as she sat down in a chair across from the foot of the bed. She looked unsure of what to say next and she felt a slight sense of relief when Erin cleared her throat to speak.

"I never got a chance to thank you."

Carol grinned. "No thanks needed, Erin - just doing my job. That cop was wrong for what he did."

"And I'm sure action will be taken against him, right?" the sarcasm dripped from Erin's voice.

"Sure - the word of a hippy and a female cop against a police vet. That will go far in the department's eyes." Carol wasn't going to hide it. She was upset over the ordeal as well.

Erin shook her head in disgust. "Why am I not surprised?"

Carol nodded. "Yeah, it's pretty screwed up. I know."

"Then why be a part of it?" Erin began. "Why be a part of a machine that perpetuates hate? I can't say I know you well, Carol, but you just don't fit. And it's not the age factor."

"I'm trying to bring order in an unruly age, Erin. I'm trying to open doors for women that have never been opened."

"And are you happy you risk your life each day, just like your partner, but make 40 cents less than he does an hour? Why not fight the powers within the establishment so people can be equal? Why not bring order through chaos?"

"Nietzsche," Carol said softly.

Erin did a double take. "That's what I mean, Carol. How many cops know Nietzsche? You're a square peg trying to fit into their circle."

"Being a cop is who I am, Erin. I don't always agree with everyone I work with. But I do my job the best I can."

"Like visiting former perps in the hospital? How many cops do you know that would be doing this? How many would rush a protestor to the hospital to begin with?" Erin grinned, slightly mindful of her bruises.

"I'm just doing my job. That's all."

"I think it's more, Carol. I think you have so much talent and potential and it's being totally wasted working for a group of narrow minded...chauvinistic pigs."

"You know, some of those 'pigs' happen to be my friends. And they're not all as terrible as you make them out to be."

"Look, I don't want to fight. I appreciate everything you've done. And the flowers are wonderful."

Carol could have pressed her point but Erin was trying to find some agreement, a sense of peace, so she let it go. "Well, you're welcome. I know I didn't strike the blow but I keep feeling a bit guilty about it all."

"Maybe it's that you really care about the condition of man and you're not just another 'uniform' . . . For what it's worth, I'm ashamed of the way I acted at the station house the day we met. I apologize. My offer to visit me still stands - more now than ever."

Carol pursed her lips and nodded. "I'll consider it. And I hope you get to feeling better soon." She stood up and walked closer to the bed. "I better get out of here before your friends stop by and see you fraternizing with the enemy," she grinned.

"You're not the enemy, Carol. If anything, I think we're more kindred spirits than opposite ends. As Nietzsche said, 'Convictions are more dangerous enemies of truth than lies.' I might be convinced the establishment has nothing to offer me but I'd like the chance to get to know you to see if that's really true."

Carol grinned. "Nietzsche also said that 'man's truths are merely his irrefutable errors' . . . You might regret knowing me," she chuckled.

"Either way, I'm willing to take that chance. It's already a tough world out there."

"Getting tougher every day. Just wait for these wounds to heal before you go looking for new ones, okay?"

Erin gave a small grin and a nod, which Carol reciprocated. Casually, Carol walked out of the room. For the life of her, Erin couldn't figure out how someone as idealistic as Carol ended up in the police department. She hoped Carol would take her up on her offer to stop by again because it felt like their conversation was far from over.

Carol walked to the elevators and waited. A woman in a granny dress exited through the opening doors passing Carol. Not paying

One Belief Away

that much attention, Carol suddenly realized that she'd seen her before. The recognition seemed to register for the stranger as well because she turned and faced the elevator as the doors began to shut.

Minos knew that woman but she couldn't pinpoint from where. With a shake of her head she walked down the hall to the nurses' station to check in. Recognizing her from the day before as 'Erin's sister' the nurse nodded her head and Minos made her way down the hall. As she peeked inside, Minos found Erin smelling her bouquet and playing with the ivory petals.

"Someone else know daisies are your favorite besides me?" Minos grinned.

"No, it was just a lucky guess," Erin grinned slightly.

It was then that Minos knew the woman she had passed. It was the cop from the donut shop. Erin's reluctance to give a name to the gift giver helped confirm that. Minos nodded toward the arrangement, "So how long did the pig stay?"

Erin sighed and put the flowers down with a little more force than necessary. "She's not a pig."

"Oh that's right. She's your savior. I forgot."

Erin pursed her lips. She loved Minos very deeply. But there were times she just wanted to backhand the woman. Usually, she could send a shot back over the net but her mind was tired and her body still ached. She opted for a different approach instead.

"Why do you say that about her?"

"Say what? She did save you didn't she?"

"Yeah, she did, but why be so goddamned sarcastic about it?" Erin retorted.

Minos sat down, shaking her head. "She's a pig, Erin. She might feel some kinda flirty chemistry with you or something but the fact remains the same – she's a pig."

"Well I saw the 'pig' stand up to one of *her own* to get me to safety. And I think you're wrong about her."

"She probably *wronged you* in another life and is trying to make peace with it now," Minos replied, her sarcasm unwavering.

"So what if she did? Everyone deserves a second chance." The words were spoken with a bit of mirth and Erin hoped that levity might help ease the tension between them. By the look on Minos' face it didn't.

"I don't know why you insist on befriending that woman."

"Because she was a friend to me. Regardless of any uniform I think she's a good person, just misguided."

"And you're going to change her?" Minos laughed. "You're going to show her our world? Let her inside? And somehow magically transform her into a free spirit who challenges the system?"

"I'm not looking to change her."

"Then what are you looking for?"

"I'm looking for knowledge. I'm supposed to hate her because she's a pig from what you say. So far I haven't seen that."

Minos chuckled again. "Perhaps you have forgotten the arrest."

"She was doing her job, Minos. I was doing mine. They just clashed."

"Keep that in mind. You befriend this woman and I see a lot more clashes in your future, for both of you. I think if you really cared about her you'd leave her be."

"I think that's a choice she should make. She's a grown woman. Just like I am."

Minos ran her fingers through her long hair. Erin had a point. She wasn't just some young high school kid she took under her wing anymore. Erin was about to graduate with her degree in journalism. She was already making plans to join the 'establishment' by interviewing with some newspapers and magazines. She thought Erin would stay a while longer but in truth, the young woman was ready to move on and make her own way in life. Minos finally relented.

"Yes, you are grown up now," she nodded. "But that doesn't mean I have to stop worrying 'bout you, does it?"

Erin grinned. "I'd be concerned if you didn't worry."

Feeling a peace settle between them Minos walked over taking a seat at the foot of the bed. The sheets were scratchy, itchy. Not like the sheets in their home that were dried in the sun and a warm breeze. She played with the end, not really looking at Erin.

"I didn't tell you yesterday but I was scared. When Marlow said he saw you beaten up and a cop leaving with you . . . " Minos paused and swallowed, steadying herself to continue. "I thought she might let you bleed to death in a cell somewhere."

Erin reached out and stroked Minos arm. "But she didn't. And I'm gonna be okay. Remember that."

"Well it's not just that," Minos went on. She stood and began to pace in front of Erin.

"What else then?" Erin asked. Her voice was soft and gentle. Like times past, she and Minos would argue on occasion but they still supported each other. Although moments before, Erin was ready to climb out of bed to give her friend a nice swift kick in the pants, now she found herself being nurturing to her friend who was obviously troubled.

"I feel like I should have been there."

"You had to work at the shelter, Minos."

"I know but I keep thinking . . . There I was working at a battered women's shelter and my best friend is getting her ass kicked because I wasn't there to back her up. It's a bit ironic if you think about it." Minos gave a slight grin. "And you know how I hate irony."

"Well, things are different now than they were a few years ago. You've graduated and moved on. Lots of our friends have. You can't keep going to the rallies and risk imprisonment."

"You mean I sold out to become 'established' so I can pay the bills and forget the causes."

"We can't stay in college forever, Minos. And you're not forgetting the causes. You do important work everyday. Only now you get paid for it," Erin grinned. And Minos had to chuckle. "I don't hold you responsible so don't hold it over yourself . . . okay?"

Minos nodded her head. "Okay, my friend."

Chapter 5

Carol checked the fraying napkin again, comparing the number she held against the number on the house. Or rather, comparing it to what was left of the number on the house. The building was in an obvious state of disrepair, needing some minor work to doors and windows and several years past a paint job. Otherwise it seemed sturdy with a large wraparound porch and well-landscaped yard.

Now that she'd selected her wardrobe carefully and made her way clear across town, she was having second thoughts. Did Erin have a sincere interest to spend time with her or was it just a casual comment like 'how are you today' but not really giving a damn? Two weeks had passed since she had visited Erin in the hospital. Would the woman even remember her? *Of course she would*, Carol told herself. *But will she actually want to talk to me is another question.*

She stood casually in her jeans, sweatshirt and a heavy denim jacket, an outfit chosen specifically to not make a statement of establishment, rocking back on sneakered heels. She was still deciding whether or not to leave when the door opened and searching hazel eyes pinned her where she stood on the top step of the porch.

"Look, cop, you gonna stand there all day or come in?"

Carol recognized Minos' piercing gaze and disdainful voice. Carol felt herself tongue tied at the speedy and blunt 'hello' but the woman at the door smiled slightly, knowing she caught the officer off guard. Minos opened the door wider, tilted her head slightly in invitation as if it was given reluctantly. Carol surmised it was.

"I'm here to see Erin," she said at last, finally making her decision and taking the few steps that brought her across the porch to the front door.

The other woman snorted. "No kidding," she said as if Carol was an idiot.

The cop chose to ignore the tone of voice and stepped into the house anyway, biting her tongue over a harsh retort that would get her nowhere.

"Skylon's room is on the second floor, second door on the left." Minos over emphasized Erin's hippie name which wasn't lost on the nervous officer.

"She has her own room?" Carol asked, surprised.

Minos shook her head. "No one has their own anything here. We share." Then the tall brunette walked away leaving Carol to her own devices.

With her hands still stuffed in her jacket pockets, Carol made her way carefully up the stairs to the second doorway which stood wide open on empty hinges. She studied the scene first, looking at the small blonde who lay curled on a mattress on the bare wood floor. She was reading something in a tattered notebook, occasionally making scribbles, often chewing on the end of her pencil. After a long moment of observation, Carol cleared her throat slightly, watching the green eyes leave paper and look up.

Erin was shocked, her mouth agape, as she saw the officer standing in the opening to her room. She felt a warm sense of joy crawl through her belly and rest heavily in her throat, causing her to cough a couple of times and blush before she spoke. "Hi," she said softly, allowing Carol once again to see the delicate side of her instead of an outspoken, brash person.

"Hi," Carol smiled gently, trying to offer the woman comfort, not wanting to make her awkward or nervous.

The young blonde set aside notebook and pencil and stood up. Today she was dressed in tattered jeans and an over sized T-shirt with a huge peace symbol emblazoned across the front. Carol couldn't help but notice the scar, although healing nicely, still visible on Erin's forehead above her right eye.

"I didn't think you'd come," Erin spoke at last, both women still standing the length of the room apart.

Carol shrugged, broad shoulders lifting and relaxing under the denim of her jacket. "You invited me. I came."

"Why?" Erin asked suddenly, surprising herself by her insecurity and the flutter in her stomach. "Not that I'm not glad," she added quickly. "I'm just surprised."

Carol grinned slightly and thought of a hundred smart retorts or teasing comebacks. Instead, she decided on honesty. "Well, it was an offer I couldn't pass up."

"Fair enough," Erin grinned back, feeling some of her composure return when presented with the officer's relaxed demeanor. "Come in, I'm sorry," suddenly realizing her manners, she stepped forward. "Let me take your jacket. We can leave it in here while I give you the grand tour. Who let you in?" she asked curiously as she took the extended jacket and tossed it on her double mattress.

"Minos."

"Ah," Erin nodded and then looked back to her guest, inquiring with her gaze. "Was she nice?"

Carol shrugged.

"Was she mean?"

The officer laughed softly, shook her head. "No, she wasn't mean. But I wouldn't have used nice as a descriptor."

Erin nodded her agreement. "She's . . . ah . . . not fond of cops. Policemen . . . um . . . policewomen," Erin fumbled.

Carol smiled. "Cop is fine, Erin. And you aren't too fond of us, either."

The younger woman shrugged, tilted her head, and said, "You're different."

"You don't know that."

"I do," Erin nodded though she didn't know from where she obtained the conviction of those words. Something about this woman called to Erin and she knew that under the tough exterior, the gun, and the uniform was a gentle person she wanted to get to know better. The attraction she felt was new and intriguing. And she'd be damned if she let it slip away without further exploration. Her world was about experiencing everything around her and she most definitely wanted to experience Carol Johnson. "C'mon," she reached out to gently tug at the woman's sleeve. "Let's go see who's around."

Erin offered a quick tour showing Carol the common rooms, waving to the shared bedrooms. They ended up in the kitchen with two longhaired men and cups of coffee. Erin introduced the men as Bill and Stan, telling them that Carol was her friend and that they'd met at the demonstration they'd all attended. She left out that Carol had been one of the uniformed attendees. Carol noticed the absence and raised an eyebrow questioningly. Erin smiled, patted the older woman on the arm and let that touch linger a little longer than necessary.

"So what are your plans for today, Skylon?" Stan asked, standing to rinse out his coffee cup.

Erin glanced at her companion quickly and was met with inquisitive blue eyes. "No plans. Maybe go for a walk, do some talking."

Bill nodded. "We're going to go down to the pharmaceutical company and sit on the steps," he grinned, teeth barely showing beneath his beard. "We're pretty sure they're supporting the war efforts so we're going to go make their lives a little more difficult." He placed his wet mug upside down on a towel covering the counter. "Wanna come? The more the merrier."

Erin looked to her hands, then to her friend's blue eyes before turning to him. "Not today. But good luck to you."

"Suit yourself," the tall man shrugged and patted his silent companion's shoulder. "Let's go, Stan. Places to go . . . people to see."

Their departure left the two women alone in the kitchen.

"If you want to go," Carol said at last, after a very long moment of silence, "I can come back another day."

Erin smiled in that over-confident manner she must have perfected years ago. "Not up to it? We could both join them."

Carol returned the grin. "I can't, Erin. You know that."

"Yeah," the young blonde's countenance turned more wistful as she looked away to study the kitchen. The water stained wallpaper curled away from the walls; the Formica counters were chipped and damaged. She tapped her toe on cracking green linoleum. "I know."

"You didn't tell them who I am." Carol watched her young friend with gentle eyes. She sensed a conflict in the other woman she could neither define nor understand.

Erin shook her head, traced a crack in the table with a blunt-nailed finger. "I wanted them to like you. If they knew you're a cop-."

"Even the cop that took you to the hospital?" Carol offered.

Erin shrugged her shoulders. "I'm not sure it would make a difference."

"So you don't think I'm likeable in uniform, Erin? It's part of me."

"I know," she shrugged her shoulders and sighed, able to meet the ice blue gaze only briefly. "But we don't look past the clothes to the person. Ironic, isn't it? That's what we claim the establishment is doing to us."

Carol nodded silently, agreeing with her observation. She also wondered why she was here and where this could possibly go. "Two different worlds," she muttered.

Erin looked up from her diligent tracing. "Yeah. But is that okay?"

"Whaddya mean?"

Erin rose from the table to pour herself some more coffee and brought the pot over to fill her friend's cup as well. She needed the brief interlude before she continued.

"Can we get past that? If I don't judge you by your uniform can you not judge me by mine?"

Carol smiled, "I think so."

"I'd like to."

"Me too," she agreed, sipping from her mug and studying Erin's features. She was lovely without make-up or a pretentious hairstyle. Her charm and looks were natural and Carol found herself drawn to them. She'd admit there were times she considered herself attracted to women before meeting the blonde. Yet she told herself she would never act on it. Now she guessed she might have to redefine that part of herself because she could easily picture romantic moonlit strolls with this woman. She could almost feel the gentle caresses and the warmth of lips. She shook her head.

In truth it was more than that. Erin excited her physically but challenged her, intellectually too. Carol never considered herself a cerebral woman but she did enjoy a good debate. On the force a good debate was usually about sports teams or auto racing. Carol could enjoy those things as well but as for philosophy or idealism, the department made for shallow waters in which to fish.

Erin was educated about many things in life. Of that, Carol was sure. And it was something that Carol realized she had missed since she joined the force. Carol most definitely wanted to get inside the mind of this young woman. Inside her mind and if she was willing perhaps inside her . . . Carol couldn't finish the thought. She felt her face redden instantly. Erin noticed her blush but kindly declined comment.

"You up for that walk? There's a park nearby, we can take Rainbow."

"What's Rainbow?" Carol asked with a raised eyebrow.

"Four legged roommate. Catches a mean Frisbee."

"Sounds like fun," the older woman agreed, downing the rest of her coffee in a few short swallows. "Let's get out of here before my true identity is revealed," Carol whispered conspiratorially to her host.

Erin laughed, finishing her coffee as well and rinsing out both cups to set them beside Bill's.

Chapter 6

"So what do you do?" Carol asked as she tossed the Frisbee. Rainbow ran with all he had to keep up with the flying disk. He was a large black mutt of some sort, probably part Lab and Shepherd. His breed was really irrelevant as it was impossible not to love him for his gregarious attitude and his large flopping tongue.

They claimed a spot under a golden leafed tree as well as a field for Rainbow's activities. The afternoon sun was bright, but not blinding in the sky's blue expanse. It was a wonderful day for outdoor activity and pleasant company - a slight chill to the air but nothing unbearably cold.

The walk over had been enjoyable. Rainbow had remained on a leash until they'd reached the edge of the park where Erin had turned him loose to bound across the manicured grass to hunt for buried 'treasures' under the fallen leaves, taking turns between rooting with his snout and rolling on his back.

"I fight for the betterment of mankind," Erin answered, tilting her head up to regard Carol and squinting against the streaming sunlight. She sat in the grass at Carol's feet, her bellbottomed legs stretching outward.

Always about the movement, Carol thought silently. "No," she corrected, taking a seat next to Erin. "I mean for a living. You must eat. Buy clothes. What do you do for money?"

One Belief Away

"I'm an artist," Erin replied, watching her companion for any sort of negative reaction. She'd found that a lot of the establishment wasn't impressed with artists or their works and dreams. "I paint. I sculpt," she continued softly, seeing nothing in the other woman's countenance to frighten her off. "Sometimes I write. About once a month I go to the Village or Soho to sell my work. All the money the house brings in goes into a large fund. That way we always have electricity and a fridge full of food," she finished with a smile.

"What about if you wanted to go to the movies or something? Don't you have spending money?" Carol asked nonchalantly, stretching out her long legs and watching Rainbow. The dog dropped the Frisbee halfway across the field and was now busily trying to scoop his nose under it to pick it back up.

"I'm usually too busy for things like that. And I rarely eat out. So it's not that much of a burden. But yes, I do have some spending money," Erin acknowledged softly, hoping that Carol was asking for another reason besides trying to understand the joint household living situation. She glanced sideways at Carol, enjoying the slope of her sharp cheekbones and the olive hue of her skin. Her black hair was pulled back in a ponytail revealing dainty dangling earrings in her lobes. Erin found her breathtaking: her eyes matched the sky and her hair was darker than night. The artist in the young woman began to plan a sketch that might reflect that beauty. She blushed at the thought and looked away again before Carol could notice.

A silence filled the space between them until Rainbow recovered the toy and made his presence known by leaping from woman to woman hoping someone - anyone - would throw his prize again. Carol took the not-so-subtle hint from the canine and rose to her feet once more, throwing as far and as hard as she could. She brushed off the seat of her pants while keeping her attention on the bounding dog and the way his ears flopped with each great leap.

"You've got quite an arm there," Erin complimented, smiling up at the officer. She shielded her eyes from the sunlight so she could see Carol's reaction, a blush that rose to her cheeks. If anything, she was more attractive with the added color.

"Well, I played softball for a lot of years when I was younger. The force has a league but I don't play now," Carol responded, rolling her shoulders with the memory of a good day on the field. She'd practiced with some of the guys from the team from time to time though she was never permitted to play in a game with them.

"Why not?" Erin asked, honestly confused. Carol's voice indicated it was something she'd enjoyed. Plus her posture and stance seemed to prove she was more than capable. "They are obviously missing out on a great outfielder with that arm."

Carol was both surprised and pleased that Erin knew something about the sport and she paused a moment before answering. "Ohh . . . I . . . the force doesn't let women play on the team. It's only recently that they allowed women on the force itself. Maybe in a few years that will change," she replied reluctantly, knowing she was cracking the door for an argument. Thus far the day had been pleasant and their time together enjoyable. She didn't want to ruin it with an abrupt reminder about how very different they were.

"So you're good enough to wrestle flower children to the ground but not good enough to catch a grounder to third?" Erin teased gently, sensing the other woman's tension but also angered at the obvious discrimination she faced.

As Carol began to laugh, Rainbow took a flying leap, sending her flat on her back. Erin scolded the animal that was now busy licking Carol's face. "I think I made a new friend," Carol said between laughs and dodging a long, seeking tongue. She put her hands on the dog's broad chest and shoved at him weakly. Erin tried in vain to pull Rainbow off, her feet planted on either side of his body and her hands wrapped firmly around his collar. But no amount of tugging was lifting the eager dog away.

Giving up on the brute force approach, Erin released her hold on the dog and tossed the Frisbee, sending Rainbow on the chase again. She knelt down beside the officer and helped pull her into a sitting position.

"I'm sorry about that," Erin apologized. "He's a little overzealous now and then." She grinned ruefully at the understatement as she helped Carol pick blades of grass out of her hair. The strands were silky against her fingertips and caused Erin's heart to flutter slightly. Her attraction to this woman was absolutely unnerving.

"No need to apologize. I love animals," Carol smiled in response, evidently oblivious to the effect she was having on the other woman.

"Even ones that plant wet kisses all over your face?" Erin questioned as Carol wiped her cheek with her sweatshirt sleeve.

One Belief Away

"Well, that depends on the animal. There are some kisses I like more than others," Carol bantered easily, trying to reroute the conversation and embarrass the brash young blonde.

"Is that so?" Erin replied with her eyebrow arched, considering possibilities, feeling her face warm again. The twinkle in the dark woman's eyes told her that she'd fallen for Carol's gentle ploy.

Carol's mind went blank except for two thoughts - one, Erin definitely had accepted the flirting and two, she really wanted to find out what Erin's kisses would be like. Though brave a moment before, the reality of it was a little more than she was ready for so Carol visibly shook the images out of her mind and moved to her feet, mumbling something about the returning dog.

Erin stayed still, soaking up what had just transpired. She knew Carol had initiated the playfulness and the flirting and she knew now by the other woman's reaction how awkward it felt to her. What she didn't know was how much Carol was playing and how much of her was seriously interested in pursuing something further. And even if she was interested, would the officer have the courage to explore it?

Erin had little doubt Carol would not be making any bold moves. That would have to be Erin's task but she didn't want to rush into things, either. Given time, perhaps the officer would come to her. For all she knew Carol might already have a special someone in her life. It seemed unlikely though. Carol had yet to mention anyone by name with comments like 'My boyfriend Steve says'. Plus, given Carol's profession of long hours and danger at every turn it seemed quite likely that Carol was living in solitude.

Carol threw the toy again as Erin came to her feet, dusting off her pants and raising her face to the sunlit sky. She wanted to find a topic of conversation that might ease the awkwardness they'd settled into. Carol could think of one that would make the silence go away.

"So what's the greater purpose you spoke of?" Carol asked slowly. "You said you would explain it to me if I stopped by."

"Where to begin . . . " Erin pondered. "It's a theory. A way of life . . . It says that our own existence isn't as important as the living condition of man. I would sacrifice my own life, if need be, for something I thought would be best for mankind."

"I'm not sure I follow you," Carol confessed, glancing away from Rainbow's continued antics to meet the gentle green eyes.

Erin paused considering the proper words. "Okay, let's take that last peace rally. I could have been killed. If I died by trying to get the message out about how messed up this country's become - then so be it. My death would cause people to stop and take notice."

"So you're saying that if you had been senselessly killed it would have drawn more attention to your cause?" None of it made any sense. "Couldn't you play a much bigger role in those same causes by staying alive rather than by becoming a martyr?"

"I would have given my life for something that I believe in. I would have made a difference unlike the soldiers in Vietnam now. All they know is death and destruction. They kill thousands of innocents in the name of 'Old Glory'. That's not the America I know and love," Erin responded, warming to the subject and wanting her companion to understand just how much she was willing to give.

"So you're a patriot? It doesn't look like it from where I'm sitting."

"No - since you get a weekly check thanks to my tax dollars it probably doesn't. You're just as jaded as everyone in the government today."

"I'm jaded because I can't see how revolting equals patriotism?"

"This country was founded by a revolution," Erin pointed out coming toe to toe with Carol. "And I think I'm more American than any sellout politician. I know I'm more American than Tricky Dick who sits in the White House and worries more about his image than he does his people."

"Okay maybe he's not Mr. Squeaky Clean but he's still our President."

Erin couldn't contain her laughter. "Oh Lord – a Republican, too. Tell me I did NOT just hear you say that!"

"Say what? I think you could give the man a little common courtesy."

"Richard Nixon considered John Lennon a 'threat' to his image so he tried having him deported. Our president went that far to try to increase his 'standing'. Lennon might have thought 'all you need is love' but he soon learned a visa card helps, too." Carol chuckled at the remark and Erin let a small grin come to her face before turning serious again. "We're getting off topic," she said, regrouping her thoughts. "Look, it comes down to this - I don't have to like what my country is doing but I'll always love what it stands for. It's just that right now I think we are straying from what's important."

'So do all you flower power types think this way?" Carol asked. Condescension crept into her voice and she regretted the tone immediately but knew she couldn't take it back.

The flower remark set Erin off. She started grinding her teeth while Carol's fists unconsciously clenched.

"For the record I'm not a flower power type. Most of them have 'tuned in, turned on and dropped out'. I consider myself still very much in the thick of things."

"In the thick of things? Or just a trouble maker?"

"The people that thought they could change the world with hearts, flowers and folk music are learning that the best thing to do when pushed is to push back."

"So you've declared war on America? How patriotic of you."

"Hey! When the government stopped listening to its people it declared war on itself. King and RFK - both of them - had visions for uniting this country. Both heard the voice of the people. Both are now dead. As a result, we have to pick up the banner. So yes, Carol, we are at war. You've got your uniform and I've got mine!"

"Thought you wanted to see past that - or was that just a drug induced hallucination you had in your kitchen?"

"I do want to get past it but I get so incredibly pissed Carol! I think the government is a controlling, bureaucratic mess that doesn't know its ass from a hole in the ground."

"If the government's to blame why are you shouting at me?"

"You subscribe to it. You believe in a government that does nothing but deceive. The lies in the White House, the lies about Vietnam, the lies about what really happened at Kent State. Why should I listen to anything the 'authorities' have to say?"

"Because without authority, there's chaos."

"How much goddamn worse could it be?" Erin chuckled sarcastically, throwing her arms in the air. "Can you tell me why we still send lower class men overseas to fight in a war while Senator's sons get nice comfy assignments in the National Guard? Are we really preserving American freedom? Or did we just get into another dick waving contest to boost our egos but got more than we bargained for?" Erin added, growing angry and taking a step away from Carol so she would be better able to look at the woman's expression without bending her neck backwards.

"Lemme guess - you spit on the soldiers who come home from the war, don't you?"

"I would never do that. I think-."

"No – you reserve that pleasure just for cops, huh?"

Erin looked down at the ground without issuing an immediate response, trying to control her temper.

"Not one of my prouder moments I assure you. And I did apologize."

Carol calmed down for a moment, too. "You did apologize and I'm sorry. That was a low blow."

Both women regrouped their thoughts in a few seconds of silence.

"Anyway, I was saying I think every man in this country should burn his draft card. But I'd never spit on those who choose to go - hell, I'm fighting to bring them back home and out of that mess."

Carol had to collect her thoughts. She was more a woman of action than words and she had to admit this little blonde had her on her toes. Erin had a lot more experience in debating and in expressing her beliefs and feelings. "Then why aren't you working within the system to change it? Let's be honest here. The lawmakers see you as nothing more than a bunch of love-crazed drug addicts making a whole lot of noise about nothin'."

"Yes. I think that's exactly how the establishment views us . . . and for that very reason I don't want to be a part of that same 'system' you hold so dear."

Carol felt the jab; she scowled slightly. "And you think I do? Is that it?"

"You tell me. Why the hell are you a cop, Carol? How could someone who's so bright, intelligent, strong and sometimes witty want to be part of a machine? A machine built on the WASP philosophy of life? A machine that says if you're not the right color, sex, age or educational background you're not worthy? How many times have you detained a black man a little longer than necessary - just for kicks? How many times have you pushed a beatnik off a street corner for a laugh?"

Carol lost what little control she had and bent down so she was mere inches from Erin. Her steel blue eyes bore into the young woman's misty emerald ones. She held her there in a silent glare for several long seconds, wanting to impress upon Erin her next words, which were absolutely true. "Never," Carol whispered, her hot breath brushing across Erin's face and moving blonde locks of hair. "I have a sense of honor despite what you may think of me."

"Oh, really?"

Erin could see that Carol was trying to do the right thing, trying to make a difference in her own way, but she was wrapped up in a machine that was confining and restricting and belonged to the brash men of society. She was shunned for her gender and her skill overlooked. *Surely she could see that?*

"Yes, really."

"But I bet you know people on the force that have - and you do nothing to stop it. Like your cop buddy that tried to rearrange my face. What's happened to him for his actions? I'll tell ya - not a damn thing. So whether you choose to believe it or not, you're part of the same hypocrisy. You choose to look away instead of taking action."

Carol flinched, backing down from the fight, knowing there was some truth in the young woman's words. She had seen it although she was never a party to it. At least that's what she told herself as she began to walk away, the uncertainty warring with her anger for control of her emotions. She left the young blonde standing in the shade of the tree, green eyes watching her every move. Erin's voice stopped her steps before she'd gotten very far.

"You know it happens, Carol. And you do nothing to stop it. And whether you choose to believe it or not, you're a good ole boy because you turn a blind eye," Erin called. But her voice was gentle and pleading, the anger having drained away. She wanted Carol to see the whole picture, to see the role she played in it.

"I don't take action, huh? Then I guess that was just a guardian angel that issued that cop a death threat if he struck you again. Maybe it was the tooth fairy that drove you to the hospital, Erin. Don't tell me I turn a blind eye. If I did he would have beaten you to death and we both know it."

Rainbow sensed the tension between the women and wisely stayed down in the sunny spot he had picked in the grass moments before. The animal watched and whimpered as Carol slowly walked back to Erin.

"Granted - but tell me why he still has a badge and he's out walking the streets when anyone else would be in lock up?"

"That's just the way it is, Erin."

"And that's just what I'm trying to change, Carol."

"Look, my father was cop."

"I knew it!" Erin laughed.

Carol ignored her and continued. "He gave me a sense of justice and responsibility to look after those that couldn't care for themselves. I joined the force to get out of a dead end job but I realized soon after that I could make a difference. I don't want to revamp the police department. I want to help people. I'm doing it my way; just like you're doing it yours." Her voice was soft, urging the smaller woman to understand. She'd wanted so badly to make a difference, to provide people like Erin a fair and honest counterpart on the force. She wanted Erin to see her in that light and not as an uncaring member of the establishment.

They continued the stand off for a few beats. Finally, Erin sighed along with Rainbow who now had his chin on his paws, eyes flashing between his two friends.

"Don't be a hypocrite yourself, Carol. Don't tell me to work within the establishment to change the world."

Carol broke eye contact first and looked to the dog, trying to lighten the mood.

"I think we've caused Rainbow emotional distress."

Erin grinned at the dog before looking up to Carol.

"I'm sorry," she apologized sincerely, reaching a hand out and laying it on Carol's muscular arm. "I didn't want to fight. That wasn't the intention of my invitation."

Since Erin had opened the door, Carol walked on through it. "And just why did you invite me?" This was the answer she really wanted. Was Erin as interested in her as she was in the hippie?

"I . . . uh . . . I just thought . . . I thought maybe there was more to you than most folks see," Erin stuttered uncertainly, having been put on the spot. *That was NOT groovy*, Erin thought silently, kicking herself in the butt. *So much for being suave and seductive.* She didn't add anything more for fear of shoving her foot farther into her mouth.

Carol couldn't tell what to make of Erin's sudden lack of grace. She was very eloquent, well spoken; she appeared to always have a solid handle on things. The innocent question left the beatnik nearly tongue-tied. Carol smiled as she assumed the other woman's behavior answered her biggest question.

"Well, whatever the reason," Carol said trying to lighten the girl's discomfort, "I'm glad you did."

Erin knew this was the only opening she would get. She had to take it now.

"Would you like to do it again sometime? Minus the arguing . . . well, maybe not as much arguing. I don't like to make promises I can't keep." She grinned faintly, her stomach tied in knots waiting for a response.

Carol saw that angelic grin and agreed immediately. "Sounds great . . . but I don't want to take up too much of your time."

"No!" Erin regretted her desperate reaction instantly. "I mean . . . It wouldn't be a bother at all. I could use some time out of the house anyway. That's if you're interested. I mean you are interested, aren't you?" She stuttered stupidly and then decided that closing her mouth would be the best approach.

Carol swallowed hard. Was she interested? She was but at this point she couldn't tell just how much. Or more to the point, she wasn't ready to admit to herself just how much. Outwardly, she grinned slightly and took a step closer, letting her body language imply as much as the young blonde was willing to read into it.

"How about this Friday?" the officer asked casually.

"Wouldn't your boyfriend like to see you?" Erin commended herself silently for slipping the question in.

"I don't have a boyfriend," Carol replied. "Or a girlfriend for that matter," she added with a chuckle. Carol disguised it as a joke, wrapping it in laughter, so as not to offend Erin. "But I understand if you do. We could set something up for another-."

"I don't have anybody." Erin said willingly, her brain still computing the answer and comment that Carol just made. *Was it off-handed or is she trying to tell me there's a chance?*

"I know you're not big into movies," Carol said, pulling Erin from her thoughts, "but maybe there's something playing you might like to see."

Erin grinned and nodded in agreement. "Sounds good. That's if you haven't arrested me again, of course," she added, bumping shoulders with Carol as they walked along.

"Of course," Carol answered in jest.

With a whistle to Rainbow, they were on their way.

Erin woke up at 4:30 AM to make her commute into the city. That hour being far too early for her to think logically, she picked out her blouse and skirt the night before. All she had to do was stumble into the bath and let the water soak her body. Once she was alert she dressed, put some make up in place and snagged Minos' van keys. The older woman wished her luck, making sure to be up to see Erin off to her first 'official' job interview.

Her resume went out to a variety of newspapers and magazines in the surrounding area, hoping her journalism degree would get her an interview. She figured she'd never hear from the New York Times but that didn't stop her from giving them a shot anyway. Being realistic, she put her name in with several other publications that were hiring. Some were named companies and some were blind ads just requesting a journalist.

As the weeks went by and not so much as a nibble came her way Erin's hope began to falter. Then one afternoon she came home from class to a message from Minos. Seems a newer magazine in New York, geared toward women and looking for 'creative, liberal writers' had tried to reach her. Erin called them back immediately.

So now she sat in one of the green fabric covered chairs in their small gray office. Her fingers played nervously with the end of her portfolio that was filled with news clips and some of her artwork. She wanted to put her best foot forward but she wondered, briefly, if she was selling out. Was she forsaking her grass roots ideology to join the status quo? No, she decided. She wouldn't go to work for just anyone. She wanted to work somewhere where she felt she made a difference. And after speaking to this business 'establishment' on the phone, she felt confident it was worth the trip to speak to them in person.

She expected to get there about an hour early and figured she'd grab a bite to eat before she headed to the interview. After getting lost, stuck in traffic and searching for a parking space, she had fifteen minutes to spare. So the nervous butterflies in her stomach and the lack of food created an annoying grumbling sound in her abdomen. She prayed the sound would subside at least for the interview. Sure, she was a starving artist but this was ridiculous.

She looked around the room and saw a host of different women there. Two looked a few years older than her and the other that sat waiting looked considerably older – older than Minos actually. Doubt began to cloud her mind. Judging by the woman's age, Erin was sure she had much more experience than she had. But she took a deep breath to keep her confidence in force while giving herself a private mental pep talk.

"Erin O'Fallon?"

Erin rose and walked to the secretary. "Ms. Rodgers will see you now. Right through those doors," the woman pointed.

"Thank you," Erin nodded politely. Once again she took a deep breath and let it out slowly. With a quick shake of her head she squared her shoulders and put a grin on her face. Confidently, she strolled inside.

One Belief Away

"Hey Johnson! Get in here! I thought you were gonna miss the kickoff."

Randell helped Carol take off her coat as she walked inside his house. Gathered for the Thanksgiving celebration were the families of both Randell and his wife, Phyllis. Everyone issued their hi's and hello's and Carol waved to the group. Randell's brother, Barry, was by the television with his wife, Molly. Seated at the dining room table were Lois and Jane, Phyllis' mother and sister. Since she hadn't seen Phyllis she could only assume the woman was slaving away in the kitchen.

Watching the Lions game at Randell's had become a tradition of sorts. Besides, Carol had to admit she loved Phyllis' cranberry sauce and looked forward to it almost as much as the 'male bonding'.

Randell's sons, Tim and Tom, moved down the sofa and patted a seat for her. They were home from college for the weekend. In fact, Carol was only 5 years their senior and they called her their adopted sister.

"So what're your thoughts, Tim?" Carol asked as she pointed to the television.

"Detroit by at least 7."

"Forget it!" Tom argued. "New York by 10!"

"Wanna put your money where your mouth is?"

Carol started to chuckle at the arguing siblings when Randell took a seat in the chair next to her.

"You want a beer Johnson?"

"Sure."

Randell turned his head toward the kitchen and shouted. "Hey Phyllis! Bring Carol a beer!"

Carol smacked Randell on the knee. "Some days you're worse than Archie Bunker," she said shaking her head. "At least you didn't call her dingbat," she chuckled.

"What?" he asked totally confused.

"I'm an adult and I won't have your wife wait on me. I'll go get it myself," Carol started to make her way to the kitchen.

"She doesn't mind," Randell called out.

"Uh huh, says you. She might tell a different story. Right, Jane?" Carol stopped at the dining room table to address Phyllis' sister.

"Amen to that," she answered.

Carol just grinned and turned back to Randell. "Don't worry. I'll be back before the coin toss."

49

As Carol pushed the swinging door open she heard Randell mutter something about 'damn women's libber crap' and her grin widened.

Just as Carol had assumed, Phyllis was in the kitchen basting the bird for the feast. Her partner's wife looked back to see who entered and upon finding Carol she smiled widely.

Phyllis was quite a beautiful woman with medium length brown hair and eyes to match. The years had been kind to her and she didn't look like a woman who had two sons in college. Some days Carol wondered how Randell ever managed to snag her. But the more time she spent around the pair she realized – they fit. Sure, they argued and debated but they also smiled and laughed a lot, too.

"He thought about calling you to see if you were alright," she waggled her finger while holding her grin in place.

"I'm not that late, am I?"

"Well, the big guy likes you a lot more than he lets on. And you're usually here to see Santa Claus arrive at Macy's."

"Sorry. I was up late last night reading. I didn't mean to worry him."

"That's okay. A little worry is good for him now and then. And for the record I would have brought you the beer. Not his but yours," she winked conspiratorially.

Carol laughed as she reached inside the refrigerator. She pulled out a brew and popped the cap on the opener mounted above the trashcan. "Did you need any help?" she said as she turned to face Phyllis.

"You know, you're the first person to ask me that all day. You're the only person to ask me that every year, actually."

"Yes and despite the fact you shoo me away every year I'll continue to ask," Carol said, raising her bottle in a toast before taking a drink.

"I just made some snacks for the game. Could you take that out?"

"Sure. Anything else?"

Phyllis handed Carol the tray filled with some meats, cheeses and crackers. She gave a gentle smile and caressed Carol's cheek. "You're a sweetheart. But no, I've got it under control."

"You're shooing me again, aren't you?" Carol teased.

"Yes, I am," Phyllis answered in a playful yet authoritative voice.

One Belief Away

Carol smiled and raised the platter in her hand. "Yell if you need any more help." With that Carol pushed her way back through the door. As soon as the tray hit the coffee table, the group dug in.

By evening's end, everyone was stuffed to the esophagus and lounging around watching 'It's a Wonderful Life' cursing themselves for eating so much. Tim was $10 richer since the Lions beat the Jets 37-20, much to Tom's dismay. And Phyllis paused long enough to eat before heading back into the kitchen to clean up. Not wanting to intrude on the family any longer Carol made her way to the kitchen.

"Are you sure you don't want any help?" she asked again.

"Get out of here, would you?"

"Okay, I'm taking off. Thanks again, Phyllis, for everything."

"You're quite welcome. Take care, hon."

"You too," Carol said before heading back to the living room.

Randell watched her walking to the front door.

"You leaving?"

"Yeah, I'm gonna take off. It was nice seeing you all again," she waved to the group. Randell got up and helped her with her coat. He knew she was quite competent to dress herself but in his eyes there were still some gentlemanly things that men should do.

"Next year, Carol, I say we get in on the bidding action and go with Tim's advice," Barry called over.

That comment earned him a throw pillow flung in his direction courtesy of Tom.

Carol chuckled. "Take care everybody," she said as she made her way out. Randell followed, closing the door behind him.

"Thanks for inviting me, Randell," Carol said as they walked down the steps toward her Mustang.

"No thanks needed, Johnson – turkey, football and Carol . . . It's part of the Thanksgiving Day tradition," he smiled.

"Well, I appreciate you taking in the orphan," she smiled.

"You always got a home here. Remember that."

Carol slapped him on the chest. "Get back in the house before you make me cry and all that women's libber crap goes flying out the window."

"You heard that, huh?" he grinned guiltily.

Carol just nodded. "You better get inside. It's cold out here without a jacket."

"Yes ma'am," he saluted and started back to the house. "Hey, you're coming for Christmas, right?"

"Yeah, I'll stop by."
"Take care going home."
"Will do."

Carol watched as Randell went back inside. From the window she could see Phyllis bring him another beer. He must have opened his big mouth because she gave him a playful swat behind the head, which only made his grin larger. She wondered if she'd ever have that – a family of her own. She was grateful that she'd been included in Randell's life yet it wasn't the same. Instead of dwelling on it she unlocked her door and climbed inside her car. As she started it up the Rolling Stones were playing 'You Can't Always Get What You Want'. She grinned as she pulled onto the road.

"Truer words were never spoken, Mick," she said out loud with a grin.

Chapter 7

What had started as a bad morning only promised to get worse. Carol had been late getting up since she forgot to wind her alarm clock the night before. So she felt half-ready when she walked in the middle of roll call, her hair still wet and pulled tightly into a thick braid. She smoothed her uniform self-consciously as she sat next to Randell in her appointed seat. He cast her a sideways glance that was a mixture of amusement and consternation. Carol ignored him and the other glances she received.

Thankfully, Randell held his tongue when they hit the road in their patrol car. Carol prepared for a verbal berating about looking bad in front of the men but she was rewarded with no such discussion. She was grateful her partner let it slide.

It was a slow morning as they drove their beat with little interference and no radio calls. Towards lunchtime they agreed to stop for some donuts. Though the pastry was Randell's delicacy and not Carol's, she felt justified in giving in since he'd spared her a tongue lashing for her tardiness. They stood in line, not speaking while they watched the patrons in front of them. Nat King Cole was singing 'The Christmas Song' on the portable radio behind the counter. Carol wasn't paying too much attention to her surroundings, opting to listen to the velvet crooner instead. That was until a young black man standing at the counter started raising his voice at Eddie, the shop's regular cashier.

"You can't charge me more for my donut than ya did for his," the college student said, shaking his head.

"Then you can't have a donut, boy. Move along, I have other customers." Eddie was not impressed by the young man's display and quickly moved his attention to the next person in line.

"Don't blow me off, man! I'm a paying customer!" He was outraged and stepped forward.

Carol grew uneasy, watching the crowd as their attention was riveted to the display. Eddie shook his head, a smug grin on his face. "I don't have time for your nigger garbage. Move along."

Carol cringed and evaluated the situation. It was bound to get out of hand rather quickly. She checked out the rest of the patrons, tried to determine everyone's position and what kind of role they may play. She needed to get the kid out of here and calmed down. Later she'd come back and read Eddie the riot act. The asshole's narrow-minded view needed a good shaking up.

The one part of the equation she'd not seriously considered in her layout of the small shop was her partner. Though often a smart-ass, Randell was a professional and she'd assumed his mind was following the same track hers was since their training had been the same. She was mistaken.

Randell swaggered forward and rested a hand on the butt of his weapon. "You heard him, move along," Randell told him.

"No sir!" the kid shouted, dancing from foot to foot. He was either high or nervous or a little bit of both as he watched his new adversary with dark eyes. "Just cause you gotta badge it doesn't make you special. I deserve to be treated fairly." Angrily, he shoved his hands into the pocket of his ratty, red hooded sweatshirt. Carol recognized it for the frustration it was; Randell saw something else.

"Knock it off, kid," the male officer growled, his voice low and threatening, his hand flexing on the handle of his service revolver though it was still holstered.

"Calm down, Randell," Carol stepped forward, touched her angry partner's tense shoulder, "He's just a kid. He wants a doughnut for God's sake. I'll buy him his doughnut." She turned to Eddie. "How much?"

"You ain't buying a doughnut for that nigger," Eddie shook his head, his lip curled in a smirk.

"Knock off the nigger remarks, Eddie," Carol said, her voice low and dangerous, her blue eyes glinting like ice. "I want a goddamned doughnut for the kid. My money's just as good as his money . . . same as your money."

"Carol, get a grip," her partner scoffed. "Kid doesn't need a doughnut."

The kid in question shook his head in exasperation and started backing up, hands fidgeting in his pocket still. "Forget it, lady. I don't want your damn charity."

Carol sighed, defeated. She was disappointed that the young man had misinterpreted her actions. "Look, I agree with you," Carol said facing him.

"Johnson-." Randell began.

"Quiet Randell!" Carol barked before turning back to the nervous man. "What's your name?"

He looked reluctant to tell her but Carol nodded in anticipation. She really wanted to know who he was. "Dan. Dan Washington," he answered, still a bit unsure of Carol's intent.

"Look, Dan. I didn't mean to insult you, okay? I'm just trying to help. But you gotta help me, agreed?"

Dan considered her words and kept shifting his eyes back to Randell who still had his hand on his gun. Carol could read that Randell was making him more nervous.

"First off," Carol began, "I need you to take your hands out of your pockets slowly. You've got my partner a little edgy so if you relax and show him your hands then I promise that he'll relax, too. Deal?"

Dan slowly did as Carol asked, showing his hands to them. Randell kept his part of the bargain by letting his hand leave his revolver, dropping it to the side. Carol could see the beads of sweat on the young man's forehead and she had to admit it was getting warm. But the unspoken peace seemed to provide a much needed break in the tension.

"Okay," Carol smiled confidently. "Now that wasn't too bad, was it?"

Dan didn't know how to take the comment but upon seeing Carol's genuine smile he grinned slightly, too.

"Now I didn't steer you wrong, did I?" Dan shook his head. "Good, just remember I'm not gonna start now, okay? Eddie behind the counter has worked here as long as I've been coming in for his coffee. He's a good worker but he can be a narrow-minded bigot and far from perfect," the insult wasn't lost on Eddie and he harrumphed from behind the counter. "He actually made a mistake with the last gentleman's order. He should have charged him 15 cents instead of 10. When you came and ordered the same thing, he was charging you the correct price, Dan. I'm not lying to you, okay?"

Dan nodded again. Carol gave a brief sigh of relief. Perhaps this will work out.

"Let's see, you wanted the cherry filled, right?" Carol asked. Dan nodded once more. "It's one of Randell's favorites, too, that's why I know the price," she smiled. "I bring 15 cents to work everyday so I can get him his donut fix. Makes my day a lot easier."

Dan's grin got just a tad wider at the confession.

"Now here's what I'm gonna do. Give me your dime," she said holding out her hand.

He watched her for a moment before giving her the money. The silver coin was shaking in his fingertips as he handed it over to her. Carol's heart went out to the kid. He was literally scared for his life and all because of a doughnut. But she knew it went much further than the simple pastry in question. She admired his strength in standing up for what he believed in.

Carol walked over to the counter and handed Eddie a dollar. "Two coffees and two cherry filled, please," Carol said calmly. *And if you don't cooperate I'll jump this counter and rip your eyes out*, she thought silently. Fortunately, Carol didn't have to act on her unspoken thought. Eddie left the counter and quickly returned with her order. Slowly, Carol reached into the bag and walked back to Dan. She pulled out a doughnut with a napkin and handed it to him.

"You paid for the doughnut and I made up the difference," Carol told him. "Next time someone in line needs a few extra pennies promise you'll help them out. It's not charity that way, okay?"

For the first time since the incident began Dan seemed to relax and gave a genuine smile. "Thank you, ma'am," he said politely.

"You're welcome," Carol said, taking a step back to let him pass. Hurriedly, he opened the glass door with the Peace On Earth/Good Will Toward Men sign taped inside it. Carol watched his retreating form. She heard herself make a cynical snort upon reading the words again.

Randell also watched the kid leave and started shaking his head. "We should have ran him in."

"For what?" Carol asked, her anger starting to rise to her cheeks making them a red hue.

"Disturbing the peace," he answered. "That kid-."

"Was denied service and was called a nigger. So if you want to go back and arrest him go right ahead but I'll tell you what; I'll drag Eddie in for vulgar language and trying to incite a riot. How's that?"

"Carol," Randell whined. "It's not the same thing."

"The hell it's not!" Carol said raising her voice. A few patrons turned to watch them and Carol lowered her voice, taking a step closer to Randell. "What makes it different? Dan's black and Eddie's white?"

"That's not what I meant," Randell replied.

Carol ignored his comment and continued, "All the kid wanted was a donut and could've gotten killed over it. Eddie had no right to egg him on the way he did. Neither of them was right but consider this Randell. The way we treat the public has a lot to do with the way the public treats each other. It has to start here."

Randell knew when he could joke with Carol. He also knew when he should just keep his trap shut and agree. This was not the time to point out they weren't the 'morality police' or that Carol could get off her soapbox now.

"All right, Johnson," he nodded. "Can I have my doughnut now?" he said cracking a tiny grin, hoping it would lighten things up. If not, it would make for a very long day.

Carol relaxed and handed him the bag. "You keep eating these things and pretty soon you're gonna look like one," she smiled.

"That's the chance I'll take," he chuckled as they walked out.

"Is . . . Skylon . . . here?" Carol asked casually once Minos opened the front door.

She stressed Erin's hippie name, waiting to see if Minos would have any disputes with her presence this time around. The name didn't help.

Minos didn't take her eyes off Carol as she yelled, "Skylon, your c- . . . friend is here."

Minos had agreed to keep Carol's police identity a secret from the house and she had to catch herself from calling Carol a cop and breaking her promise. Carol could hear Erin's feet racing downstairs and she had to smile at the thought of seeing her new friend. After such a bad day, she'd been looking forward to spending some time with the gregarious activist tonight.

"Thanks, Minos," Erin said arriving at the door, almost winded from her quick journey. Minos stood still, sizing the two of them up. The younger woman realized that Minos wasn't about to give them any privacy so she pushed her way between the doorway and her friend so she could slide onto the porch with Carol. "I'm not sure how late we'll be so don't wait up, okay?" Erin told her.

"I'm not your mother, Skylon," Minos grinned.

"Oh yeah?" Erin responded, returning the teasing smile. "Then why have you stayed up every other time I'm out after dark, huh?"

"All right, all right," Minos confessed. "So I worry about you."

"Well don't worry tonight," Erin said wrapping her arm playfully around Carol's. "I'm quite well protected."

"You better be," Minos said in a warning tone that wasn't lost on the dark cop. Carol grinned sheepishly, still wanting to be friends with Minos if for no other reason than the older woman was obviously important to Erin.

"She will be," Carol said sincerely, nodding her head for emphasis. With a slight tug from Erin, the two left the house and proceeded to walk down the street that was decorated with the twinkling colored lights of the other houses.

"It's a nice night out tonight. Care if we just walk a-ways? Look at some of the light displays?" Erin asked.

"Not at all," Carol answered with a smile, secretly grateful that the younger woman had left their arms hooked. "Any idea about what you want to do later?"

"The local theater is putting on a production of 'Hair.' Of course, it's nothing more than an attempt to commercialize my life but it's got some good music. Did you want to go?" Erin asked.

"Have you seen it before?" Carol questioned, not knowing much about the play except it seemed to popularize Erin's counter-culture.

"Yeah," the blonde answered with a grin. "But I don't mind seeing it again. It will be a great educational experience for you so you know what NOT to expect from the hippie lifestyle."

"Sounds good to me," Carol agreed with a chuckle. She figured she might as well relax. It could distract her from today's events. However, she really didn't want it to spark an argument between the two of them.

A small silence fell until Erin asked, "So what happened in the doughnut shop?"

"You mean the kid today?" Carol asked just for clarification, knowing that was exactly what Erin meant.

One Belief Away

"Yeah – Dan Washington," her companion replied.
"You know about that?" Carol asked with a raised eyebrow.
"What can I say? Small town," Erin smiled.
"Do you know him?"
"Sure, I've seen him at the student union once in a while. Nice guy. Can't imagine him giving anyone a hard time."

Carol shook her head and chuckled grimly. When Carol didn't voice her thoughts Erin dragged them out of her.

"What is it?" the flower child asked.
"I can't believe this town could be THAT small," she answered.
"Well, I am rather 'connected' in these parts," she answered with a mock smugness. "Seriously, what happened?"
"The clerk got testy. The kid got lippy. I really don't know, Erin," Carol answered. "You don't mind if I call you Erin, do you?" she asked. "I mean I've been assuming it's okay but if it makes you uncomfortable..."

Erin considered the options of her name. No one had called her by her actual birth name since high school. She was ready to graduate soon with her political science/journalism degree this spring. For some reason her hippie name just didn't fit when Carol said it. Besides, she liked the sound of her actual name from the other woman's lips.

"Erin is fine," the honey-blonde grinned but she began to digest Carol's words, not sidestep the real issue. "Anyway, mouthing off doesn't seem like Dan's style. I'm not saying that he's an angel or anything since I don't know him that well, but he was always very mild-mannered when I saw him."

Carol shrugged, averted her eyes. "Well he wasn't too mild-mannered this morning. He was downright pissed. The shopkeeper called him a nigger so I really can't blame him for getting upset. Things got pretty tense when Randell reached for his weapon."

"So the ole boys club was in full swing at the coffee shop, eh?"
"No, actually . . . The kid put his hands in his sweatshirt when he started yelling, which was the worst thing he could've done. I could tell he was just nervous and trying to make a stand. Randell thought he might have a weapon. I didn't blame either of them actually. The sad part is it was just a misunderstanding that totally got out of hand."

"Did you set things right then?" Erin asked proudly.

"Yeah . . . I guess I did. I mean I really didn't think about it until now but in the end Dan got his doughnut, Randell didn't open fire and everyone finished the day in one piece."

"Sounds like your partner's a bit of a hot head."

"He thinks it's generational. He and I rarely agree on anything but he's good at what he does," Carol said. "Someone else might have done more than put his hand on his service revolver. With someone else that kid might have been dead as soon as he reached into his jacket. Randell knows his job well."

"So he's a defender of human civil rights? Lobbying for you to join the baseball team?" Erin pressed with a wily grin, trying to ease the pressure though dying to get the entire story out of her somber companion.

"I didn't say that," Carol responded with a very slight smile, hoping that this was a sign Erin was ready to let the topic go. She hadn't sorted it out in her own mind and wasn't prepared to analyze it out loud yet.

"Well you would know him better than I would, right?" Erin asked flippantly.

"Right," Carol nodded, relieved that the radical was willing to drop it after all. She was also a little surprised that Erin had sensed her awkwardness and willingly backed away. Perhaps tonight wouldn't be a night of fighting.

"Here we are," Erin announced, going to the ticket window and propping her elbows on the wooden counter. "Two, please," she told the clerk.

"No, Erin," the officer insisted. "Let me get it."

"Think I can't pay my own way? Is that it?" Erin prodded with a glimmer in those green eyes of which Carol was growing so fond.

"No," Carol argued, drawing her voice out slowly with the explanation. "But I do know I make more than you so it's only right that I pay."

"Carol?"

"Hmm?"

"Take your ticket."

Carol didn't quibble further as they made their way inside. She did however whisper into Erin's ear, "I am going to buy dinner later - no arguments."

The blonde couldn't help but love that protective, forceful nature of Carol's. She nodded silently, taking the other woman's large hand in hers, using the dark as an excuse to guide her. "I know the best seats. Follow me."

"How can you say that?" Erin asked before sticking another french fry in her mouth, chewing quickly. "It was a remarkable play. A landmark in our own time!" she joked.

Carol smiled and shook her head sadly, blue eyes twinkling in the artificial light of the burger joint Erin had chosen. It was far enough away that they'd gone back to the house to retrieve Carol's car and driven here. The cop was pleasantly surprised with the quality of the food and had already told her companion so.

"It was a bunch of people running around on stage . . . naked . . . singing about masturbation," she said in critique.

"You got something against masturbation?" Erin asked, trying her best to look serious. Her resolve fell apart and she found herself grinning with embarrassment from asking such an impulsive question. The flush from her cheeks, however, came more from the standpoint of imagining Carol masturbating than from the assertiveness of her words. "I'm sorry. Really I am," Erin said turning twenty shades of red and studying her plate with infinite concentration.

Carol realized this was the first time they had even come close to discussing sex so she didn't want to just drop it. She wanted to plunge deeper into it and explore her friend's thoughts a little more closely. "In response," Carol said smugly, "I have nothing against masturbation. I think fantasy is healthy. Would you agree?"

Erin wasn't quite sure where this was going but she nodded slowly and cleared her throat, risking a brief glance at Carol's probing eyes. "I . . . would . . . agree," she answered, straining to get the words out.

"So tell me, Erin . . . between you and me, no holds barred, who do you think of?" Carol asked mischievously, warming to the subject readily. She'd never been this invasive before and had she stopped to consider it, the audacity would have startled her.

"What do you mean?" Erin asked slowly, raising her head only slightly. She tried to nonchalantly chew a fry but she nearly gagged on it.

Carol smiled. She was sure the activist was aware of exactly what she meant but if she wanted it spelled out . . .

"You know what I mean. Who do you think about? Is it you in your fantasies? Or do you close your eyes and imagine someone? Or maybe you're a good girl and you don't do that kind of thing, huh?" Carol hadn't noticed how husky her voice had gotten but she did feel the temperature in the room go up considerably.

Erin found herself starting to giggle nervously, not quite sure from where it came. "I think you know well enough by now that I'm not a good girl," she admitted, not looking at Carol but giving up any attempt to finish her food.

"Well then," Carol said before pausing to drink more of her chocolate malt. "Who is it? Lemme guess . . . some big rock star like Roger Daltrey, right?"

Erin listened to the words but her attention was focused on saying what needed to be said. Saying what she has wanted to say for quite some time as she'd been getting to know this woman seated across from her.

"No," she answered when Carol stopped and waited for some sort of response. "I don't think of rock stars. It's usually people that I know."

"Okay, lemme guess again. Bill?" Carol said with a grin, hoping her attitude of levity was taking some of the seriousness away from her inquiry.

"No," Erin said with a small shake of her head, finally looking up to meet Carol's eyes, seeing in them a mixture of gentle humor and sincere affection. That look gave her a little courage.

"Stan?" Carol tried again.

"Nope," Erin shook her head.

"Minos, perhaps?" Carol smiled flatly as she tried to disguise that this was the answer she most wanted to know. Was Erin attracted to women? Was this even possible? The name made Erin look away again.

"You," Erin said just above a whisper. She didn't look at Carol. She couldn't. The embarrassment and the fear of admitting the truth were almost too much. Instead, she watched her fingers as her french fry made lazy trails in the puddle of ketchup on her plate. "I think about you," she said a little more loudly when Carol hadn't responded.

"I heard you the first time," Carol finally acknowledged, trying to shake herself out of the shock caused by her friend's statement. It was ironic, really. That was exactly what she'd been fishing for but she hadn't thought the blonde would come right out and answer her unspoken question. But then again that was part of Erin's style and one of the many facets of the young woman that had her captivated. Besides, she did say no holds barred, didn't she?

"Maybe you should drive me home now," Erin offered. *Great job Erin. Ya had to go a little too far, didn't you?* For all of Carol's brazen teasing, the reality was more than she was ready for. Erin regretted the silence across the table and her own admission, which had ended their blossoming friendship. Erin nervously wiped her fingers in her napkin. It felt like forever but finally Carol answered.

"I think that's a good idea," the officer agreed. She had to think about this and here really wasn't the place to do that. So lost in her own emotions she didn't notice how glum Erin appeared as she stood and waited for the blonde to rise from the table and turn toward the door.

They drove in absolute silence. Erin still hadn't met Carol's eyes. As the car pulled to a stop in front of the house Erin watched Carol put the car in park. As Carol turned the ignition and headlights off, Erin couldn't figure out why on earth Carol was stopping. She watched as Carol's hand tentatively reached out, the back of Carol's fingertips stroking her cheek.

"What are you doing?" Erin asked, finally looking over at the object of her fantasies.

"This," Carol whispered as she leaned over and kissed Erin gently on the cheek. It was soft and lingering. Reflexively, Erin closed her eyes, soaking up the tenderness. "Would you tell me your fantasies some time?" the cop asked cautiously. "I'll share mine if you'll share yours."

Erin didn't know how to respond so she nodded mutely, overwhelmed by the move that Carol had just made and how closely it matched her own desires. Carol started to laugh softly, feeling giddy with her admission and Erin's warmth so close to her side.

The younger woman tensed. Had Carol been playing with her feelings? Was she now going to kick her out of the car shouting a few unpleasant names at her in the process? Surely she hadn't misjudged the other woman so completely.

"What is it, Carol?" Erin asked, confused. She wasn't sure if she wanted to hear the answer but she needed it just the same.

Carol paused a moment and saw how nervous Erin had become. The young woman looked like she was on the verge of tears. Carol quickly explained her change in behavior.

"Oh sweetheart, it's not you. Well, in a way it is you, but it's really me," Carol smiled, bringing the back of her fingers up again to stroke Erin's face. That helped the young woman relax somewhat. "I wish I had some way of telling you how you make me feel. I'm not good with words - never have been. There's so much I'd like to be able to say. You make me feel so many things. Things I've never felt until now. I've never been seriously interested in a woman. I mean I've noticed women but I never thought I might have a real relationship . . . one that.... I - I'm rambling so I'll just shut up." The officer shook her head weakly, frustrated at her inability to share her feelings with the one person that needed to hear them.

Erin paused and took a deep breath. "When you wake up do you think of me?" she asked. Carol nodded silently. "Am I the last thought you have before bed?" Another nod. "Do you see things or hear things and wonder what I might think about them?"

"Yes," Carol finally said aloud. "All those things."

"Well, I feel them, too. You're in my thoughts constantly, Carol. It scares me because . . . oh man," Erin paused; she wasn't sure how much to confess and it showed. But Carol gently prodded her to go on with a slight nod of her head.

"Your voice," Erin continued, "it's...it's like a siren's call and those eyes are the bluest blue I've ever seen." Erin paused a moment to choose her words carefully. "You keep me centered by questioning my direction in life and I light up when you're near me. I miss you when you're gone ... and I count the minutes until I can see you again." Erin paused and started to shake her head. "Jesus, I sound like a Karen Carpenter song," she chuckled. "How bad is that?"

Carol smiled too but waited for her to continue. Erin's smile slowly faded as a look of intent washed over her.

"I'm scared, Carol. I'm scared because I've never felt like this before either...Nothing ever seemed this important to me."

"Nothing?" Carol teased, knowing how much the greater good meant to the young woman.

Erin's face held no laughter, only sincerity. "Nothing," she replied honestly and hoped the earnestness showed in her features and in her eyes. "The way I feel about you . . . let's just say it's pretty far out."

It was Carol's turn to feel nervous but she spoke after clearing her throat.

"I know what you mean. It's . . . intense. You're so full of life. I wish I could find some way to capture the way I feel right now, at this moment." She wanted to kiss Erin but she didn't know what to do. Erin didn't recognize the look on Carol's face but it made her grin foolishly, the tenseness of the situation lending to her silliness.

"What?" Carol asked, tilting her head against the headrest of her seat, a lazy smile on her lips.

Erin just shook her head and shrugged, "Nothing really. You just looked perplexed there for a moment."

"Oh that," Carol's smile grew. "I wanted to kiss you but I didn't know how to go about it. I mean should I just kiss you? Do I ask first - very friendly and very politely? I mean, what's the proper etiquette here so I won't offend you?" she finished with a chuckle.

"I wouldn't know," Erin confessed. "You're the first woman I've wanted to kiss. But-"

"Really?" Carol asked, her head shooting up from its resting spot. She'd assumed that Erin had been with other women because of her cavalier attitude. She'd even gone so far as to assume Minos had been one of them.

"Well yeah!" the blonde said in mock defense.

"I'm sorry. I just thought you were . . . experienced," Carol finished for lack of a better word.

"Well, I'm not a virgin," Erin laughed. "But I've never had a woman."

Carol looked a bit concerned as she considered her smaller friend's words. Did she really want to be the 'first' in Erin's life? Could she risk losing her heart to a woman who might decide it was just a 'crazy mistake'?

"I'm sure if we put our heads together, as well as a few other body parts, we can figure things out," Erin offered.

A small rumble of laughter filled the car but quickly died down. Carol gently cupped the back of Erin's head and brought her closer. Both women felt the explosion go through their bodies upon impact of the kiss. It was soft yet searching. Both wanted to know if the depth of the other's desire was real. Once Erin was satisfied that Carol's intentions were true, she moaned. The vibrations it sent through Carol invoked a similar response. When they finally did separate, both women inhaled sharply. Erin soon found Carol's neckline and began planting little nips and kisses along a path up to an enticing earlobe.

"Why don't you stay tonight?" Erin whispered in Carol's ear, licking where her breath had warmed. She thrilled at the shudder than ran through her companion's body.

Carol's desire to take the young woman was unbearable. But gently she grasped Erin's shoulders and disengaged her from her activities. It was just too soon. Carol still held the younger woman in place as she rested her forehead against Erin's.

"I . . . I'd love to, but I . . . I need time, Erin," Carol said sincerely, hoping she didn't hurt the girl's feelings.

"I understand," Erin confessed honestly. "I'm not sure if I'm ready yet, either. I just have a habit of letting my emotions get the better of me."

"That's not a bad trait," Carol replied with a very tender grin. "A few minutes ago it felt pretty wonderful," she chuckled dryly again before growing serious. "Honestly though, I think we both need more time before, well, you know."

"Yeah, I know," Erin grinned. She kissed Carol delicately on the forehead though she had to restrain herself from doing more. "See you again this weekend maybe?" Erin asked hopefully, wishing her voice didn't sound pleading.

"Count on it," Carol answered soundly, nodding. She was glad to hear that Erin wanted this as much as she did.

"I should be here so just drop by if you get the chance," Erin said calmly with a shrug of slim shoulders. *No big deal, right?*

"Hey, Erin." Carol caught her attention. "No more playing it cool and casual. I'll be here this weekend. Tomorrow at six sound good?"

"Sounds great," Erin answered with relief, a gentle grin playing at her lips. She got out and closed the door. She blew a kiss to Carol, which the officer caught, making her smile. Watching the Mustang pull away, Erin almost ran right into Minos.

"I thought I told you not to wait up?" Erin teased and avoided her friend's inquisitive gaze. She knew the look in her own eyes would reveal everything.

"Is that lipstick I see on your collar?" Minos teased back, having no intention of letting the small blonde off the hook so easily.

Erin didn't reply immediately. Instead, she asked simply, "How much did you see?"

"Enough," Minos wore a teasing grin and put her arm around her friend. She closed the door behind them. "So did you decide on the ivory or the floral pattern?"

Chapter 8

The weather was warmer than normal for mid-December. It reminded Carol of another atypical climate day - the day that she and Erin 'met' on the campus steps three months before. Why on earth Randell chose to eat outside after getting their food from a drive-in burger stand was beyond her. If they stayed in the restaurant or the car they would have protection from the elements, no matter how mild. But as always she figured she'd buck up and make the best of it. Besides, the food was fairly decent and reasonably priced. In the sunshine it was rather warm. She couldn't complain too much.

"Can I ask you a question?" Carol asked, her voice breaking up the quiet that had fallen between them.

"Shoot," Randell responded before stuffing his face full of greasy french fries. Carol couldn't believe anyone's mouth was actually that big . . . but then again it WAS Randell. Instead of commenting on the size of Randell's mouth, which she often did but for totally different reasons, she turned her attention back to the question she'd had on her mind all day.

"What do you think makes a relationship last?"

Randell didn't answer immediately. He was still in the process of chewing and trying not to smile at the question. He washed down the fries with a swig of root beer. "Gee Johnson," Randell smirked, wiping his fingers with a napkin. "Did you find yourself a special fella?"

Carol grinned at the irony of the question. "No," she answered. It wasn't a lie. "I'm just curious. Do you think opposites attract?"

"Hell yeah, opposites attract - but that isn't what you asked. You asked what makes a lasting relationship," he replied.

"Well you've been married to Phyllis for what, 20 years? How did you manage that?"

"Pretty amazing, huh? A guy like me actually stickin' with something that long. Or is it more the fact that she's put up with me for that long?" he chuckled.

"I didn't mean it as an insult," Carol remarked, growing a bit agitated. She wanted an answer, not games.

"I know Johnson – hey, lighten up- I'm teasing you here," he said as he tossed his paper napkin at her, trying to lighten her mood. When he got a scowl in response he knew that wasn't going to work. He'd be better off just answering the question. "Let's see, what makes it all work? It's true Phyllis and I are opposites in a lot of ways. She loves sappy romance and comedy movies. I'm more of an action kind of guy myself. She likes to read. I'm lucky if I pick up a newspaper once a week. But when it comes to things that really matter - we always see eye to eye."

"Such as?" Carol prodded.

"You know - life, morals, beliefs- the foundation," he replied. "You can build any kind of house you want, Johnson, but if you don't have a solid foundation it's not gonna last. That's how relationships work. You find the things that matter to both of you and you grow from there. So you can make any kind of house you like but you better be sure it's sturdy when the flood comes . . . And the flood will come at some time. Believe me," he chuckled.

"The philosophical cop," Carol snickered. "I must admit. I'm impressed. Didn't think you had that in ya."

"That did sound pretty impressive, huh?" Randell nodded, quite pleased with himself. He paused a moment taking a drink from his overly frosty mug. "Nah - you wanna know what really makes it work?"

Carol nodded. She did want an answer. Since meeting Erin she began to question everything in her life. She knew she was totally attracted to her – the young woman was a virtual magnet and she found herself unable to break free of thoughts about her throughout the day. As Randell watched the bob of Carol's head he could see something deeper in the woman's eyes. This conversation wasn't just idle chitchat even if Carol said she hadn't found Mr. Right.

One Belief Away

"My wife believes in being honest," Randell began. "She thinks it's better to say what's on your mind than to sacrifice your soul in silence. She thinks laughter is the best medicine and she opens up her heart to anyone who needs help."

"That's it? It's that simple?" she asked.

Randell chuckled. "It's far from simple, Johnson. But we've built the same foundation-together, with time and patience. We're not one of those couples who make small talk. We talk about the important stuff. She's my lover, not my roommate."

"Okay," Carol joked. "That's a little more information than I need."

Randell smiled but continued. "Point is we deal with those little things that we both do that drive each other insane, like leaving wet bath towels on the floor. We communicate. We speak the same language. We may not always agree – I mean I still can't see why putting my towel on the bathroom floor is a crime . . . But that's what makes it work."

"So even though you go about things differently - you can still build a lasting relationship as long as the 'foundation' is strong?" *Please say yes,* Carol thought silently.

"Absolutely. My wife and I love our kids, our country, our God. We think helping people is what makes the world go round - but she still can't drag me to a Woody Allen flick. So yeah, I think it's possible."

Carol beamed on the inside but only gave Randell a slight smile. "Speaking of the kids," she said hoping to change the subject before she got *too* deep into the discussion. "Are the twins back at school?"

"Tim and Tom?" he replied conversationally.

"Are there some I don't know about?" Carol laughed.

Randell chuckled, too. "They're doing fine. Getting good grades. But don't ask how I manage to send both of them to college on my salary," he laughed.

"You're not on the take, are you Randell?" Carol teased.

"No," he answered, taking another drink. "But I'll never go on another vacation until I'm 65 and retired," he smiled. "Even then I might have to scrape some pennies together for gas money...But they're worth it. And I hope when it comes time to take care of me they remember who sent them to college. What comes around goes around," he grinned at her.

Carol stood on the dilapidated porch again less than twenty-four hours later. She stuffed her hands in her sweat jacket and rocked on booted heels, lips pursed, glancing at her surroundings slowly. She'd already knocked twice and checked her watch three times; she was beginning to get a little worried that she'd been confused.

Suddenly the front door swung open a crack and Erin shimmied out, pulling the door closed immediately behind her. This action didn't permit Carol to see anything going on inside though she had heard music and laughter.

"Hey," Erin said softly, running a tender hand down Carol's arm. "It's good to see you." She felt a little awkward, torn between kissing the older woman or moving on with the conversation. This confusion wasn't abated when Carol tilted her head sideways, allowing her long raven hair to drape over one shoulder.

"You okay?" Carol asked curiously, glancing at the closed door and her nervous friend. One whiff of the air that had escaped the house with Erin gave her a clue as to what was going on.

"Yeah. Good," Erin replied with a tight grin, giving up on the welcome kiss. She edged her way around Carol and toward the walk, hoping her tall companion would follow.

"Am I interrupting something in there? Did you want to stay?"

Erin eyed her love interest cautiously, unable to tell from the stoic expression and shadowed features what she was feeling. "No. I want to be with you."

They stared at each other in silence for a long moment until Carol sniffed dramatically.

The blonde dropped green eyes to study her companion's polished boots. "I didn't, Carol. I swear." She looked back up, pleading with this woman to believe her.

"Ever?"

"Tonight," Erin clarified, her heart thumping double time. Though she certainly didn't have a problem with recreational use, her tall companion was an officer of the law. The blue eyes revealed nothing.

"I see."

"Carol? I . . . let's not talk about this, huh? Let's just go somewhere and they can do whatever they're doing."

"Why didn't you join them? You did last time."

Erin closed her eyes, remembering the smoke she'd had just before meeting Carol the night before. But that had been different; she was just going out for a good time. Now she wanted more and Carol had admitted to the same. She didn't want to mess things up by advertising the differences between them. She shrugged, answering Carol after a long silence. "I knew you wouldn't approve . . . I . . . I wanted you to like me." This time when she studied the face before her she thought she might have seen a twinkle in those icy eyes.

Carol decided to let her fidgeting friend off the hook. "Relax, Erin," she whispered gently, allowing a smirk to claim her lips. "I'm just teasing you. I'm not gonna run you guys in. You can do what you want."

Erin studied the features silently before releasing a nervous chuckle. "Don't worry me like that."

Carol laughed out loud this time, her face appearing less angular when making the sound. "Didja really think I'd draw my weapon and bust in there?"

Erin shrugged sheepishly because part of her expected that. "Not used to dating a cop."

"Not used to dating an activist," Carol returned gently, bumping shoulders with the smaller woman's. "We'll have to play it by ear. And for the record Erin...department procedure says if I witness illegal activity I have to make an arrest."

Erin suddenly looked concerned.

"But," she said holding up her finger. "If everyone my age turned over their friends for a party they wouldn't have friends anymore," she grinned. "They're just having fun. They're not hurting anyone. They're not running a chop shop or a bordello so you don't have to worry, okay? Now if Minos becomes a madam," she added, playfully. "then you can be concerned."

"Well I don't think that will happen," Erin chuckled.

"Then put your mind at ease, my dear." The endearment flowed naturally from Carol's lips and the sound of it brought a smile to Erin's face.

The night was already starting to put Carol on edge again. She spent most of the day, discarding outfit after outfit and finally deciding on something daring like jeans and a black T-shirt. She wanted something that didn't *stick out* – something that showed she could be a civilian once in awhile.

Erin wore bell-bottoms and a colorful sweatshirt. Her blonde hair was pulled back into several thin braids, revealing perfectly sculpted ears and freeing her pale features of cumbersome wisps. A blue scarf hung around the neck outside her blue jacket bringing the jade of Erin's eyes out even more than normal. Carol admired her quietly.

"Where are we going?" Erin asked at last. It had taken her several minutes to even come up with the question. It seemed right somehow to just be riding in a car with this woman, enjoying a companionable silence.

"Movie okay? Then I thought maybe some ice cream or a walk in the park if it's not too cold?" The officer sounded hesitant, unsure if her young friend would approve of such a plan.

"Ice cream? It's a week before Christmas."

"I like to eat ice cream in the winter. It doesn't melt all over the place like it does in the summer. I hate being sticky," Carol retorted.

Erin gave a lecherous smile but opted not to make a lewd remark about the sticky comment, although deep inside she wanted to. *Take things slow* she told herself. Instead, she reached over to lay a warm hand on her companion's well-muscled thigh. "You know, I never considered that before but you're absolutely right," she nodded. "Movie and some ice cream it is."

Erin told Carol about the discussion she had earlier in the day in her English Lit class when they learned that the US resumed the full scale bombing of North Vietnam. Chaucer, it seemed, took a back seat to Ho Chi Minh.

Carol added little about her day. The words that Randell gave her about love seemed to come back to her as she drove along listening to the young woman chatter. She loved the sound of Erin's voice and the enthusiasm behind it whenever she discussed something she was passionate about.

Soon they arrived at the theater. Standing outside and reading the information on the marquee proved only how very different these two women were. They decided against 'The Godfather' because of the crime theme. Across the street from the first movie house, the second offered 'Deliverance' which intrigued Carol but Erin had seen it and had no desire to watch it again, especially with Carol, imagining the conversation that might follow. That left 'The Poseidon Adventure'. With quick looks exchanged, both turned on their heels and headed back to the Mustang.

"Ice cream, did you say?" Erin asked gently, humor in her voice.

Carol nodded, pursing lips, which poorly disguised a wry grin.

They sat silently on the warm hood of Carol's car behind the now closed soda shop. It was a pleasant night for Upstate New

York; chilly enough for the jackets they each wore but warm enough to avoid frostbitten fingers.

Erin finished her cone first, and then settled back on elbows to watch the starry night sky. "Orion," she said gently.

Carol had been too busy examining the young blonde to notice the stars. Now she directed her attention upwards and saw the sparkling jewels. "They're beautiful," she acknowledged.

"So are you," Erin whispered, pulling the dark woman's gaze back to her. Carol tossed her cone and stretched out next to her young companion.

"Thank you," she smiled slightly, leaning in close, her face inches from the blonde's perfect ear.

Erin felt the hot breath on her lobe and it sent shivers through her.

Carol's grin turned slightly evil. "You, on the other hand, are gorgeous."

The blonde blushed, tucking her chin into her left shoulder as she turned her face to observe the woman beside her. Carol was smiling easily, her ice blue eyes dancing with merriment and deepening with desire. But Erin pulled back slightly and started to watch the stars again. Carol didn't comment. She knew the young woman wanted to say something so she gave her the space but didn't look away.

"Tonight makes me wonder," Erin finally muttered in a small voice.

"About?"

"Us. I mean . . . will we ever see eye to eye? We can't even agree on a movie."

"There's more to life than movies. And I think what you said at the hospital was correct. I think we are similar in many ways."

"Who'd have thought that a radical and a cop could be so . . . " Erin let the sentence hang, not quite sure what to use.

"Connected?"

That fits, the radical considered with a growing grin. "Yeah. Connected . . . You saved my life, after all."

"I guess we do see eye to eye. And there is a Chinese proverb that says once you save someone's life-."

"You're responsible for them forever."

"You've heard of it?"

"Yeah - philosophy class. But I gotta ask. How did you know it? That's not something they teach at the police academy. Last I heard they never taught Nietzsche either."

"Promise you won't laugh."

Endeared by Carol's look of vulnerability, Erin nodded. "Not even a giggle," she promised crossing her heart with her long, slender finger.

Carol gave a deep sigh before speaking. "My dad couldn't afford to send me to college. I was a good student but I lost the shot at a scholarship. So while I was training at the academy and working as a rookie I'd read textbooks. I was never gonna have the time to sit in a class so I just got the books . . . But I had a problem."

"What?" Erin asked, getting involved in the story.

"I had all this knowledge and all these names but I didn't know how to pronounce any of them," she chuckled. "So after I read the books I went up to the campus and found a professor. If I used my knowledge I didn't sound like an idiot. Pretty crazy, huh?"

"Sounds rather inspiring actually. Out of curiosity, who was the teacher?"

"Dr. Orlando," Carol answered. "You know him?"

Erin grinned. "I have him this semester actually."

"Well, if I had questions after I finished a book, he'd help clear things up. He didn't have to do it but the man loves to teach and make a difference. So even though I couldn't pay for classes he'd give me an hour or so of his free time to make my life better. I really admire him."

"He is one of the best ones out there. You picked a good one," Erin complimented.

"I know. I'm a cop. It's my job to investigate now and then." A small silence passed between them. "So do you think that's silly? I go to school but I don't . . . go to school?" Carol laughed nervously as she finished the statement.

"All the more reason I can't see why you continue to be a cop. You have so much potential."

"Ah yes, but so little time and money. Girl's gotta do what she can to survive and be able to sleep sound at night."

"I must confess," Erin said before licking her lips at the idea of having Carol. "I'd love to be able to watch you sleep."

It took only a moment of silence to lead to the inevitable. They met somewhere in the middle, tasting soft lips with velvet tongues, exploring, teasing, wanting more.

Slowly Carol moved closer, reaching her arms under Erin's raised back and lowering her gently to the hood, which buckled slightly under the pressure. The change in position allowed Carol to kiss the young woman more deeply, one large hand tangled in blonde braids, the other between the girl's lower back and the steel. Carol's long hair draped over both of their faces, closing the world down to several inches and hot breath.

Erin moaned, feeling her body react. Her hands wandered over broad denim clad shoulders and a muscular back as she sought more from the woman above her, pressing her tongue deeper, involving teeth and lips. Carol withdrew first, breathing hard. Erin chased her still, raising up to reclaim those lips.

"Easy," Carol whispered her voice dark and husky, her desire clearly evident.

"Oh God," Erin moaned, still searching. Her small hands applied pressure at the back of Carol's head, tangling in raven tresses, trying to bring her target closer.

"I know," Carol chuckled softly. She stroked the flushed cheek in front of her and waited for those sparkling green eyes to blink open.

The blonde's brow wrinkled. "Then why stop?"

"Not here."

"No one can see us back here," Erin grinned rakishly, sliding her hand down to cup the dark woman's jean clad cheek.

"I can't Erin," Carol added. She shook her head slowly, completely uncomfortable with it.

Erin moved away, giving Carol space. Besides, Carol did have a point. As liberal as the campus town was she couldn't say for certain it was that liberal. And being beaten to a bloody pulp by a group of bigots was not her idea of a fun night out.

"It's okay, really. I understand Carol and I won't push. But I must admit you're a great kisser."

Carol chuckled deeply. "Never in a million years did I think I'd be lucky enough to hear another woman tell me that."

"Yeah. It's pretty amazing where life can take you if you free your mind."

Carol sat for a moment admiring Erin. She wanted to share so much of herself with the beautiful woman now splashed in moonlight. A thought occurred to her. "Well right now I'd like to take you back home. To my place."

Erin was obviously confused by the offer. "I thought you wanted to take things slowly."

"And I do. It would just be nice to show you my place. I've seen yours," Carol paused as she watched Erin deciding what to do. "You're not 'promising anything' by coming with me."

"I wouldn't mind."

"Seeing my place?"

"Promising."

Carol felt herself grin. "One step at a time, remember?"

"To your home?" Erin still seemed surprised that Carol wanted to let her inside her inner circle.

"Don't you think I have one?" Carol teased, brushing at the blonde's lips with one of her own thin braids.

Erin laughed softly. "Sorry . . . no. I just didn't . . . "

"Didn't what?" Carol thought for a moment that perhaps she offended Erin in someway.

"I didn't think you would want to take me there," she admitted sheepishly. "Really," she added softly.

"Why not?" Carol stood bringing the shorter woman up with her. "Maybe I'm sending mixed signals here, but I'm pretty serious about you."

"Not mixed signals, no," Erin grinned wryly. "I just wasn't sure you wanted . . . well . . . more than this," she blushed. "Do you?"

Sex just for the sake of release hadn't really crossed Carol's mind. She wanted a lot more from this vivacious person before her. She wanted to know Erin, to understand her, to find out what was on her mind and in her heart. It dawned on Carol that Erin might only want a roll in the hay. The young hippie lived in a world where sex was exchanged freely, where one's body was an expression of life. Maybe this was all the blonde had intended and Carol fumbled with an answer, "I . . . I think so. I mean . . . I know so. I guess I never asked what you really wanted. I just assumed-"

Liquid green eyes peered at Carol as Erin placed a finger over her lips stopping her. "Not just one night, not just sex. I want more."

Carol felt herself give a sigh of relief at the answer she wanted.

"Good, then let's take things slowly," Carol responded, dropping her lips back down for another warm kiss. "We've got plenty of time to get closer," she repeated, her lips brushing seductively against the blonde's. "But I would like to take you to my place; show you a piece of my world." Carol's lips found Erin's if only for a brief moment.

Her answer was given when Erin pulled back from the kiss only to hold Carol more tightly. Her embrace was steady and sure, as was the whispered agreement when it reached Carol's ear, traveling right to her heart. "To your place then."

Chapter 9

The blonde remained silent for the trip, so involved in her thoughts of what they might do once reaching their destination that she wasn't sure how long the vehicle was stopped before she noticed.

"This it?" she asked, peering across the darkened driver's seat.

"Mmm hmm," Carol agreed softly, nodding.

It wasn't what Erin had been expecting. It was a quaint cottage-like home with a white picket fence and intricate latticework adorning the shuttered windows. Even in the pale moonlight Erin could tell it was well kept, the lawn neatly manicured. Although it was dark she could see a flowerbed along the front. Carol just didn't strike Erin as the gardening type.

"C'mon," Carol said at last, breaking the silence. "You get the nickel tour."

Erin felt oddly out of place as she entered the neat home and stood in the entryway, waiting for Carol to close and lock the door behind them. Sensing the other woman's distress, the officer leaned forward and kissed Erin's lips gently. "S'okay," she assured her, reaching for her hand and squeezing it.

"We're so different," Erin whispered, as if her normal speaking voice might break something. This was nothing like her busy old house with people crawling out of the woodwork and someone always up and about. Her home was filled with laughter and music; it smelled of pot and incense, not wood polish and bleach.

She felt horribly out of her element here, as if she wasn't upper class enough to stand on this hardwood floor and be encased in these shining white walls. She tugged at her sweatshirt as Carol walked further into the living room and plugged in her Christmas tree.

Carol nodded, smiling encouragingly, thinking back to her conversation with Randell.

"Doesn't matter," she said confidently. "We're alike where it counts."

She turned on the hall light and guided Erin with her. She showed her everything, turning on all the lights as they moved deeper into the small square home. "Kitchen, dining room, living room. Those stairs go down to the basement. That's where the television is. And there's a bathroom down there. Down this hallway," she tugged the small form behind her, "is my dad's office" she pushed the door open to reveal walls lined with bookshelves and a large roll top desk.

Erin froze and started to back pedal. "Your dad? I shouldn't be here. How will you explain-."

"Shhh," Carol wrinkled her brow slightly. Whatever false bravado this young woman had been parading around with had all but disappeared when she was removed from her own environment. "No one's here, Erin. It's just you and me. My father's gone."

"Gone?"

"He died about five years ago. My mother died not long after I was born."

"I'm sorry," Erin dropped her eyes. "You must miss him."

"I do." Carol smiled gently. "I keep this room as he left it. Partly because I still want to feel him around here. Another part is because I haven't had time...Are you close to your parents?"

The sudden question startled Erin. She smiled self-deprecatingly and shook her head. "Nah. I don't need them."

"Where are they?"

"Probably where they were when I left."

"Did they kick you out, Erin?" she asked gently, studying her smaller companion's profile in the poorly lit hallway.

She shrugged one thin shoulder. "It was by mutual agreement. There's not much to tell. Minos took me in and helped me finish high school and apply to college."

"I'm glad," Carol said softly, brushing soft lips against softer blonde hair. "C'mon. Tour's almost over."

One Belief Away

She led her to the back of the hallway, showing her another bathroom and the unused bedroom of her father. Erin stepped through the open door without prompting and grinned suddenly. It was as if the atmosphere changed in this room, it felt warm and safe.

There was a double bed covered in a beautiful hand-stitched quilt whose bright colors matched the blues twisting through the fabric of the curtains. There was a well-used desk in a corner, covered with loose papers and writing utensils. A bookshelf proudly displayed a myriad of reading selections along with several Police Academy awards. The long low dresser was covered with framed pictures of a dark man and a little girl. Erin stepped forward and examined them more closely.

"He loved you very much," she said softly, fingering a large photograph of the man lifting an obviously squealing girl above his head. Carol was all pigtails and smiles.

The older woman simply nodded.

"How did he die?"

"Killed in the line of duty," Carol answered, her response automatic as if she'd said it a hundred times before. "A riot downtown. He was trying to help a young black couple and their baby make it to safety. He was off duty and got mistaken for a looter. Another officer shot him."

"I'm sorry, Carol."

Carol nodded silently. "You know that couple came to the funeral and despite all the stares they got they sat through the entire service. After it was over they came to me and told me how my father gave them something they could never repay – their lives. A lot of officers overlooked them that day. But my dad stopped to help. So I get offended if someone says I don't care about all the people I protect." Erin grinned warmly in response. "I didn't mean to get up on the soap box, as Randell calls it," Carol added with a smile.

"Why not?" Erin asked. "You look good from down here," she complimented.

"Well thank you . . . but I apologize anyway."

"He was a brave man, Carol," the blonde whispered gently, looking at the picture. "He believed in a greater purpose."

Carol grinned and laughed. "Yeah . . . he did. I'm sure he would have liked you." A small silence passed between them as Carol adjusted the picture. "So what about your parents? Did you get your beliefs from them?"

"I got my ideals because of them – there's a bit of a difference," Erin replied.

"Do you speak to them?"

"My attitude is fuck 'em," she said quickly and with great confidence. "So where's the rest of the house?"

Erin walked out of the room and Carol knew she hit upon a sore topic. She decided to let it drop as she followed Erin out into the living room and to the kitchen in silence. Erin took it all in, absorbing it all. Carol admired the way even the smallest detail didn't escape Erin's senses. But even in her admiration Carol wondered what had happened to the young woman in her past.

The officer walked over to the sink. "How 'bout some coffee?"

"Sounds good," Erin grinned.

The table in the well-lit kitchen was green tile banded around the edge with ribbed metal. Erin ran her fingers idly along the cool raised surface, shifting to get more comfortable in the matching green vinyl chair. There was a more formal wooden table in the next room but it seemed cozier here in the gentle colors of the kitchen, listening to the coffee percolate.

Carol hadn't said a word since pulling out the chair for Erin. She was lost in thought over how to get her to open up.

"Coffee smells good," Erin spoke softly, trying to break the tension her aloofness inadvertently caused. She could feel the awkwardness and uncertainty in Carol from across the room. They'd argued before about Carol's profession, and though Erin didn't agree in any way, shape, or form with the establishment that had sucked up her friend, she knew this silence was much more personal. Carol seemed worried, confused. Erin prided herself in her ability to be a friend to this woman who was her absolute opposite. Maybe if she changed the topic entirely it would help.

"Did you decorate the house?" Erin tried another conversation starter, letting green eyes wander across the wallpaper border and eggshell paint.

"No," Carol said, turning her back again under the ruse of searching for something in the cupboards. "My mom did. My dad kept the place up as she'd designed it: the picket fence, the shutters, the wallpapers."

Erin nodded, then vocalized since her companion was still facing away. "It's nice."

Carol shrugged. "It's all I know her by . . . her decorating tastes. Isn't that funny?"

"No," Erin disagreed, finding it more sad than funny, but knowing the dark woman would bristle at her sympathy. "You can tell a lot from a person by the way they dress or how they surround themselves."

"Yeah?" Carol poured the mugs and sat in the chair opposite her friend.

"Sure."

"What can you tell about me?"

"You wear a uniform," Erin grinned recklessly. "I sense some sort of authority about you."

Though she tried not to, Carol grinned as well. "No. This me," she indicated herself with a wave of one large hand.

"Ah. You're a strong person who thinks independently. You don't love often, but when you do, you do it deeply and remember it always," Erin whispered, reaching a hand out to squeeze the other woman's muscular forearm. "You're lonely sometimes. There are moments that you feel you don't fit in at the station or here. This place is more your parents and very little you, but you feel like it would betray their memories to change it. However, there's something comfortable about it. You're not into change and this suits you just fine."

Carol's sapphire eyes widened with surprise. "Wow," she stammered. "You're pretty good at that."

Erin smirked, shrugged a slim shoulder. "What can I say? I'm gifted."

"And humble," Carol teased.

"Artists rarely are."

Carol smiled and nodded, dropping her gaze to the slender pale fingers contrasting against her tanned arm. "I'd love to see your work."

"I can arrange that," Erin said softly, withdrawing her hand to wrap it firmly around her mug. She took a sip, letting the biting warmth course easily down her throat. It felt right somehow, to be here with this woman, sharing their souls.

"So what's your story? If I was gifted, what would I see in you?" Carol asked at last, letting the silence string between them for several long seconds. It was a bold question, really. People didn't like to evaluate themselves, it was hard enough to hear what others saw in you, let alone admit your weaknesses yourself. She thought Erin might decline. She should have known better.

"I'll fight to death for what I perceive as another's rights but I won't pick up the phone and call my mother," she shrugged sheepishly, her voice low and rich while unraveling the tale. "I believe in what I stand for . . . but I don't quite fit in, either, not in that big loud house with the peeling paint and the crumbling people, half of whom don't even know or care about the cause they fight for . . . as long as they get to fight. I like a lot, love very little. And when I don't like where my feet are, I move them," She finished her assessment and glanced to the searching blue eyes before her. She saw undeniable affection in them.

Carol smiled. "You make it sound easy. Change can be a frightening thing."

"You don't like change, do you Carol?" Erin asked rhetorically.

"Name one person that does and I'll tell you they're lying."

Erin chuckled, "I didn't say people liked it. I just think it's inevitable. Sometimes change can be the best thing for you . . . but taking that first step is what's scary as hell. That's why I take note of where I'm standing. If I don't like where my feet are planted I just move."

"Wild and carefree, huh?"

Erin shook her head, after taking a sip of her coffee. "Just the opposite. I do have goals and I care very much. That's why I need to know where I am. And if I don't like where my life is at any given point – I start walking."

"Is that how it was when you left home?" Carol asked with a careful grin.

"Wondered how long it would take for you to work in another question," Erin grinned.

"What can I say," Carol replied. "It's the investigator in me." Carol reached out and took Erin's hand in hers, feeling the softness of it. It was almost as if she were memorizing it for a moment somewhere down the road. "Seriously, I won't press. But I hope you'll share the story with me when you're ready."

Erin's fingertips squeezed around Carol's and she took a deep breath. Erin wondered silently what made her feel so comfortable around Carol. If her friends could see her now – perched on the edge of telling some 'cop' her life story. Stories that some of them didn't even know.

"My father died when I was very young. My mother married a man who liked to drink more than work. And since I was never 'his child' I never did quite fit in. When I was old enough I left. Not much of a story huh?" Erin grinned.

One Belief Away

Carol could tell it was entirely for show. Something much deeper, much larger lay beneath the simple facts. Carefully she pressed on.

"How old were you when you left home?"

"17," Erin answered. "I met Minos when we were in high school – she was a senior and I was a freshman. When she finished college she and her friends bought the house. She asked me to live there and I said 'yes'."

Erin's free hand traced the top of her cup in a nervous gesture. For someone so outspoken, Carol could tell that Erin rarely opened up to anyone. She looked frightened, like a small child who was waiting to be scolded. But even in light of Erin's appearance something else shown through - her determination, her resolve to live on her terms. And Carol admired that greatly.

"So you didn't like where your feet were planted so you just packed up and moved on?" Carol received a small nod. "You make it sound simple."

"It was far from simple," Erin answered. "It was probably the hardest thing I had done. I left my comfort zone. Even though it was hell to live there, it was still my home – the only home I knew. But I had to take the chance. I couldn't keep on living my life there for all the wrong reasons."

Carol wanted to give Erin a respite from her disclosure so she pulled away and walked to the refrigerator. "Are you hungry at all? I could make you something," Carol offered.

"Actually, I'd like to see the best room in the house – the only room you haven't shown me – your bedroom," Erin grinned lecherously.

Carol began to fidget with the refrigerator door and a small shuffle of her feet started. Erin could sense the apprehension wash over Carol by her flirtatious comment.

"Look, we promised slow so slow it will be. I just want to see it. After all, I showed you mine, it's only fair you show me yours?" Erin teased.

Carol grinned and took Erin by the hand leading her back to the hallway. With a flick of the light switch her room lit up for Erin's inspection.

"Here it is," Carol announced, leading Erin inside. "Is it all you dreamed it would be?"

The room looked similar to Carol's father's with a hand made quilt on the bed. A maple dresser sat across from the door with a matching nightstand next to the bed. Erin released a small chuckle, which Carol didn't know how to compute.

"Yeah, I know it's not much," she answered.

"I don't know. I think I half expected to still see teddy bears and rag dolls from your childhood in here," Erin teased.

"Shh," Carol said, placing a finger across her lips, "They're in the closet sleeping. You don't want to wake them."

Erin looked up at Carol to see the light expression on her face. She had to admit she was falling for this woman – very hard and very fast. Her fingers reached up and stroked Carol's cheek, making their way over to Carol's lips. Gently Erin brought down Carol's head, kissing her tenderly on the lips she'd just outlined.

"Thank you," Erin said quietly as she pulled away.

"For what?"

Erin looked deep into Carol's eyes. "For sharing."

Carol leaned in and planted a delicate kiss on Erin's forehead. As she looked up she noticed the clock. "Jeez, is it that late already?" she said out loud.

Erin looked over at the clock now as well. "I better get going," she remarked.

"No," Carol answered, silently scolding herself for chasing Erin off. "I didn't mean to imply anything."

"It's okay. I have class tomorrow and you have to work. I can take the bus back."

"Don't be silly. I can take you home. I mean if that's what you want," Carol answered. "Do you want to go?" she asked hesitantly. Had she frightened the smaller woman off? Was the reality of being with her suddenly too much?

Erin took a breath. "I'd like to stay," she said softly. "But I'll understand if you need me to leave. I can get back to the house on my own."

Erin started to make her way from the room but Carol reached around the smaller woman, gently pulling her back to her. Then she leaned forward and pressed her forehead to the fair one. "I would love it if you stayed with me tonight. No strings attached."

Erin sighed and closed her eyes, feeling the heat of the woman's breath and the warmth of the skin of her forehead. "I wouldn't mind being attached, you know."

"I thought all radical hippies believed in free love," Carol teased.

"Well, this radical hippie would make special concessions for you." Erin smiled but Carol knew deep inside that Erin was committed to their blossoming relationship. For a brief moment her plea to take things slowly seemed to disappear. But before she could act on it, she kept any comments she felt compelled to make to herself. Instead she nodded toward the living room.

"Let's close up for the night." Carol tugged gently at Erin's hand, leading the smaller woman through the house. She brought a glass of water for the tree and began turning off the lights throughout the house as they went back to Carol's bedroom.

They changed quietly, Carol turning her back to undress and slip on a nightshirt. Erin slid off her jeans and replaced her sweatshirt with the T-shirt that Carol had provided. Given their height difference it made a good nightshirt for the shorter woman. Then they slipped into the bed and Carol flipped off the lamp on the nightstand. The silence was nearly deafening.

"Can I hold you?" Erin whispered at last. Carol chortled softly, scooting closer and gathering the smaller woman in an embrace.

"Better?"

"Yeah." Erin turned into the older woman's arms, resting her head on Carol's shoulder and her arm across a well-muscled stomach.

Carol could feel the hot breath on her neck and realized her heart was pounding and she wasn't nearly as sleepy as she thought she was.

Erin took a deep breath and resituated, her legs rustling faintly against the sheets as she tossed her right leg over her companion's thigh.

Carol jumped slightly at the warm sensation.

"Sorry," Erin whispered and began to withdraw but Carol stopped her with a large warm hand on the small woman's thigh. Subconsciously, Carol began to rub the appendage that covered her.

"S'okay," she murmured. "I like it." She dipped her head and was not surprised when Erin lifted up slightly to meet her seeking lips.

It started chaste, just as it had before. Slowly, it turned into something more with each shared breath, exploring more deeply.

"I can't believe how you make me feel," Erin murmured between kisses. She shifted her weight so she lay more fully atop the longer woman.

"Mmm," was all Carol could manage but it was obviously agreement. The T-shirt Erin wore was too big and canted off one shoulder at a pleasing angle giving Carol easy access to the smooth, fair skin from just above the blonde's breast to her collarbone. She kissed there lavishly, applying tongue and teeth until Erin was moaning and squirming restlessly. Then Carol returned to the tempting open mouth to kiss her again.

"Carol," Erin muttered. It was more of an affirmation than a plea or a query. The confidence of it allowed Carol to gain the nerve to run a large hand from where it had been resting at the small of the blonde's back, up her side, and towards her front where she cupped Erin's breast.

The hippie gasped, arching her neck back and giving Carol access to the column of her throat. The dark woman took the invitation gladly, sucking on the throbbing pulse point.

Carol savored each moment. She relished the salty taste of Erin's skin, the musky scent that was part her, part fresh linen and all arousal. The breast in her hand was pliant and warm, the tip of the nipple screaming forth into the T-shirt fabric and wanting more attention. She'd never imagined making love with a woman, in fact hadn't really put much thought into making love at all. Her attention had always been on doing well in school, and then at the Academy, and then proving herself to her father. But now, suddenly, holding and touching this woman was all that she'd hoped for and more.

For her part, Erin was lost in sensations and emotions, melting into the warm body beneath her, getting lost in the delicate touch. She slid her hands down Carol's front and under her shirt to rest on the well-muscled abdomen she found there, the heels of her palms laying lightly on the elastic waistband of the other woman's underwear. The dark woman's skin was warm and soft, the muscles twitching under Erin's searching fingertips as they ventured upwards to stroke the underside of Carol's breasts.

First the covers were too restricting and were discarded to expose their intertwined bodies to the slatted moonlight coming in through the blinds and curtains. The pattern was delicate on the blonde's hair, striping her with gold-laced silver. Then clothing became too much and Carol tugged at the T-shirt and broke away from her partner with a raised eyebrow, requesting permission.

Erin hesitated just long enough for the answer to be clear to the officer. They had wanted to slow down. They'd both agreed to it. Carol smiled warmly, not wanting Erin to feel awkward even though this reaction was somewhat surprising after the blonde's readiness at her car only hours before. The cop smoothed the shirt back down and tightened her embrace, settling Erin snugly against herself. She tucked her head into the nape of her neck and stroked the golden hair as they both fought for breath.

"I'm sorry," Erin murmured, her lips moving against Carol's neck, pausing to place a kiss there.

"Shhh," the dark woman countered, squeezing her young friend even closer. "Nothing to be sorry for. We agreed to go slowly, right?"

"Yeah," Erin whispered. "God . . . it's so much. Feeling you, touching you. Like I'm alive for the first time."

Carol chuckled softly, bouncing the slight body on top of herself and parting blonde tresses with a snort of air. "Me too."

I never thought I could feel this way, Carol thought, not quite having the courage to voice the words yet.

"Can you sleep with me here?" Erin queried softly. Her small body was only touching the bed at her legs, one between the dark woman's thighs and the other on the outside. The lengthy body beneath hers wholly supported the rest of her weight.

Carol considered the question, finding the firm weight quite comforting. She felt safe here in this small woman's arms, felt the world couldn't touch them here where their differences were irrelevant in the darkness and the warmth each provided the other. In that respect, she would have no trouble sleeping with the blonde's slight weight on top of her. However, the fact that her blood was singing and her body incredibly sensitized to the woman's touch assured Carol she would remain sleepless for quite some time. The longer she stayed awake the more she could relish this gentle girl's presence. "Yeah," she said at last. "I've never been more comfortable."

"Me either," Erin murmured, snuggling more deeply into the arms surrounding her, inhaling great breaths of Carol-scented air.

"Sleep, sweetheart," Carol crooned, stroking the woman from the top of her blonde head to her lower back. The motion was completely soothing to both of them. After several long moments, Erin's breath evened in sleep. Carol sighed. "Good lord, I think I love you," the dark woman murmured, surprising herself both with the emotion and the admission.

Chapter 10

Carol stopped at the grocery store on the way home after a long and tedious day. One car crash, one lost Christmas gift – someone's puppy - and one speeding motorist were all she could handle on Christmas Eve. She felt pretty proud that the yellow lab had been located and she saved Christmas for one young family. Watching Randell crawl around on all fours trying to coax the pup from under a parked car was true comedy in its highest form.

She let herself into the small house while juggling two brown paper bags. She'd never thought to ask what her young friend liked or didn't like but knew a couple of safe items from their few meals together. So she'd planned on baked chicken and a pasta salad. With that thought in mind, she went right through the house, placing the bags on the kitchen counter first, and then setting the oven to 350. She went back to her room to change out of her uniform and into jeans and a T-shirt before placing a small package under the tree she'd removed from one of the bags.

She still had about thirty minutes until Erin was due so she went to work boiling pasta and cutting up fresh vegetables after putting in the chicken. It was difficult for her to concentrate. Her thoughts kept coming back to Erin, who had agreed to stay the night yet again. Before committing, however, Erin asked for a run down of the 'ground rules' for what was 'off limits' since they agreed to continue to take things slowly. Carol was certain Erin would keep her word but also knew the woman would drive as close to the line as possible without going over it. The thought made her grin wickedly.

A part of her was as nervous as she was anxious to see the young woman. While she was out shopping she decided to get Erin a gift. They hadn't known each other that long and she wasn't sure if Erin would see the gift as being too commercialized or establishment driven. Carol knew that she got the gift for Erin as a sign of affection. In her eyes, it was only right. Christmas was a time to show those you loved your feelings by giving them tokens of love, commercialism aside. Did she truly love Erin? Carol wondered as she looked through the glass display case in the store, picking out something she thought would fit the free spirit perfectly. By the time the gift-wrap was on the package she decided that she did...very much. But the nagging fear that she would offend Erin in some way overshadowed the joy of the purchase.

The doorbell rang not too much after Carol began cooking. Wiping her hands on a convenient dishtowel, Carol walked down the short hallway. She opened the door to reveal Erin standing on the stoop. A light snow had begun to fall and the crystal flakes rested on her young companion's honeyed hair before quickly melting away from the heat radiating off the woman. Carol realized that this angel was the best gift anyone could give her. The blonde grinned and held up a small, brown paper bag as Carol motioned her inside.

"Hey there, Angel," the officer said softly, vocalizing her thoughts.

"Hi," green eyes flashed a smile as Erin placed her palm on Carol's taut stomach. "Smells great."

"We'll see later if it tastes good," Carol smiled. "Come on in. There's iced tea in the refrigerator. Help yourself." Walking behind the woman to the kitchen, Carol looked at Erin's small bag. "What did you bring?"

"Dessert," Erin said handing the bag over. "Better put it in the freezer."

Carol grinned as she placed the four individually wrapped ice cream sandwiches next to the ice cube trays. "Great idea."

"Looks like we're gonna have a white Christmas," the blonde said lamely, grimacing slightly at her awkwardness as she poured herself a tall glass of iced tea and topped off Carol's.

"Sure does. Did you have class this afternoon?"

"Nah, I'm off for the next two weeks but I go back on the 4th," Erin said with disdain.

"Graduation isn't that far away though," Carol added optimistically, resuming her position at the counter chopping vegetables. "Chicken's about ready," she motioned with her knife to the bread, "Why don't you get us a few slices?"

Erin nodded silently, taking the loaf to the small table.

Suddenly, Carol realized that Erin had only been carrying the bag of ice cream sandwiches. *No clothes. She must have changed her mind.* She couldn't help the feeling of disappointment and it must have shown because Erin's brow wrinkled slightly.

"What's wrong?"

Carol tried to shrug it off. It wasn't a big deal if had changed her mind. "It's nothing."

"Nah ah. Tell me."

Erin was beginning to know her all too well. The officer grinned sheepishly, pausing in her slicing to avoid losing a fingertip due to her distracted state.

"I thought you were staying the night. But you didn't bring anything."

Erin chuckled dryly, before taking a drink of tea. "I brought myself and a toothbrush," she patted a large pocket on her jacket. She unzipped her coat and pulled something from the waistband of her jeans. "I've got something else, too, but you can't have it until tomorrow morning. Santa doesn't come early, you know?" Erin waved a thin package in front of Carol, pulling it away before Carol could touch it. "Nope," Erin teased. "No peeking, no shaking, no touching."

"Where's the fun in that?" Carol answered slyly.

"I was talking about the package, not me," Erin grinned before giving a suggestive wiggle of her eyebrows.

Carol smiled as she watched Erin make her way to the living room to put the gift under the tree. Once there, Erin noticed another package.

"And what's this?" she called back to Carol.

"Something you can't peek at, shake or touch," Carol answered as Erin walked back to the kitchen.

"That's not fair."

"I thought turnabout was fair play?"

"Not in my world," Erin grinned.

One Belief Away

Carol smiled. She was glad Erin had decided to stay with her and how empty the prospect of being alone seemed a moment ago. It showed on her face.

"What's the matter now?"

Carol smiled again and brushed it off. "When I didn't see an over night bag I just...I just thought you might have changed your mind is all. It was disappointment."

Erin paused a minute while she looked around the clean room, taking in again the decorations she'd seen over the weekend. "Have you changed your mind?" she asked suddenly, turning her attention back to Carol's long form where the woman had resumed slicing a cucumber. "I mean if you don't want to spend the holiday with me then-."

"No," Carol chuckled. "I do want you here. I was disappointed when I thought you wouldn't be staying, not because you said you would."

"Okay – just checking."

Carol began to shake her head. "Talk about insecurities, huh? We're pretty pathetic, aren't we?"

Erin laughed, nodding. "I've never really cared before . . . if someone liked me or not...not like this," she admitted hesitantly. She found her fingers examining the vegetables that Carol cut, unable to look up at her companion.

"Well, relax," Carol said reaching over to pull Erin's chin up to make eye contact again. "Because I think you're wonderful...I'm lucky to share the holidays with you."

"You relax, too," the blonde responded, finishing her tea quickly and walking to get more. "Because this is where I want to be."

Carol grinned and glanced over her shoulder at the boiling pasta. "Few more minutes," she decided after some thought.

With a nod, Erin continued to the refrigerator to refill her glass. After she was seated again, she asked, "How was your afternoon?"

Carol paused a moment in her slicing before she continued. She finished the cucumber and moved the pasta to a cold burner before she responded. "Coulda been worse."

"Could've been better?"

She shrugged. "It really wasn't too bad. I did manage to locate someone's escaped Christmas puppy. It was just one of those rookie days."

"Rookie days?" Erin asked with a raised eyebrow.

"Nothing too exciting. Just some ho-hum stuff," Carol responded with a grin. "It makes for a long day." She drained the pasta in a colander and ran cold water over it, tossing the tight curls to let the water run through.

Erin let out a sigh of relief. "So it was pretty mundane then?"

Carol just cast her an awed look. "You're good at that."

"At what?"

"Word nuances," Carol replied, tossing the pasta with the freshly cut vegetables and then an Italian dressing.

"Thanks . . . I think," Erin looked at her in puzzlement.

"So to answer your question, yes, it was mundane. And all I could think about was you," Carol confessed with a sly smile.

"Looking forward to some stimulating conversation were you, Officer Johnson?"

"Anything has to be more stimulating than listening to Randell try to sing old Elvis songs all day."

"Oh my god," Erin grimaced.

"Exactly."

"Could've been worse you know . . . He might have tried to sing NEW Elvis songs like Kentucky Rain," Erin offered, trying to look at the 'bright side'.

Carol stopped what she was doing and turned to Erin. "I'm not sure you'd have that opinion once you've heard 'Teddy Bear' sung by a 40-something year old cop," she chuckled.

"Put a chain around my neck and lead me anywhere," Erin recited the lyrics, coming up behind Carol, wrapping her arms around her waist.

Carol leered at Erin behind her. "Don't tempt me," she warned.

Carol slipped from the embrace and knelt in front of the refrigerator to clear a spot for the salad. Then she slid the large glass bowl inside before standing.

"We can always sing Kentucky Rain," Carol answered before starting to sing, "Kentucky rain keeps falling down, down, down-."

Erin put a finger over Carol's lips. "Please," she begged. "Don't go there. I might just lose all respect for you."

Carol smiled and moved across the kitchen to the living room. "Come out here and sit," she called.

Erin obliged, taking a spot on the sofa, cradling her glass of iced tea in her palms. Silence reigned for several long minutes as Carol rested her head on the back of the sofa, eyes closed.

"What are you thinking?" Carol asked at last, trying to start a conversation.

Erin quirked a grin and looked at her companion's profile before looking across the living room to the twinkling Christmas tree. "I'm trying to think of a stimulating topic to engage your mind."

"We could talk about you," Carol offered softly, opening her eyes yet keeping her head tilted back to welcome the colorful rays. "You engage my mind."

"And with any luck I'll engage your body sometime soon," Erin let slip out. Immediately, she made up for it. "Don't get me wrong. I love our relationship and I promised we'd go slowly. And I meant it so just...forget I opened my mouth, okay?"

"Forgotten," she muttered.

"You really are brain dead today," Erin said, running her hand across Carol's face, not getting the slightest reaction.

"Mmm." It was the only response Carol could offer.

"Okay, how about this statement: I've decided not to be anti-establishment. I won't participate in demonstrations or sit-ins or do anything to hamper your colleagues," she grinned recklessly. "I'm not an idiot. I'm not one of those potheads looking for a cause. I'm educated and down to earth."

"Who are you and what have you done with Erin?" Carol murmured.

"Ah, you have been listening," she answered before pausing a moment "Of course, a good toke has its benefits," she added, attempting to lighten the mood.

Carol laughed and raised her head. "I know you're not an idiot, Erin. You're intelligent and creative; you have a great depth of understanding and acceptance. But what I can't figure out is how you ended up with Minos and the others."

"It's where I want to be," Erin shrugged, puzzled. "I mean . . . I love Minos and the house and the classes I take. What I do, I do for me, not because I don't have a choice. I've chosen this - all of it: the drugs, the rallies, the lifestyle. I'm happy where I am."

"What about your parents?" Carol asked carefully.

"Fuck 'em," the blonde replied flippantly. "Is that chicken done yet?"

Taking the not-so-subtle hint, Carol let the subject drop again. She felt rather like an open book to Erin whereas she still knew very little about the radical.

"Lemme check," the officer said, rising to her feet and moving toward the oven. On her way by, she felt a feather light touch near her elbow. She glanced down into vibrant green eyes that flashed apology. Carol simply smiled and ran her fingers gently through the woman's bangs before resuming her trip to the kitchen.

"I'm just not ready to talk about them . . . " Erin said slowly.

Carol waved her off with one hand while poking the meat with a fork in the other. "No sweat, Erin. You don't owe me any explanations. We're here for dinner and some company, right?"

"Right," Erin nodded. She paused a moment. "It's not you, Carol. In fact, I can talk to you more than anyone. It's-."

"Erin," she began, cutting her short. "I said you don't owe me any explanations and I meant it. When you're ready, you'll tell me . . . Okay?"

Erin gave a thankful smile and walked toward the kitchen. "So how goes the bird?"

Carol watched as Erin strolled over confidently and picked up a fork. She poked at the fowl like an experienced cook. Erin was a mass of contradictions. At this very moment the woman looked like she was capable of doing anything.

After dinner, they sat on the couch in the downstairs TV room where the cement basement walls kept the room pleasantly chilled. Carol had scrounged up a notebook and pencil for Erin and watched the young woman intently as she sketched everything from daisies to city high-rises. It turned into a game of sorts, Carol calling out items and Erin drawing them in sure, gentle strokes. The officer was completely astounded by the young woman's talent.

Erin was tucked solidly into Carol, the taller woman having one arm across her midsection and the other in her lap. Carol's mouth was only inches from Erin's ear, the soft breath when she spoke all but distracting the young artist.

"Horse."

"Easy," Erin chastised, sketching the lines quickly and fluidly, giving her horse a diamond on his forehead and some spots over his haunches. "Challenge me," she said, putting some final wisps into his tail.

"Umm . . . a field in the winter," Carol replied smugly, quite proud of herself. How did one draw a field of snow with a pencil and nothing else?

Erin nodded slowly, flipping the page and set out to work. Carol watched the pencil tip dance across the paper, tilting her head when the image didn't make sense and she couldn't follow the young woman's train of thought. Then, slowly, she saw it: a field with a tree dripping icicles, patches of snow mingled with dead grass, an overturned wooden wheelbarrow blanketed in a carpet of snow. The young artist even sketched in the wood grain of the wheelbarrow and footprints from it. She penciled in the bark of the tree and finished by adding her short signature across the bottom corner.

Carol gasped softly, causing the blonde to grin. "You are amazing."

"Thanks."

"This is what you should do for a living."

The activist shrugged. "Nah. This is what I do for my heart. Give me another one." She was enjoying the challenge and the camaraderie.

Taking the hint that harder subjects were better, Carol pondered a moment. "Here we go: a football team of young boys who've just lost their first game."

"Good one," Erin nodded approvingly and dove into the request.

They passed the evening like that, wrapped around each other and listening to the television drone on while they merely absorbed the sense of belonging they'd both been missing so terribly.

Later, they made their way to Carol's bedroom, changing into nightclothes and crawling into bed. Hesitantly, they snuggled into each other.

"Thank you for coming over," Carol murmured, tightening her hold on the blonde, relishing the feel of her body touching along the length of the smaller woman.

Erin grinned and rolled her head slightly so she could kiss Carol's shoulder. "Thank you for asking me."

"I didn't sleep well last night," the officer admitted sheepishly.

"Neither did I," Erin acknowledged.

"And I missed you," Carol whispered, having trouble confessing the feelings.

"I missed you, too," Erin responded. "We'll both sleep better tonight. Scout's honor."

"I never knew you were a scout," Carol grinned, snuggling closer. "See? I learn something new about you every day." The poke in the ribs from Erin made her jump a little.

"It's an expression," Erin chastised playfully.

"I'm glad you're here to tell me these things," Carol retorted.

"Carol?"

"Hmm?"

"Go to sleep."

"Yes ma'am."

After a few relaxing moments, Carol looked over at the clock. It was a minute after twelve.

"Merry Christmas," she whispered. A light snore and a small stir were the only response she got. She smiled and lightly kissed Erin's forehead. "My angel."

"Santa came last night. You must have been a very good girl this year."

Carol smiled as her mind regained consciousness. Slowly, her eyes focused to find Erin above her waving the gift from the night before.

"You mean I didn't get coal as usual?"

Erin smiled and thrust her gift forward with a little hop on the mattress. "Well, after you open it you might wish you had gotten coal. At least coal you can have some use for."

"Don't be silly," Carol said taking the gift and placing it next to her. "Where's yours?"

"Still under the tree."

"Go get it," Carol shooed her.

Erin giggled like an excited schoolgirl and Carol had to chuckle. She darted from the room only to return to the bed moments later with a flying leap.

Erin settled herself in front of Carol. "You first," Erin nodded.

Carol picked up the package and held it for a moment before tearing into the paper like an impatient child. Erin held her breath as she waited for a reaction.

It was a frame. That much Carol knew and when she turned it over she found an 8 x 10 sketch of two women lying naked together, their bodies hidden by each other's as if they were merged together. It was erotic yet tasteful and filled with passion. Erin licked her lips waiting for Carol's reaction.

Carol's fingertips glided over the image as her eyes consumed everything about the picture. It was beautiful. It was positively beautiful. How long has she wanted something like this in her own life? And now here she sat, on Christmas morning, with a woman who would someday make all her fantasies come true. Carol felt a swelling in her heart. She bit her lip, hoping she wouldn't turn into a blubbering idiot as she gave into her overflowing joy.

Erin, however, took it as something else.

"I'm sorry," she began. "You don't like it. I knew I should have gone with something more-."

"No," Carol said softly. "I do like it. I cherish it actually...You don't realize how much this means to me. Really."

"You don't have to say that to make me feel better, Carol."

"Honestly, Erin. This is truly beautiful...It's not disappointment at all. If anything, it's disbelief." Carol leaned over and kissed Erin softly on the cheek. "I never thought I could be this lucky." She didn't want to start crying so she quickly nodded to the package that Erin held in her hands. "Your turn."

Erin grinned and worked the ribbon and paper free from the small box. Upon opening the lid she carefully pulled away the tissue paper to reveal a silver bracelet with a small charm. An engraving read 'E + C'. Slowly, she turned it over and examined it further.

"I wasn't sure what to get," Carol said, nervously clearing her throat. "It's the yin-."

"And yang," Erin replied. "Two halves that make one whole. E and C," Erin examined it in silence before clearing her throat. "I really should have bought you something," she said shaking the bracelet.

"Why do you say that?"

"Look at this, Carol. This had to be expensive...And all I can manage is a few doodles in a frame – a cheap frame at that."

"You mean you didn't draw this picture with me in mind?"

"Yes, of course I did. Why would-."

"Then I love it," Carol grinned, cutting her off before she could go any further. "If I had talent to share," she explained, " if I had a gift to create something this beautiful that showed how I felt about you, I'd give you a picture, too. But with my ability I don't think you'd find two stick figures with straw hair very appealing."

Erin grinned. "If that's all you could give me I'd love it anyway."

"Right," Carol nodded. "So what makes you think I'm any different?"

"Oh fine. Go ahead and throw logic at me why don't you?"

The two women grinned at each other before Carol looked down at her gift again. "Wish I could hang this up at work but it might raise a few eyebrows," she chuckled. Her mood turned sober and her eyebrows crunched in thought. "I wish I could tell the world how I feel about you. But people would hate me – a few might even kill me...Do you think that will ever change?"

"I don't care about what the world thinks. I only care about you," Erin answered.

Carol managed a grin and brought the frame to her chest, clutching it tightly. "I really do love it. Thank you."

Erin smiled and held the bracelet out to Carol, followed by her left wrist. "Give me a hand?"

Carol took the jewelry. For some reason it began to shake in her grasp as she tried to hook it around the small wrist before her. Carol wondered how many other lovers would be doing this same thing this morning. Would they realize just how precious a moment like this could be? Or would they simply take it for granted, thinking the snapping of a bracelet was just a 'typical' act of love? For Carol, it was a first time experience and she savored it all. The coolness of the silver, the way it sparkled against pale skin, the clamminess of her own hands – even the small sigh of contentment that came from Erin as she locked it into place.

Carol felt Erin's other hand cover hers as she finished the task, their fingers soon locking together.

"Does this mean we're officially going steady?" Erin asked with a mischievous grin on her face.

Carol smiled in response and looked up to see that grin. She had to admit she fell into it even deeper than when she had woken up that morning.

"Yeah. I'd like you to be mine. And I want to be yours, if you'll have me."

"I would love to have you."

Erin crawled over the covers and gently took the picture from Carol's lap, resting it beside them. The kiss upon her arrival was soft and delicate. Carol's hands reached up and her fingers took up residence in the hair at Erin's temple, ever so gently pulling her closer, deepening the kiss.

She didn't know how it happened but soon her back was on the bed with Erin's weight upon her, the blonde's lips moving to her earlobe. With a soft sigh Erin settled next to Carol's side, her hand resting on the older woman's abdomen.

"It's almost 6 am," Erin remarked as she made lazy figure eights on Carol's nightshirt. "You said it would only be a few hours?"

"Yeah. We're all working short shifts today. Gives everyone the chance to enjoy the holiday. I have to figure out how to explain to Randell why I won't be over today."

"Tell him you've got a hot date with a gorgeous dame," Erin chuckled. "That should go over big with him."

Carol chuckled. "Oh yeah. I'm sure it would . . . I should be back around one if everything's quiet…Will you be here when I get back?"

"Yeah. I figured I'd pop out to the house, wish everyone a Merry Christmas and then come back if that's okay?"

"Sounds wonderful," Carol grinned. "I'll leave the door unlocked for you."

"Well, you'd better get going."

Erin began to rise but Carol pulled her back down to the bed. "Just a few more minutes? Unless you're in a hurry?"

Erin smiled and proceeded to let her fingertips knead Carol's shoulder. "No hurry. I just don't want to make you late is all."

"I want to enjoy this awhile longer."

"No arguments here, Officer Johnson."

"See? You're agreeing with the establishment more and more. There's hope for you yet."

"It's not too late for me to get my hands on some coal you know," Erin retorted, giving Carol's side a poke for good measure. Carol simply chuckled and let Erin's warmth spill over her.

After a long silence Carol looked down at the blonde crown settled above her breast. "Thank you, Erin."

"For what?"

"For making this my best Christmas ever."

Erin snuggled in closer. "The pleasure's all mine."

A week later Erin was having serious doubts about her sanity. The gang was gathered at the commune house. They jumped between watching Dick Clark broadcast from Time Square for the New Year to listening to the stereo. No one had the desire to see any of the guests singing on the Rockin' Eve broadcast but they did all take time out to periodically watch the drunks in Manhattan.

It was 11:46 pm and Erin was expecting Carol any minute. Actually, Carol was sixteen minutes late but who was counting. She knew Carol had to stop by Randell's house to wish everyone a happy new year and then find some way to escape before midnight.

One way or another, Carol had told the young woman she was determined to get there in time for a New Year's Kiss.

Minos set her drink down on the table next to Erin, making the young woman physically jump at the sound.

"Feeling edgy?" Minos teased.

"No," Erin lied.

Minos saw through it and bent down to Erin's ear. "Wouldn't have anything to do with the fact you invited a COP to the festivities, would it?"

"Actually, it's not the cop I'm worried about. I'm more concerned with my friends making asses of themselves in front of someone I happen to care about."

Minos knew perfectly well she was one of those friends in question. She reached down and played with Erin's bracelet for a moment.

"This must have set her back a few bucks."

Erin pulled her wrist away.

"What?" Minos asked. "I like it."

"Like hell you do."

Minos took a drink, setting the bottle back on the table before turning to Erin. "Do you really think this little romance is gonna work out? Especially when she busts in here and arrests everyone tonight?"

"She won't do that," Erin answered.

"You know this for a fact?"

"Yes."

Minos got a wicked grin. "To quote you, like hell you do."

Erin was exasperated. The two of them were having these types of conversations more and more lately. "Why are you giving me such a hard time about this?"

"About what?"

"You know what!"

"The pig?"

"She's not a pig!"

At that moment Bill walked in the kitchen for another beer. "Who's a pig?" he asked innocently.

"Minos at the moment," Erin answered before the older woman could say anything.

"Come on girls. Don't fight," he said putting another beer in front of each woman. "It's New Year's Eve. Get blitzed and fight tomorrow."

He walked away chuckling but Erin just wasn't in the mood. She heard her housemate Marlow call from the front door. "Hey Erin!"

One Belief Away

She looked over to see Carol standing there. She lit up brighter than Carol's Christmas tree. She had to admit she liked Carol's tree. Minos refused to put up decorations since doing so would be 'supporting the dictation of organized religion'. Erin saw Christmastime as a means of fellowship to mankind and not necessarily a celebration to any God. So being able to spend time with someone who enjoyed the holidays was a nice change of pace. Erin would have reveled in her delight a bit longer but the oinking noise that Minos made put an end to that.

Instead of chastising Minos, which would get her nowhere, Erin made her way through the ocean of people to the front door. Marlow excused himself and left to go mingle again.

"Hey, you made it!"

"I'm sorry I'm late," Carol apologized. "Randell had a thousand questions – where was I going, who was I seeing – you'd think the guy was more my dad than my partner," Carol said softly as she took off her coat.

"Well that doesn't matter, you're here now and," Erin paused to look at her watch, "You've got 5 minutes to spare. Let me take your coat upstairs. Come on."

They made their way back through the living room, elbowing and shouldering their way through. When they got to the foot of the stairs Carol spotted Minos at the kitchen table.

Carol politely nodded. "Minos."

Minos mimicked her actions. "Pig."

Erin rolled her eyes and took Carol by the hand. They climbed the stairs and Erin opened the door to her room. Carol followed her inside.

"You got a door I see." Carol remarked.

"You remembered I didn't have a door?"

Carol shrugged. "The pig in me I guess – always observing."

Erin sighed. She didn't know why Minos had to be so confrontational. "Don't let her bother you, Carol."

"It's hard not to."

"Why do you care what she thinks?"

"Well, she's important to you. I know you think a lot of her. I could see that the first day we met."

Erin paused, "Yeah, well we seem to be growing apart lately. Or I'm growing apart. I mean that's why I got the door, so I wouldn't have to be surrounded by all these people in the house on a continual basis. I wanted to have some privacy."

At that moment Bill yelled up the stairs, "Dick Clark's dropping the ball on the drunks Skylon! You're gonna miss it!"

"Now you don't want to miss that, do you?" Carol smirked.

"I'd rather stay right here," Erin said, pulling Carol closer by the hips. Erin rested her head on Carol's chest, listening to her heartbeat. Reflexively, Carol's arms encompassed the smaller woman. Her cheek took residence on the top of Erin's golden locks as she held her tightly.

Downstairs the countdown began. Ten. Nine. Eight. Seven. Six. Five. Four. Three. Two. One. Happy New Year!! The crowd below screamed, rattled their noisemakers and blew their whistles with tremendous force. Carol pulled back first and raised Erin's chin so their eyes could meet.

"Happy New Year," she said softly.

"Happy New Year."

Carol's lips claimed Erin's with reserved passion and hopeful promise of what might lay ahead for them, disregarding the ruckus going on in the living room. Carol kept her promise and got the New Year's Kiss she was after. As they pulled away they could hear everyone downstairs singing Auld Lang Syne.

"May I?" Carol asked, posturing herself to dance.

Erin smiled. One hand took Carol's while the other rested on her shoulder. In the dimly lit, musty room they danced to the song that drifted up to them. Soon they too began to join in the singing softly, alone in the room. Erin knew that whatever might happen between them – whether they grew old together or drifted apart - one thing would remain. She would remember and savor this moment for the rest of her life.

The intrusion of reality came crashing back with the sound of Bill pounding on Erin's door. "Hey you missed it! You okay in there?"

"Yeah, we're on our way out," she shouted back.

"Sorry you missed Dick Clark," Carol grinned.

"Ah that's okay. I'll watch American Bandstand this weekend in lieu of tonight," she chuckled. "Come on. Let's go before Bill organizes a search party."

Erin started to leave but Carol snagged her by the waist before she could open the door.

"Hey," she said softly, giving her a light kiss on the cheek. "Happy 1973."

Erin took Carol's hands from her hips giving them a squeeze in commitment. "It will be a good year . . . I can feel it."

One Belief Away

"This, my partner, is a mess."

As Carol examined their cruiser stuck in a snow bank, with more flakes coming down, she had to agree with Randell's appraisal of the situation. The southeastern US was getting hit in a major way – almost 2 feet in the Carolina's. Since the eastern US was 'used to' getting this weather they didn't make the national broadcast. It was a few days before St. Valentine's Day and she didn't feel much in the mood for love at the moment. It was days like today that Carol had to admit she disliked the job. She was certain she'd be aching and tired after helping motorist upon motorist out of the banks and ditches in the area. But then again if Erin would rub her shoulders her mood might certainly change for the better.

"Should we call for back up?" Carol joked with a grin, looking at their disabled cruiser.

"What? And have them either get stuck too or laugh at us? I think not."

Carol smirked and opened the trunk to see if they had anything they might be able to use to get them in motion again.

"Any sand in here?"

"No, we used it for the last motorist."

Randell gave a defeated sigh. "Don't these people ever turn on a radio? You know a snow advisory means they are advising you NOT to be in the snow. If I have to help one more nitwit today..."

"Including us?"

"Very funny . . . We have to be out here. The majority of people don't. They could stay home, watch television, bake some cookies but no. They come out here, get stuck and need all of our sand."

"You're awfully chipper today."

"I hate winter."

"And snow," Carol added.

"And snow. And Valentine's Day, too."

Okay you lost me, Randell. "What?"

Randell rubbed the back of his neck. Whenever he grew uncomfortable talking about something he'd rub his neck nervously. "I'm in the dog house and Valentine's Day is coming and I'm sure Phyllis will hate whatever I get her."

"Why are you in the doghouse?"

Randell looked at Carol and shook his head. "I can't tell you because you'll probably be mad at me, too."

Okay now I'm totally lost...unless he..."You didn't cheat on her did you?"

"Hell no! It's nothing like that." He paused, thinking of how much he could get away with telling Carol without her getting pissed, too. "We got into a discussion about the ERA. Needless to say she and I don't see eye to eye. I said something. She said something. I said something else and now . . . "

"You're sleeping on the couch."

"And I've got the bad back to prove it."

Carol gave a hearty chuckle and slapped Randell on the arm. Slowly a grin worked its way to his face and he began shaking his head. "You're a woman, right?"

"Last time I checked."

Randell turned beet red. "You know what I mean, Johnson. You understand women. So what can I say that would make it better?"

"Apologize. Say you were wrong. And quit being an ass."

"That simple, huh?"

"Yep. Buy roses, too. That will help."

"You know how much roses cost this time of year?"

"Think of how much a doctor would charge to fix your back if you keep sleeping on that sofa."

Randell pursed his lips together and nodded.

"Good point."

Carol grinned. "Glad I could help."

At that moment a microbus rounded the corner moving way too fast.

"Oh boy, here we go again," Randell elbowed Carol as they watched the bus slide. "Five bucks says they're not gonna make it."

Sure enough, another vehicle was then swallowed up in Mother Nature's snow bank across the street.

"Come on," he nodded to her. "Maybe if we get them out they can pull us out."

They walked up to the vehicle - Randell taking the driver's side and Carol going to the passenger's side. He motioned for the driver to roll down the window.

"Looks like you got yourself into a little bit of trouble," Randell said conversationally. It was then that Carol saw the passenger. It was Erin. Quickly, she rolled down the window as Minos addressed Randell.

"Yeah, you gonna give me a ticket?" she answered smartly.

"Well, that wasn't my plan. I was going to help you but if you'd like one I'm sure I could think of some violation to write up."

"Carol!" Erin said excitedly.

"You know each other?" Randell said to Carol between the two windows.

"Yeah, this is the friend that I spent New Years with. The one I took to the hospital after that riot."

Recognition crossed Randell's face. "You look much better this time," he grinned.

"I feel better, too," Erin grinned.

"So," Carol asked. " . . . how've you been?"

Erin blinked. Carol had just seen her last night. What the hell is she ...ohhh..."Good. And yourself?"

"Oh Jesus. You're not foo-" Minos sighed.

"Failing History," Erin said cutting her off. "I managed to pick my grades up this quarter."

"That's good to hear," Carol nodded, playing along.

Minos knew it was all a charade but for whose benefit? They all *knew*. But wait . . . maybe they *all* didn't know. Randell. Carol's partner. He obviously didn't know. With a cheshire cat grin at the prospect of spilling it all, Minos turned to Erin.

The grin fell from Erin's face upon seeing Minos' 'twinkle'.

*Don't you dare say anything. Don't you dare say a God damned word Mino*s, Erin's mind screamed.

"Why don't we try to get you ladies out of here?" Carol said quickly. "Randell, let's go to the front." Carol didn't wait for a reply. She just prayed he would follow her lead. She gave a small thanks to God when he met her there.

"Okay," Randell said. "We're gonna rock it a bit so hit the gas after we get some momentum." After a few pushes, Randell told Minos to hit it. Her tires spun for a moment but it was enough for her to get traction and get back on the road.

"Think you could give us a pull?" Carol called to Erin. She knew if she asked Minos the answer would be no. Carol pointed over to their cruiser. Erin leaned out the window. "We don't have a tow."

"We've got one. We could hook up our bumpers."

"Okay," Erin answered. "Get ready and we'll pull around."

She rolled up the window and Minos shot her a glare. "This is MY car you know?"

"It's the house's car which means it's part my car, too. I'm using my part to tow Carol and her partner out of the snow bank because they were kind enough to help us even though you were extremely rude to them for no reason whatsoever." Erin took a deep breath after her long rant.

"He doesn't know, does he?"

"No he doesn't and it's going to stay that way," Erin shot back.

"Boy, you must feel proud," Minos snarled. "She won't even tell people that she loves you."

"You don't understand."

"You got that right, sister."

"Then let's drop it."

"Fine by me."

Minos turned around and backed up to Carol's cruiser. Carol waved for her to stop but she kept coming back, tapping Carol with the car.

Minos leaned out the window. "Sorry," she smirked.

Carol didn't say anything. She just went behind and hooked Minos bumper, hoping the woman wouldn't suddenly have another accident and pin her between the two cars, leaving her a bloody mess. After they were both hooked, Minos hit the gas as Randell and Carol pushed the front of their cruiser out of the bank.

Carol unhooked Minos' car and gave a wave. "You're all clear. Thanks a lot."

"Anything for you, Officer Johnson," she replied sarcastically, blowing a kiss before taking off down the road again. Carol let out a long breath. *That was a close one. Thank God she didn't say anything.*

Randell walked up and tapped Carol on the arm. "You hang out with these people?"

"Well, not her," Carol answered. "But it's not my place to dictate who my friend's other friends should be...You know?"

"Yeah, I suppose so," Randell nodded. "Shift's almost over. Want to head back in?"

"Sure...Besides you have to make a trip to the florist," Carol grinned.

Randell just groaned.

Chapter 11

"Are you sure about this?" Carol asked, looking over her shoulder on several occasions. Easter break for Erin was two days away. Suspicious eyes watched their every move in the college cafeteria.

Three days had passed since they had seen each other and Carol had to admit it felt like an eternity. They agreed on lunch but as they stood in line to pay for their food she wondered if it was such a good idea, especially since she was still in uniform.

Erin claimed the food at the cafeteria was the best in town. The place was packed as they stood in line, waiting to pay for their sandwiches and sodas. The officer could feel all eyes upon her. She could honestly say she had never felt more uncomfortable in her life. Even the mundane traffic routine this week was fun compared to the eyes of the students boring into her back now.

"Relax," Erin soothed. "They don't bite. Honest."

Carol smiled. Erin's soothing presence steadied her rattled nerves. When they reached the cashier, Carol started to dig into her pocket.

"No," Erin insisted. "You made dinner the other night." She handed over the bills to the cashier who now had a raised eyebrow. "Is there a problem?" Erin asked the cashier bluntly. It was obvious the woman knew that Carol didn't 'fit in' with the usual patrons and Erin wasn't about to let it go by without comment.

"No. No problem."

"Good, then you can keep the change," Erin smiled. "Come on. Follow me," she told Carol.

Carol obeyed. They were on Erin's turf now and it was best if she let the honey-haired woman lead. They walked down a long corridor, paper-sacked lunches in hand. Posters lined the wall promoting the upcoming Spring Dance the college was having the next week. Erin would love to have Carol on her arm but she knew that wouldn't be a possibility. Instead they would spend a quiet evening at home, she surmised. That was fine by her, since she did love to 'steal away' with Carol. But some times, she wished that things were different, that it didn't matter that Carol was a woman or a cop. In the real world, she told herself, it just doesn't work that way. So she told herself to be content with what she did have – a woman who seemed to truly adore her and someone that wasn't afraid to question her or make her think about her course in life.

"Here," Erin said as she came to a lazy stop. She pointed to a framed picture on the wall. The colors were brilliant and the contrasts had no distinguishable features.

"What's this?" Carol asked.

"It's one of my other works."

Carol didn't know what to make of it and she cocked her head from one side to the other - wondering just what the hell it was. One thing was certain, it wasn't like the other paintings she'd already seen or the sketches they'd played with just a few nights before. Finally, she decided to ask.

"What the hell is that?" Carol chuckled dryly, shaking her head.

Erin joined in her laughter, not offended in the least. She'd expected such a reaction after Carol had seen her other work.

Erin chuckled again. "It's modern abstract art . . . Kind of like Warhol's work . . . if you like that shit," she swore under her breath.

Carol laughed. She'd never heard Erin swear outside of topics concerning her parents or her causes. It was kind of endearing and humanizing. "I take it you don't like Andy's work then," Carol responded with a grin.

"Oh I'm sure many people love his work but I can't say that I'm one of them. I mean a bunch of soup cans. How original is that?"

"You mean the Campbell thing with the-."

"Yeah! Makes me wonder how many other artists out there are striving for notoriety with their own creations while he comes up with 'mmm, mmm good'. As a sketch artist and painter, I find it lacks merit."

"Ya got a point," Carol said going back to examining the work. After a few moments Carol turned back to Erin, "I like it," she announced.

"Oh really?" Erin asked skeptically.

Carol paused a moment before sighing. "No, I'm just trying not to offend you," Carol laughed nervously. "Look I'm sure it's a wonderful abstract painting. I'm just . . . "

"Not into abstract art?" Erin offered.

"Exactly!" Carol answered, relieved that Erin didn't take it personally.

"Good, cuz neither am I," the radical grinned. "I did this piece in my sophomore year and my instructor just loved it. Many famous painters line the walls here," Erin added with a wave down the corridor. "He wanted to hang it. So who was I to say no? I gave it to the University. Maybe someday the fact that my name is on this will mean something."

"You said before you didn't want to do this as a living?" Carol asked, indicating the painting with one large hand.

"I'm majoring in political science and journalism. I have dreams of my art being something someday, but I'm not a dummy," she grinned.

Carol reached out and stroked the length of Erin's arm. "Dreams are wonderful. I think if we stop dreaming, we stop living."

"Honestly?" Erin questioned with a raised eyebrow.

"Oh, absolutely." Carol replied quickly. "Why do you ask?"

"You don't strike me as a dreamer, Carol. You seem so deep in reality is all."

"Perhaps, but everyone should have dreams," Carol answered.

Erin came within inches of Carol looking up into the deep blue of the officer's eyes. "And what about you Carol? What are your dreams?"

Carol let out a ragged sigh. "To be the best cop I can be. To be a leader of men and women. To make new strides that haven't been made within the department. But you know what I'm dreaming right now?"

"What's that?" Erin asked playfully, trying to keep to the course Carol was setting.

"I'm dreaming of a ham on rye," she said, waving her bag.

Erin gave a breezy smile and took Carol by the hand, leading her to the exit. "I know a perfect place at the student union. Come on."

Moments later they were in a cellar eating their lunch, sharing their sandwiches. It was well lit with a jukebox and a pool table and various tables and chairs throughout. It was a relaxing place where students could unwind. *Well at least they could if you weren't around* Carol figured after the hundredth set of eyes had examined her presence yet again.

Carol had to commend Erin's assessment of the cafeteria's quality. It was pretty damn good for school food. Heck, it was even better than the deli she and Randell often frequented during lunch. They sat finishing up the last of the meal when they noticed Stan making his way over. Erin tensed at first but pushed it down. Carol was the woman she was falling for, uniform or not, and she refused to let the officer's exterior be a problem for her in front of her friends. She certainly didn't want Carol to think that she was embarrassed to be seen with her.

"You okay?" he asked suspiciously as he walked up, his eyes shifting between the officer and his friend. He thought perhaps Erin had found herself in another pair of handcuffs.

"I'm fine, Stan," Erin replied with a smile. Suddenly her expression shifted to questioning. "Hold on. Aren't you supposed to be in World Geography now?" Erin realized, looking at her watch.

"Yeah, but Minos sent me to find you. I've been looking all morning," he replied. He did a double take on his next glance to Carol. Realization washed over his face - it was the same woman that was in his kitchen. "Oh my God, you're a cop?" he exclaimed.

Carol and Erin looked at each other and burst out laughing. "No Stan, she's just got a thing for dressing in police apparel," Erin said sarcastically between chuckles.

"But don't worry," Carol added calmly, taking a drink of her soda. "It's not contagious."

Erin and Carol looked back at each other and started to laugh again.

"Whoa, man, that's heavy. A cop, huh?" he sighed, shaking his head. He looked up to see two sets of eyes burning into him. "I mean it's not bad or anything. I think . . . nah, it's kinda groovy –

fighting the establishment of our establishment by befriending the establishment. It's a pretty deep statement," he said nodding his head repeatedly.

"It's not a statement," Erin said shortly. "It's a relationship."

"A relationship? So are you two kinda . . . " He let the sentence hang, not sure where he wanted to go with it or what he really wanted to say.

"Kinda what?" Erin challenged. She figured if she had to make him say it then he wouldn't and he'd let the subject drop. When he didn't add more she continued. "She's the officer that took me to the hospital the day of the riot. But don't you dare tell anyone. I'm not ready for the heat this will bring yet," she added in after thought.

"No problem," he said holding up his hands. "I told you I think it's cool so I'll keep my mouth shut."

"Anyway, you said you had a message or something," Erin said impatiently.

"Oh yeah! Minos said your mom called about your dad. Or was it your dad called about your mom? Shit, I don't remember. I was half toked when she told me to find you." Stan froze, realized what he just said and in what company he had said it. Erin didn't notice. She was too deep in thought. "Anyway, you're supposed to call home. Gotta run. See ya."

Stan made his way from the pair as Carol grinned and shook her head at the now paranoid message boy. She might have been in the uniform but she wasn't always a cop. Carol was going to make some joking comment to her young companion but the expression on Erin's face altered her words.

"What's wrong, Erin?" she found herself saying instead. The girl had grown as white as a sheet in the course of the thirty seconds it had taken Stan to deliver his message.

Erin came back from her thoughts at the sound of Carol's voice. "Do you think you can find your way back without me?"

"Sure," Carol answered, rising up along with Erin. "Is everything all right, sweetheart?" Carol could see Erin was shaken by the message and not just emotionally. Her young love interest was physically vibrating.

"I don't think so," Erin said, a sob teetering on the edge of her voice. "I can't explain now. Can I call you at home later tonight?" The question sounded like a plea.

Carol smoothed large hands over Erin's arms, hoping to calm the young woman's jumping nerves. She'd never seen Erin this unsettled before and it frightened her. She wanted to demand that the blonde tell her everything right then but she kept her voice flat and even.

"You can call me any time."

Erin nodded and started to make her way home but Carol couldn't let her leave like that. She stopped Erin and brought her into a tight embrace, nearly crushing the young woman against her.

"I love you," Carol whispered into the honey-hair.

She wasn't sure how it slipped out but it felt so natural and she hoped the confession didn't cause Erin more distress. She hadn't spoken the actual words before to Erin but she felt the young woman might need to hear them. She was relieved when she felt the woman's tension ease just a bit and her returning grip get firmer. But soon, Erin pulled back a few inches, her hands gently tugging Carol's head down.

"I love you, too," Erin returned the whisper. She reaffirmed her words with a light, affectionate kiss to Carol's cheek. To the outside observer it could be considered platonic in nature. But to the both of them it was larger than the universe. "I'll call tonight. I promise."

With that, Carol let Erin leave her embrace. Only after the girl was out of sight did she make her way back to the station house.

After Carol met up with Randell again, the desk sergeant had given them another assignment.

"You've got to be kidding me?" she groaned, looking at the slip of paper she held in her right hand. She glanced from the script on the page to the sergeant.

He smiled gleefully, his grizzled appearance actually seeming to soften with the smile. "All yours, Johnson. Do us proud."

"C'mon now," she complained. "This is rookie stuff."

The sergeant raised one bushy eyebrow. "Are you refusing an assignment, Johnson?"

"Of course not," she replied softly, promising herself she wouldn't complain again. She waved Randell along and they checked a black and white out of the car pool and made their way to the address on the page. Pulling up in front of the corner store, she shook her head ruefully before sliding out from behind the wheel and closing and locking her door.

"Mr. Barnes?" she called as she opened the door to the small grocery store with Randell right behind her. "It's Officer Johnson.

One Belief Away

Hello?" The tall woman closed the door behind her, the jangling of bells disturbing the silence of the store. "Mr. Barnes?"

"In here," he called from the back room and Carol made her way through the main aisle and around the cash register to the storage room beyond. A cold breeze floated in from the back door, which opened out onto an alley. It was in this open doorway that she found Mr. Barnes and his latest unfortunate victim.

Mr. Barnes was an elderly man who gave every appearance of being fragile but he had a hot temper that immediately flared any time he thought someone might be insulting him. Apparently, the milk deliveryman had offended him today and had found himself in an unpleasant position. Wiry Mr. Barnes had the tall white uniformed man backed against the wall just inside the door, a broad mop held across the taller man's throat.

"What's the story, Mr. Barnes?" Carol said coolly, trying not to sound as bored as she was. They got a call about once a week from the cagey old man and it was always something painfully ridiculous.

"Young lady," he began, glancing away from his prey long enough to run a discerning gaze up Carol's lanky form. "This thief tried to trick me out of two quarts of milk! I run an honest business here and I won't be taken advantage of!"

Carol ignored the slimy feeling of being leered at by a seventy-year-old man and instead turned her attention to the guy in the uniform. "What's your name?" she asked shortly.

"Ben. Ben Casings," the man responded. He sounded more annoyed than frightened and that humored Carol slightly.

"Okay, Ben. I'm Carol Johnson. This is my partner Randell Stevens. The station sent us down to see if we could help you guys work this out peacefully." She turned her attention back to the elderly man still wielding the mop. "Put down your weapon, Mr. Barnes. Ben isn't going anywhere. Are ya, Ben?"

"No ma'am," the man agreed affably. Carol guessed him to be in his early thirties. He was calm and collected in his white uniform with his short hair and clean-shaven face. He didn't look like a thief. Of course, none of Mr. Barnes' victims had been proven a thief yet.

"Officer Johnson, I won't be made a mockery of," Mr. Barnes declared.

Too late, Carol thought to herself, biting back the sigh at the edge of her lips. "Of course not, sir. Put down the mop and we'll get to the bottom of this."

It took nearly two hours to go through the inventory on the truck, in the store, and the delivery orders to determine that the elderly storeowner had not, in fact, been cheated out of anything. Luckily, once the man saw all the proof and paperwork in front of him he had the good sense to back down and apologize to the unfortunate delivery man who was now well behind schedule. After bidding Mr. Barnes goodbye, Carol walked out into the alley with Ben as Randell made his way to the squad car.

"Sorry about that," she said with a slight grin. "Happens about once a week. Didn't your company tell you?"

"Nah. Started new just yesterday. I think they were trying to initiate me."

Carol laughed, shaking her head. "We do the same to rookies . . . send them to Mr. Barnes here for a day of counting stock. Unfortunately, we had no rookies who could reply to the call so here I am. Hope it wasn't too painful for you," Carol added.

"Not at all," he smiled softly.

"Well Ben, you can press charges if you're so inclined. He did hold you at mop point."

Ben shook his head with a grin, opening the door to his truck and climbing up inside. "I'll just pay more attention next time I work with the old man," he sighed.

"Most do," Carol agreed, her thoughts already wandering back to her house and how empty it would be. She'd hoped Erin might be able to come over tonight but the mysterious phone call from home could very well prevent that. She checked her watch.

"Get off soon?" the man asked, leaning an elbow on the steering wheel.

"Huh?" Carol looked up. "Oh . . . yeah." It wasn't until her eyes met his that she noticed how the man was looking at her. His expression was gentle and hopeful and while Carol certainly didn't find him unpleasant, she couldn't see herself spending any free time with him.

"Interested in a cup of coffee when you get off? I have to deliver quite a bit more but I could meet you around, what, six?"

She found herself blushing at his attention as she smoothed a wayward wisp behind her ear where it had escaped from the French braid. "No thanks," she smiled.

"No really, just a cup of coffee. I find you really intriguing." He made an obvious glance at her finger. "You're not married."

"No, I'm not," she agreed. "But I'm involved with someone. I do appreciate the thought," she assured him, trying to let him down easy, flattered by his gentle attention. "If you change your mind about the charges, c'mon down to the station."

Not waiting for his response, she waved at him slightly and then made her way down the alley toward the parked patrol car. *Involved with someone*, she mused. *And she told me she loves me.* She realized the grin on her face probably made her look plain goofy but she didn't care.

Chapter 12

Hours later, Carol moved quietly around the house. She'd put on a TV dinner, not wanting to make a meal for just herself, and was now walking through her father's office, tilting her head to read the spines of the books on shelves. She wanted something to curl up with, to distract herself from the fact that she was lonely. She'd been alone a large part of her life, never making close friends or having lasting relationships, but this was the first time she remembered feeling lonely.

Part of her was also concerned for her young friend's well-being. When Erin had left, the hippie was obviously nervous or upset about something. Carol realized she knew very little about the spunky blonde aside from her arrest record, her big heart and her zeal for life. She couldn't even begin to imagine what had caused her friend such concern.

Finally, Carol settled on an old favorite of her father's, one she had read many times herself and carried her selection back with her to the kitchen. She tossed the paperback on the table and cracked the oven to peek at her dinner. The ringing phone startled her.

"Hello?"

"Hey," the soft voice was immediately recognizable.

Carol sat down, relieved to hear Erin but also immediately concerned by the defeat she heard in the now familiar tones. "What is it, hon?"

"I . . . uh . . . " the young woman sounded like she had either been crying or was about to soon. "I may not be around for a few days. I wanted you to know."

"What's wrong?" Carol inquired gently, wishing the blonde was here so she could hold her tight and comfort her.

"Something at home," she sighed, obviously struggling with how much to share.

"Erin," the dark woman said softly, her husky voice lilting warmly into the phone. "You don't have to tell me anything you're not ready to. I promised that. But know that nothing could change how I feel about you."

The blonde laughed dryly with little humor actually in the sound. "God, I wish I were there right now."

Carol hopped up. "I'll come get you, Erin. We can talk for a while, or let me just hold you," she wondered if she sounded as desperate as she felt. "Are you at the house, sweetheart?"

"No . . . no," the blonde stammered. "I mean, yes I am. No, you don't need to come here. I'm packing some stuff and then Minos is going to take me to the bus station. My bus leaves at eight."

"I could take you there myself," Carol offered. "You wouldn't have to go by bus."

"That's okay," Erin replied.

"Then can I come by and pick you up? I'll sit with you until you need to leave."

Her request was answered with a ragged breath.

"Erin, I know I'm pleading . . . and maybe I sound too desperate. But I can tell how much you're upset. I love you and I want to help," Carol's voice was no more than a whisper when she finished and she could hear across the line that Erin was crying now.

"I don't feel right dragging you into this mess," she said at last. "It's something I started a long time ago and it's not right for you to have to be involved."

"I love you so that makes me involved. I want to help you, Erin. Let me do that." Had it always been so hard for this woman to accept someone's assistance? How had Minos ever gotten in?

Erin was quiet for a long moment before she took a deep breath. "I'll be ready to go in twenty minutes. That would give us time for a coffee while we wait."

"I'll be right there," Carol promised. "Bye." She barely waited for Erin's response before she hung up and turned off the oven. She dragged the aluminum dish out and set it on the cold burners before finding her keys and coat and heading out the front door.

Erin and Minos sat side by side on the top step of the dilapidated porch. Carol parked the Mustang right in front of the house and made her way cautiously up the walk. The two women sat very close to each other, the older one's arm around the slight blonde's shoulders, her head tilted as she spoke to Erin in muffled tones.

The night was clear and cool, the April breeze doing little more than ruffling Carol's bangs. She walked up silently, kneeling in front of the two on the step. Minos looked up first and for the first time since they'd met, Carol saw gentle acceptance in her gaze.

Minos grinned meekly, murmured something to Erin, then kissed her cheek warmly and went inside, leaving the two women on their own. Carol took up the recently vacated seat.

"Hey," the officer said softly, reaching out a large hand and stroking her young friend's hunched back.

"Hi," Erin looked up and smiled weakly, wiping her sleeve across watery green eyes.

"I . . . I want to ask you some questions, Erin," Carol said slowly. She'd thought about this the entire drive across town. "If you don't want to answer, that's okay."

Without comment, Erin nodded.

"Are you walking into a dangerous situation by going home? Will they hurt you?" the officer asked carefully.

"No," Erin sniffed, wiping her eyes again. "They won't hurt me. Probably tell me how worthless I am and how I'm an embarrassment," she let out a watery laugh. "They'll try to make me stay . . . but they won't lay a hand on me."

Though she spoke the words with a certain amount of conviction, she couldn't help but wonder if it was the truth. Her mother had never physically hurt her and never would, of that she had no doubt. Of course, the state of her stepfather's health would be the determining factor in his own ability to hurt her. She decided to leave that out, easily sensing her dark companion's concern.

"Are you afraid to go back?"

"A little. I never planned to. I kinda burned some bridges, ya know?" *Or the bridges were burned for me*, she thought. *But I never tried to stop the flames.*

"Yeah," Carol agreed, using her large hand to rub up and down the small woman's back.

"If I stay too long, I might not be able to graduate."

"How long do you think you'll be gone?" Carol asked moving her hand up to smooth away long strawberry blonde hair. The smaller woman's cheeks were wet and glistening in the porch light.

She shrugged, tilting her head to meet concerned blue eyes. "What do you see in me?"

It was such a sad, insecure question from this young woman who had an uncanny ability to exude confidence. The question that seemed to come out of nowhere nearly broke Carol's heart. "I love you," she said gently. "You're warm, funny, brilliant and witty. What's not to see, huh?"

Erin grinned slightly before looking away, letting her emerald gaze travel across the darkened front yard to the street beyond.

"No matter how they make you feel, Erin, or what they say . . . they can't take away what you are inside. You know that."

"Yeah," the blonde chuckled softly. "Yeah. It took me a long time to realize that . . . what I could be without them, in spite of them. The skin's still a little soft sometimes."

Carol slid closer and wrapped her arms around the small woman, relieved when Erin relaxed in her embrace. "A couple days, you think?"

"Probably," Erin's response was muffled by the dark woman's shoulder. She sighed. "Maybe sooner. Maybe even tomorrow. My stepfather is really sick. My mom asked me to come back."

"So it could be awhile?"

"Maybe. But I have to graduate, Carol. I didn't come this far not to."

The officer nodded, pulling the smaller woman around so the blonde straddled her lap. The new position allowed Carol to embrace her companion more tightly. "How far away is home?" Carol questioned, tilting her head into blonde tresses.

"This is home," Erin responded without hesitation.

Carol smiled softly, kissing the head tucked beneath her chin. "How far away is your mom?"

"Four hours by bus."

"If you need to come home for final exams, I'll come get you. Okay? And then take you back to your mom's."

"You would do that?"

"Of course, Erin. You have to graduate. You've worked too hard."

"I love you," Erin murmured, snuggling deeper into the strong arms.

"C'mon," Carol began to disentangle herself. "Let's go get that coffee?"

"Yeah," the blonde wiped at her tears one last time, using Carol's broad shoulders to push herself to a standing position. "Thank you for coming over," she smiled shyly.

The officer returned the smile and gently ruffled her companion's hair. "This your bag?"

Erin nodded silently and followed Carol down the walk and toward the waiting car.

No one had met Erin at the bus stop, not that it had surprised her necessarily, but the inconvenience of hitching a ride across town had slowed her down considerably. When she'd arrived at the house, there was only a housekeeper there. It wasn't the large Hispanic woman, Maria, she remembered from her youth but instead was a svelte, young bleached blonde. She imagined her stepfather had had something to do with that change. Maria had been a wonderful woman with a huge heart, raising Erin and caring for her as if she was blood. In fact, it was Maria that Erin had cried for on the nights after she had left. Never once had she shed a tear for either of her parents.

The new housekeeper had been rude and disdainful, her brown eyes looking down an aquiline nose at the young hippie before her. Staying there for the night was certainly out of the question. Hell, the woman wouldn't even let her in the front door! She knew there was no chance the maid would let her wait for her mother to return, either. Had Erin not been so out of sorts from the long bus ride and the hassle of getting there, she would have launched a few choice words in this woman's direction. Instead, she simply asked which hospital they were at and then began the mundane duty of hitching another ride across town.

Once downtown and within close range of the hospital she found a musician on the street corner playing guitar and singing Joni Mitchell songs. The first thing Erin noticed about her, beside the fact she had a really good voice, was that she resembled Carol. The similarity she saw made her ache for her officer back home even though it had only been hours since she saw her last. Erin chastised herself for not letting Carol help her when she offered.

When the woman finished 'Big Yellow Taxi' and collected her money from her guitar case she walked over to Erin. "Hi there," she said softly with a warm grin. "You've been standing there quite awhile," she commented.

"I was enjoying your music," Erin replied honestly.

"Do you play?" the woman asked.

"No, I'm an artist," Erin answered.

"Really?" the woman replied, obviously interested. "What do you do?"

"Lots of stuff with brushes and pencils," Erin smiled. "Been playing long?" Erin asked, nodding to the guitar case the woman held.

"Why? Does it sound like I just started?" the woman laughed.

Erin chuckled at that reply. There was something about the woman, as if she was a kindred spirit. "No, in fact you sound better than Mitchell," she complimented.

That earned her a smile from the woman and the offer of a handshake, "I'm Terri."

Erin didn't know how to reply. Was she Skylon or was she Erin? Her identity had begun to change so much since meeting Carol. The officer always used her given name when she referred to her. Erin realized she had to give an answer soon or the woman would think she was a total idiot.

"I'm sorry," she apologized, taking the hand offered. "Erin," she added, making her decision.

The woman released her hand and pointed up the street. "There's a late night coffee house up the block. Think you might want to grab a cup of coffee and chat? You don't look like you're heading anywhere in particular."

"Sure," Erin answered. "Need any help with that?" she said motioning to the case.

"Nah," the woman replied starting to walk. "Come on. It's not far."

The two walked the short distance and took a seat at a table for two. Terri leaned the case against the wall behind them and went to place their order. When she returned with two steaming mugs, Erin asked how much she owed but Terri told her not to worry, adding that she should just return the favor to someone else someday. Erin could tell, that if given the chance, this was someone with whom she could have a really great friendship. However, she knew her time was limited. Soon she'd have to find

121

a place for the night and in the morning, make her way to the hospital.

"Are you from around here?" Terri asked.

"Originally," Erin replied. "I'm going to State now but my stepfather's sick so my mother asked me to come home."

"I'm sorry to hear that," the singer apologized.

"Don't be," Erin grinned. "My family isn't the Brady Bunch."

"Whose is?" Terri answered. "I know I'm not the little girl my folks wanted me to be," she added. "Living in a commune house, playing music on street corners, chasing eligible women." Terri paused to get Erin's reaction.

Erin chuckled, "We sound a lot alike – I've got my commune, my art . . . as for chasing women…there's only one woman I'd like to chase."

A silence fell between them and Erin could feel Terri's eyes examining her, wondering if she should proceed. Terri was certain that she wasn't offended by the fact she was inclined to spend 'quality time' with the fairer sex. *What the hell*, Terri considered. *Go for it.*

"You're free to chase me. Are you an eligible woman?" Terri asked, easing her way into perhaps making a proposition to Erin.

"Actually, no," Erin answered, quite certain in her resolve. "I've got a wonderful woman back home. I should say I caught a wonderful woman."

Terri smiled at the fact she called it right. She let out an exaggerated sigh. "All the good ones are taken . . . Well, you can't blame me for trying," she added.

Erin smiled and sipped her coffee. "Not in the least," she replied. "So you never answered me before – how long have you played?"

"About 10 years now," she answered. "My parents thought it would help if I learned an instrument. Now they are cursing the days they paid for lessons. My 'artistic talent' was going to impress their friends and any of my future beaus. They had no idea I'd someday be doing protest music and spend my free time ogling beautiful women," she chuckled.

"Nothing ever goes as one plans," Erin offered, a knowing grin on her face.

"You can say that again," Terri agreed, raising her mug in toast. Erin softly clinked hers against Terri's before taking a drink. "Ahhh," Terri hummed. "Good coffee," she sighed.

One Belief Away

"Yeah it is," Erin nodded. "Not as good as Carol's though. Carol makes the best coffee," she added.

"I take it Carol's your lady?" Terri asked.

Erin nodded. "She wanted to bring me here but at the time I thought this was something I had to do alone. But the more I think about it, the more I wish I had brought her with me . . . Now I've got no money, no place to stay and the hospital won't let me in until tomorrow morning and I miss her . . . But it's more than that. She doesn't know the whole story about my upbringing and I think I should have shared that with her; opened up to her."

"What about your parent's house?" Terri asked. "They won't let you stay there?"

"Mother wasn't home. Stepfather's in the hospital. New maid won't let me in," Erin said in a choppy, short recap.

"That's cold," Terri told her.

"That's life, or as we just said . . . things never go as planned."

"Well you can stay with me tonight," Terri offered. Erin rolled her shoulders and the singer could feel her reluctance. "No, seriously. Forget what I said earlier. Remember I said 'eligible women' and I know you're not one of them. You're off limits," Terri smiled. "You can crash at my pad. I've got other roommates but they won't mind an extra body there for a night or two."

"I don't want to put you out," Erin replied politely.

"Don't be silly," Terri answered. "People come to our place all the time. Some call it the hippie haven in these parts. I think they even took in a circus act one day last week. Monkeys and all," she teased. "I'm sure one little artist who's going to 'State' won't be a problem." Erin considered it. Terri could tell by the expression on her face. "You mean to tell me your house has never taken anyone in?" she added.

Erin smiled. They took people in all the time that needed a place to rest their heads for a few days or, sometimes, a few weeks. "Okay," she answered. "But if I see anyone playing 'Helter Skelter' I'm outta there," she warned, waving her finger.

Terri laughed but slowly turned serious, "Hey, I know. Manson gave us a bad rap but we're not a fanatic cult - just a group of folks who live by their own rules and want to help where we can."

"Well, thanks for the offer Terri. I'm sure your place is much better than the bus station," Erin smirked.

"Well," Terri said rising and picking up her guitar. "I'm not sure about that. We're still trying to get rid of the monkey smell," she joked. "Come on, let's head outta here."

Chapter 13

The evening had passed and Carol had to admit she had a fitful night's sleep – if it could even have been called sleep. She kept having dreams of Erin all night – some happy and some very dark with the young girl crying in her arms. Carol tried repeatedly to get her to open up but the girl refused to do anything but cry. When the alarm rang at 6 it was somewhat of a relief for Carol. She could finally start the day and with any luck be able to talk to Erin at some point.

But for now, she and Randell pounded their beat just as they had always done.

"Kid busting windows. This is real challenging police work," Randell said as he and Carol walked the back alley of a strip mall. "You know I don't expect undercover stake-outs and high speed pursuits but you gotta admit these last two weeks have been dull."

"We're serving and protecting, Randell," Carol chuckled. "Serving and protecting, remember that."

Randell grinned and tapped Carol on the arm. "We should have taken an extra hour for lunch today. Jones and Peterman could have answered this call instead of us," he conspired.

"Actually, I wouldn't have minded. A friend of mine got some bad news and I haven't heard from her since yesterday. I would have been able to call her house and see how things are going," Carol said in agreement.

"A friend?" Randell teased. "I didn't know you had 'friends' Johnson. How can anyone stand to be around you that long?"

"Very funny," Carol smiled. "But I'll have you know I'm a very warm and caring person. Underneath this tough exterior beats the heart of a saint."

"Don't tell me. Your phone just rings off the wall at night," he replied. He looked around the alley, found some broken glass and kicked it away.

"Well, I'm not sure if my phone rings off the wall but my little black book is just overflowing," she teased.

Randell began to chuckle but the sound of breaking glass stopped him abruptly. The two looked at each other and picked up their pace toward the noise. They watched as a young man, probably in his late teens, early 20's, swung wildly with a baseball bat.

"Looks like he's juiced up," Randell whispered to Carol.

"Let me do the talking, okay?" she answered.

"Sure thing. You do much better at speaking the language of the insane," he teased with a grin.

Carol let the comment go by without a retort and took a deep breath as they stepped out to face the man who wore a white collegiate sweatshirt.

"Hey buddy," Carol started conversationally. "What seems to be the problem here?"

"Stay outta this, pig!"

The young man swung again, shattering yet another window. Randell put his hand on his gun but Carol kept her hands up, showing she was no threat, as they stepped closer. The young man started to grow more agitated and repeatedly mumbled something unintelligible. Carol was convinced he was tripping pretty badly. Drugs, a lot of anger and a hard wooden bat could be a lethal combination and Carol took it all quite seriously.

"I don't want any trouble," Carol told him. "I just want to talk to you a minute so put the bat down."

He swung violently at Carol and she leaned back to avoid him. "Fuck you, pig! Go to hell or you're next! You hear me?"

Randell watched Carol's back while she crept closer to the young man, still trying to find a way to reason with him. He was sweating and shaking. More obscenities and disjointed words flowed from his lips. Soon he got very quiet and started to pace erratically.

One Belief Away

"Let's talk about this," Carol offered again. "I'm not sure what those windows did to offend you but they sure are taking a beating, wouldn't you say?" Maybe a bit of levity would work.

"Like you're gonna help me, right pig? Who do you think you are? Big bitch with a badge? I can take you out ya know. Just like that I'd take you out." His speech was quick and his movements even quicker. Suddenly, he started to spit at Carol and laugh wildly. With a mighty swing he went after Carol again. This time taking three swipes but not hitting his target. Randell pulled his gun and Carol pulled her nightstick. She didn't want to shoot. She figured she'd still try to reason with him on some level. It was obvious the kid had no idea what he was doing. Randell sensed it too, which was why he didn't fire. When the kid got so close that Carol couldn't lean back to avoid him she ducked and worked her way behind him. Levity was certainly out of the question now.

The young man grew even more irate when he realized he was trapped. He swung again and Carol connected with her baton, hoping to knock the wooden weapon from his hands. It didn't work. Instead of making Carol his target he decided to take on Randell who wasn't quite as far away now. The kid swung once and connected with Randell's arm, the force of it knocking him against the alley wall. He reared back to hit Randell again.

"Drop the bat!" Carol yelled. The baton was now at her feet and the service revolver was planted firmly in her grasp.

What transpired next only took a few seconds. Randell regrouped and raised his arm to fire. The man looked back at Carol as if taunting her with the fact that he was going to strike again. He reared back. She knew she couldn't let that happen. She fired once and everything seemed to stop. The bat fell from his fingertips and the young man staggered back against the wall, a crimson mark growing on his sweatshirt. As he fell to the ground, Randell managed to soften his impact.

"Call an ambulance," he barked. "Now!"

Carol felt dazed by what had happened. But the sound of Randell's voice jarred her feet into action. She ran to the black and white car and radioed for help. Everything seemed to blur. Her head was swimming from moment to moment. She could remember Randell trying to help the young man and the paramedics taking the man away.

Suddenly, she was in the captain's office but for the life of her she couldn't remember how she got there. Once more the sound of the Randell's voice brought her back from her confusion.

"You can't do that, sir!"

"Don't tell me what I can and can't do. She's on desk duty until internal affairs say otherwise. And if you don't want to join her, you'll keep your trap shut," the captain warned.

"But sir," Randell sighed in frustration.

"Didn't you hear me?"

Carol's mind lifted from the fog it was in to look to her partner. "Don't. Let it go."

"But Johnson, it was a clean hit. I was there. That kid-."

"Has turned into an explosive situation!" the captain shouted, cutting Randell off. "I've got the mayor's office breathin' down my neck to suspend, and even fire, both of you. And I wouldn't be a bit surprised if that damned campus doesn't tear down these walls for shooting an unarmed student. So get the hell out of my office - NOW!"

Randell tried yet again to speak in Carol's defense. "He wasn't unarmed. He-."

"Enough!" the captain yelled. "Get out of here. Both of you. . And don't say a goddamned word about this to anyone. God knows we don't need the press all over this!"

"Yes sir," Carol nodded.

The captain then looked to Randell to hear his agreement. Randell paused a moment so as not to give him too much satisfaction.

"Yes sir," he answered, "Loud and-."

"I expect you both to be back here in this office for review at 8:00 a.m. sharp. Got it?"

Randell was even more pissed. The office door almost came from its hinges as he ripped it open. The tremendous rattling noise that followed could be heard throughout the precinct. Quietly, with much less commotion, Carol followed him back to the locker area. She heard the slamming of a locker door repeatedly as she entered. She walked around the corner to find Randell now pacing.

"Thank you for defending me," Carol told him sincerely.

"You know, I've been on the job for nearly 20 years now. I've seen just about everything. But this tops it!" Carol watched him walk back and forth in front of her as she took a seat on the wooden bench in front of the lockers. "I can't believe they're doing this to you. If it had been me and that kid had charged you I would have done the same thing. You're a damn good cop, Johnson. I know I tease and harass you but that's because I respect you. Your old man did a good job of raising you and you don't deserve this kind of shit."

"There's no sense in getting yourself demoted over this, Randell. Besides, he didn't say this was permanent. When things cool down then maybe I'll be back on the street."

Randell's pacing had now become annoying and Carol grabbed him by the arm, making him sit on the bench next to her.

"It's not right, Carol. We didn't know what the hell that kid was gonna do. Hell, he hit me first. I was gonna fire but you beat me to it. It could just as easily have been me that shot him. And you know what . . . if it had been me I bet . . . well, the situation would be a lot different. As much as I hate to admit that, it would . . . Jesus, this really sucks," he said in defeat.

"In any case," Carol said with a pat to his back, "thank you again for defending me."

Randell looked over at Carol with an expression far more serious than Carol had ever seen before on his face. "That's what partners do - which is exactly what you did today in that alley. Don't let them make you think any different."

Carol gave a weak smile and stood up, taking Randell with her. "Go home. Go see your wife. We'll come in tomorrow and turn in our reports. Okay?"

"I don't like it," Randell muttered.

"I know," Carol agreed. "But we do it by the book from here on out, okay? Please? No going to the press. No going back to the captain. We come in tomorrow and we give our statements. Alright?"

Randell gave a reluctant nod before he answered, "By the book, I promise."

The desk sergeant poked his head inside the door and Randell turned to him. "What is it?" he asked.

"Just thought you should know . . . The hospital just called. That kid Johnson shot died about a half hour ago."

Erin hadn't gotten much rest the night prior, either. Terri's place was wonderful and her friends just as gracious as she was. But it still wasn't 'home' which made for a fitful sleep. Terri offered Erin the chance to return if need be but Erin declined saying she'd probably be heading back to the university soon. They wished each other well and Erin started on her way to the hospital. It was only a few blocks and before she realized it she was standing in front of the tall white building. Her images of

Carol, her past with her parents and the worry of what might be said clouded her thoughts, making the trip seem much shorter than it was. She took an unsteady breath, raised her head and squared her shoulders. *You can do this*, she told herself.

After checking with registration, she made her way up to the room. Erin crept silently inside, looking right and left. She spotted her mother on the far-left side of her father's hospital bed. Tubes, wires and machines were littered around his area.

She was weary from her lack of sleep and emotional turmoil. But all of that seemed to leave her now as she peered at the two people in front of her. How long had it been since she saw them last? Five years, perhaps? The gray in her mother's hair had shocked Erin for a moment. Breathing hard, heart pounding, she crept closer.

"Mother?" she approached cautiously. She didn't add more, instead waiting to see what move, if any, her mother would make.

"I didn't think you'd come. Busy with your own life 'n all," her mother replied.

Erin let the comment go. She could tell that her mother was just looking for a fight like always. But instead of letting it provoke her she simply let it slide off her back. "What's wrong with him?"

The tone of the word 'him' didn't go unnoticed by mother or daughter. Erin didn't mean to let her disdain out but it just tumbled forward before she could stop it. She wanted to chalk it up to how tired she was, how drained, how much she longed for Carol's comforting presence. But the reality was that she could never think or speak of this man fondly.

"I know how you feel about David. You never-"

"If you say the words, 'got a chance to know him' I swear I will walk right out of this room," Erin barked, any pretense of being friendly jumping out the window into the sunlight beyond. "And I will never look back. I'm tired of the rhetoric, Mother. It's trite, clichéd and not worth listening to anymore - as you pointed out . . . I have my own life and all."

"Why do you hate him so?" her mother pled.

"You have to ask?"

She was an older version of Erin with darker hair. She still had the same green eyes and fair skin. Her light brown hair was streaked with gray and pulled back into a tight bun, so fitting for the woman herself. Erin tried, but she couldn't remember a time when she'd looked at her mother and felt anything but distaste.

One Belief Away

The distaste was for a woman who couldn't stand on her own two feet and say enough is enough - a woman who wouldn't defend her daughter from a man's brutality because she was afraid he'd leave her. She'd had nothing to fall back on; no schooling, no skills. She was raised to be a wife and a mother. She knew no other tasks and gave up her maternal responsibilities to support the man who put bread on her table.

Erin took a moment to consider her next words, tilting her head in thought, trying to rein in the overflowing emotions that threatened to break the dams of her restraint and come pouring forth in a vicious lashing.

"He always thought he was someone he's not, like my father. That man is not my father." She spoke the words neutrally, stepping closer so she was close enough to touch her mother but not daring to do so.

"He was the closest thing you've had to a father for years, Erin. People lose parents but you have to move on. You can't blame us for everything in your life." Her mother sounded weary and her words appeared rehearsed. Had she stayed up nights having imaginary conversations with her missing daughter? Had they looked for her? Had they cared? Obviously, her mother hadn't had too much trouble finding Erin this time. Did that mean she'd never even tried before?

Erin started to chuckle cynically, not believing for a moment that either had done anything but celebrate her disappearance.

"Who's blaming anyone here? Do you have a guilty conscience, Mother? Do you finally see that the years that man spent drinking have caught up to him?" Erin crept closer to get a better look at his face. "I'm surprised he's lasted this long," she smirked defiantly, hating the cold side of her that was coming forth but unable to control it. The hatred she felt for the man was thick and heavy in her stomach, the bile that rose scratching her throat and coming out in heartless words.

"That happens to be my husband you're talking about," her mother argued, still not raising her voice, still appearing weary and defeated.

"And I happen to be your daughter," Erin spat harshly, taking a step back, shaking her head. "But that didn't seem to matter to you, did it? You did every single thing that drunk told you to do because you had no backbone, no spirit to stand up for what was right. You never stood up for me, not once. In all the drunken battles I had with that man, and I use the term loosely, you never stood up for me. You were never there for me. Now the SOB is on his way to the other side and you need me to prop you up? Well, sorry Mother, it just doesn't work that way."

She willed herself not to cry, not wanting her mother to see how much she hurt inside. She felt the salty prickle of tears against the corners of her eyes and she pinched the bridge of her nose in an effort to hold them off.

"I asked you here because I thought it would be your last chance to make amends," her mother answered beginning to tear up She let go of her husband's hand to reach towards her daughter. The irony of that gesture was not lost on Erin but it simply wasn't enough. Not after all this time and all the heartache.

Erin's face was dark. Cold. Unreadable. "I love you, Mother, but I don't like you. And if a final peace with him is what you're looking for, well, let's just say that any hope of that was dashed with this scar," she said revealing her arm.

She didn't have to explain. Her mother remembered quite well how Erin had gotten it and she could no longer meet her eyes. All Erin could do was sigh in defeat and drop her arm to dangle by her side - nothing had changed after all these years she thought glumly.

"Look, Mom," Erin began, her anger deflated when she realized how pointless it was. She couldn't change things, never had been able to. "For what it's worth, I hope he pulls through for your sake. But don't ask me to do the 'Leave it to Beaver' scene. That just isn't gonna happen." With those final words, Erin turned her back on her mother and began to make her way to the door until the other woman's plea stopped her.

"Wait!" she exclaimed softly. Erin slowly turned to face her mother, wondering what would come next. She watched as the older woman struggled for something to add, some reason to keep her there a bit longer. But instead of words, she heard her mother sigh in defeat. "Take care of yourself, Erin," she stated softly.

Erin tried her damnedest to grin through the pain. It was the end of a chapter in her life and she could almost hear the book slam closed with harsh finality. I have no family. "Always."

She walked out without a backward glance.

Chapter 14

Erin sat on the bus heading home. She knew it would be late when she got in but she didn't care. It was better than staying up most of the night like she had the day before. Without money for a motel and not wanting to take advantage of Terri's generosity, heading home seemed like the best option. She was nearly asleep when a news report came over the radio about a university student being shot and killed by police earlier in the day.

Her head shot up and she looked around. She was only a few blocks away from Carol's. She was sure the officer would know what happened.

"Stop the bus!" she yelled up front.

The only other passenger looked up from the magazine he was reading as Erin grabbed her bag and moved to the door. The light rain from earlier that day had become a downpour by this time but she didn't care. The driver pulled to the side of the road and Erin sprinted down the street. By the time she made it to the house she was soaked all the way through. She tried to catch her breath even as she rang Carol's doorbell.

Carol had spent the evening sipping on a beer and staring out the window of her kitchen. She kept replaying the shooting over and over in her mind again. To make matters worse, she worried about Erin's predicament. The young woman was certainly shaken by the news she had received. Given the beatnik's resistance to questions regarding her family, Carol knew things in Erin's world weren't so rosy, either.

They had shared coffee at the bus station in relative silence that night, Carol reaching out constantly to stroke the other woman's arm in quiet support. Though she had never been a woman to show physical affection, her need to touch and reassure Erin was palpable and Carol found herself responding to that need without questioning how it would appear to the public. She hadn't cared.

Besides, it wasn't anything she wouldn't have done if Erin was just a friend instead of a love interest. Erin's slight shoulders had been hunched in agony and though the tears had stopped flowing, her green eyes had remained haunted. They'd hugged as Erin climbed on the bus, Carol murmuring gentle endearments that were returned in kind. Carol had stood silently aside and watched the bus pull out into the dark night and disappear on its journey toward the highway.

That haunted look had stayed with Carol constantly during her menial tasks and she hoped her young friend was coping with whatever horrors being home had wrought. As the officer finally decided to change out of her uniform she heard the doorbell. Glancing at the clock, she realized it was just past eight and she hadn't been expecting anyone. In her oversized shirt she went into the hallway and looked out the peephole. She was more than a little surprised to see her petite flower child standing outside.

"Erin?" she asked as she opened the door. The shock was evident in her voice.

"Heard about a shooting. Bad time?" the hippie asked still breathing hard, totally drenched. "I can come-"

"No! No!" Carol said gently pulling her inside. "I wasn't expecting to see you so soon. I've been so worried. Come on in, sweetheart."

Erin was edgy, fidgety. But she soon sported a devilish grin when she saw Carol's state of half-dress.

"Didn't mean to catch you with your pants down," she teased.

Carol quickly realized just what Erin was referring to and promptly blushed. "Yeah well, maybe I was in the middle of something when you knocked." She tried to tease with a suggestive tone while heading to the bedroom but Erin sensed something amiss in the comment.

"Fantasy is healthy," Erin retorted, following behind the officer. "At least that's what a beautiful woman told me once."

One Belief Away

Carol turned to see Erin beaming at her - full and bright. But even though she carried a smile Carol could tell the young woman carried something greater underneath it. Perhaps not sorrow so much as . . . frustration? Carol's curiosity got the better of her and she had to ask.

"So what brings you home so soon and so wet?" Carol tried to pose it conversationally as she pulled on a pair of bell-bottomed jeans and snapped the waist. Erin shrugged at first and Carol threw her robe on the bed so Erin could get out of her wet clothes. Carol turned and faced her closet as she removed her uniform shirt revealing the T-shirt underneath. Soon that slipped away as she readied another one to put on. Erin still hadn't spoken and Carol proceeded to search for something more comfortable to wear.

"You have a wonderful back," Erin replied as she stripped out of her clothes to don the robe. "Great definition in your shoulders - very firm, very strong."

"Very evasive." Carol turned back to Erin, smiling softly to take away any sting the words may have carried.

Erin knew she'd been busted and had to grin in response. "Okay, I'll give you a point for that one . . . I am being evasive." She bundled the robe around her as she took a seat on the bed.

Carol wasn't sure how to approach her growing sense of despair. She decided honesty was best.

"It worries me that you won't tell me," Carol confessed.

"Why?" Erin asked, leaning forward a bit to give Carol a little more of her attention.

She took a seat on the bed as she threw a sweatshirt on.

"I'm not sure," she answered. "It just feels like you don't trust me. Like you can't open up to me. I wish you could see that there isn't anything you could tell me or do that would make me love you any less. It just feels like . . . you won't let me in sometimes. But maybe you shouldn't trust me."

Carol's mind went to the shooting. How would Erin take the news? Maybe this entire conversation was moot. Erin would walk out and never come back. As it stood now, however, she was more concerned about the young woman than her own sense of guilt and wanted to find out just what had happened since she last saw her.

Erin considered the comment. It was the last thing in the world she intended. She valued Carol's trust in her and she thought she had been doing well to convey her feelings in return.

Apparently that was not the case and the longer she considered it the mistier her eyes became. Carol noticed Erin's discomfort.

"Hey!" Carol exclaimed tenderly. "Please don't cry. I didn't mean to hurt you."

Carol's concern was Erin's undoing and the tears began to flow freely. Carol gathered the young woman in her arms, pulled her tightly against herself and began to rock her gently.

"Shhh, it's okay," Carol reassured. "I'm not putting any pressure on you here, Erin. I just want you to know you have a place to go. That's if you want it, that is."

Erin knew Carol was right. She had finally found a home. A real home. Someplace where she could just be herself. Something she was never permitted to do before - not even in Minos' house - because even there she had a role she was expected to play.

Erin took a few gulps of air and wiped her eyes. "I'm sorry," she said, managing a grin. "I need to stop crying on you. Looks like I got your new shirt all wet," she added, pointing to the tear spots by Carol's breast.

"Yeah, but it will all come out in the wash," the officer teased, trying to relieve the young woman's tension a bit. "So how 'bout it? Think you can tell me?"

Erin smiled but soon felt her lip quivering. She loved Carol so much. And Carol obviously loved her, too. It was a unique situation - one that brought a caldron of emotions forth. Emotions Erin didn't even know she had. But instead of giving in to the tears again, she took a deep breath.

If Carol wanted to know all, she would tell all.

"My . . . stepfather is in the hospital," Erin began. "We never got along. He liked to drink. I liked to wear flower child clothes. We clashed quite a bit. He knocked me around sometimes, was very physical. But the worst of it was how often he told me I was nothing. That if I was worth something, they would love me. He said my drawings were wasteful scribbles . . . " she trailed off, looking up to meet gentle blue eyes. "I believed him, ya know? I was young and stupid and I thought that I was a bad person and that I deserved his words and his abuse. It went on for years. I was young when my father died and my mother remarried shortly after. I started hanging out with a kinda rough crowd at school, came home less and less. Maybe did some things I shouldn't have done, which made me believe that he was right all along: I was worthless."

One Belief Away

Carol didn't dare fill the silence but instead waited for Erin to continue. She could sense the sadness in the other woman and imagined the horror of her upbringing. Carol's father had been warm and supportive, always encouraging her and loving her despite any mistakes. It was obvious Erin had never had that. Not only had the man abused her physically, but he'd belittled the girl, crushed her spirit. Minos must have done a lot to bring back the vibrancy that Carol witnessed now daily. Only occasionally did the cop get any insight into the insecure girl hiding behind the brash woman. Despite her obvious differences with Minos, Carol was grateful to the other woman for what she had done for Erin.

Finally, after some calming breaths, Erin bared her arm to Carol. "I got this from a broken beer bottle - Miller by the way, in case you're curious," she added, trying as always to keep things light. "I got in late one night, senior year in high school, and he started in with his patented tramp speech. I was slutting around with the boys, so on and so forth," she waved a hand as if the whole thing were negligible. "Truth be known I was with Minos helping her move out of her house so she could come here to where we're at now. He hit me some, yelled at me a lot," she realized she was downplaying it. She remembered vividly cowering on the front porch of her childhood home, tucked into the corner. She'd covered herself with her arms, feeling the toe of his boot connecting with her ribs. She'd wondered vaguely why she'd even come home. "He broke the bottle over the porch railing and tried to slice off a part of my anatomy," Erin chuckled nervously, no humor in the rasping sound.

Carol didn't buy into it; she just listened intently and sorrowfully to Erin's tale.

"That night had been the final straw. In all of his abuse, he'd never done anything so violent. I moved and he sliced my arm instead. I ran into the house...Packed a quick bag...Got my schoolbooks and left. I never went back. I went to Minos and she took me in. I think she'd been waiting for me to make that decision. She knew what he was doing to me but I was so stubborn, even then, that she knew she couldn't tell me to walk away. I had to make that decision myself." She sighed, shrugged her shoulders and brought the story to the present. "Seems all his drinking has caught up to him. The nurse said he had a heart attack. His liver is shot to hell. Maybe she thought he and I could make amends . . ."

Carol didn't speak as Erin paused. She felt her anger for a man she never met brewing deep inside but she didn't dare let it show. She didn't want to frighten Erin since she had made such big strides in opening up. When Erin didn't continue, Carol knew she would have to speak so she tried to pick her words carefully.

"I don't know what to say," Carol answered honestly. "I'd say I'm sorry but you're not a woman who accepts pity. That much I know. I guess all I can say is that it's in the past. You've moved on and you're a very bright, talented woman who's got a cop who's crazy about you in every way."

Erin began to cry again and Carol immediately apologized, shaking her head at her own apparent insensitivity. Her apologies, however, were soon stifled as Erin put her hands up to stop her.

"I'm not crying now because I'm sad," Erin said, swallowing tears. "I'm happy for the first time in my life. I feel like I've found what I've been looking for." Carol wasn't sure where Erin was going so she held her tongue. "It's you," Erin chuckled. "All my life," she whispered as she met Carol's eyes. "It's you."

Carol realized that perhaps Erin wouldn't be as certain of her feelings if she knew of the shooting. She also knew she couldn't hide it. In fact, she didn't want to hide it. She wanted to share it with Erin and tell her how much she was aching inside. Erin could feel Carol retreat within herself even though she still sat only inches away.

"What's wrong?" Erin asked.

Carol felt her bottom lip start to quiver. "You're gonna hate me."

"What?" Erin asked, totally thrown by Carol's comment. Fear began to grip the young woman. Maybe Carol had changed her mind. Perhaps yet again she'd lose a home she thought she had found. "Why do you say that?"

Carol took a deep breath and regained herself. "The shooting . . . It was me . . . I killed the student."

Erin opened her mouth as if to say something but for once the articulate woman could find no words. Shock was an understatement. She shook her head trying to digest what Carol just said. How could that be possible? How could Carol kill someone? None of this made any sense.

"You killed a student?" Erin finally muttered.

"His name was Jimmy Watson," Carol answered, slipping into 'cop mode', sticking to the facts. "Did you know him?"

One Belief Away

Erin gave a small nod, still not able to trust her voice just yet. She watched as Carol began to pace in front of her, her arms folded across her chest as if she was closing herself off from the conversation. "He was in my American Lit class last year . . . You killed him?"

Carol just nodded.

Erin watched the woman pace in front of her a few more moments. Finally, Erin felt steady enough to speak. "Why did you kill him?" she asked.

"He came after me and Randell in an alley, behind the strip mall on 7th Street. He was breaking windows, shouting bizarre stuff at us . . . He must have been high," Carol explained.

"So you shot him? For breaking windows?" Erin asked. There had to be more to this story. She couldn't have been this far off the mark in judging Carol's character.

"No, I tried to talk him down," Carol said, coming to kneel in front of Erin. "He started to come after us. I pulled my baton to stop him. He swung at me a few times and when he hit Randell I pulled my gun and just . . . I warned him first but it didn't make a difference and I had to fire . . . I didn't want to kill him. I just wanted to stop him."

"Is Randell okay?" Erin asked.

Carol nodded. "Yeah, the kid hit his arm. It's bruised pretty bad but he was gonna go back to hit him again and I . . . just . . ."

"Protected your partner," Erin finished.

Carol looked surprised at first. She expected Erin to walk out and never return but instead the young woman seemed to understand the situation. Perhaps, even better than she understood it.

Carol felt relieved but she also berated herself. Erin was much more understanding about all of this than Carol had given her credit for. Without realizing it Carol began to sob and Erin pulled her close. Soon, the little murmurs telling her everything would be fine along with the gentle caresses on her back put Carol more at ease. In fact, she felt better than she had all day. She wondered if the weight of what she had done would ever be lifted. But she had to admit, things felt a bit lighter at the moment just having Erin near.

"What does Randell say about all this?"

Carol swallowed hard, pulling herself together as she rested her head in Erin's lap. "He said it was a clean shot. The captain says it's excessive use of force. And tomorrow I get to go before internal affairs to give my side of the shooting. Until they make a decision I'm on desk duty and I might be there the rest of my career – and that's if I even have a career."

"I'm sorry," Erin replied honestly. "I really am."

Carol let out a deep sigh. "What's worst of all is that poor kid will never see his parents again. He won't graduate, get married, have kids, buy a house in the suburbs . . . "

"That was his choice," Erin said softly. "I'm sure you gave him every opportunity to walk away but he didn't take it."

"You weren't there," Carol answered. "How would you know what I did?" It almost came off as a challenge, as if their entire relationship hung in the balance of the answer. Carol's azure eyes looked up into Erin's green pools.

"Because I know you," Erin answered. "Like I said, you're not like the others. You're special and you'll always be special."

"Well, I don't feel very special right now," Carol answered, putting her head back down. "And for the record I did try to reason with him but he was flying so high, Erin."

"Sometimes people get on bad trips," the blonde replied. "It happens . . . He made the choice, Carol. Not you."

Carol stood up long enough to take a spot on the bed next to Erin. She took the young woman's hands in hers. "I didn't mean to unload on you," she said sincerely. "You've had a terrible time lately, too."

"Sounds like we've both been through terrible times in the last day. So don't worry," Erin grinned trying to give Carol a ray of optimism. "Terrible times aren't as bad if you don't have to go through them alone. I'm learning this slowly."

Erin's fingertips found Carol's tear-stained cheek and wiped it dry, the digits cool on the brunette's flushed skin. Carol tilted her head slightly to capture the blonde's fingertips with her lips, lightly and lovingly. The kissing of the fingers soon led to the kissing of the palm and then of the wrist. Erin could feel where Carol was going, the heat was radiating off of her in huge scorching waves, leaving no doubt as to her partner's intentions.

"Erin," Carol sighed, reluctantly pulling away, meeting emerald eyes. "We're both very emotional right now and I think-"

"Make love to me, Carol," Erin whispered, cutting her off. She didn't want excuses or pity or to be protected from her own heart. She wanted to be loved and to give love. She needed the physical manifestation of the emotions she felt thick and heavy in the room.

Carol didn't respond immediately, torn between listening to the thrumming in her body and the nagging voice in her head. She wanted this, knew Erin did, too. They hadn't actually been subtle about where this relationship was going but she'd wanted the first time to be perfect and she wasn't sure this qualified. Erin's gentle features were streaked with dried tears, the dark circles under her eyes told of great tension and little sleep. She looked weary and frazzled, as if she might shatter at any moment. But Carol knew that wasn't true. Erin had more strength than she did, certainly, and had spent years building walls to protect herself. This latest development would not be her undoing.

The passion in the jade eyes was unmistakable, however. The pupils had dilated, leaving the surrounding irises to darken and sport flecks of gold. Carol looked deeply into Erin's eyes, realizing what she was being offered, and rationalized with herself that their first time would be perfect regardless of the events leading up to it. With that conviction, she leaned forward and captured coral lips that parted easily for her, inviting her in.

"You make me feel alive," Carol whispered sincerely as their lips parted. "I want you so much but-."

Carol never finished her sentence. Erin snared her lips once more with intent, making sure to show Carol that stopping was not an option. The kiss Erin stole made Carol's heart skip a beat and the result was a great wetness between her legs and an overwhelming need for pressure there. Some kind of pressure. Any kind of pressure.

The urgency of her arousal was intense as Carol, gently yet swiftly, laid Erin back on the bed. She settled herself softly on top of the smaller woman so their legs intertwined. When Erin began to ready herself for the next series of kisses her leg shifted accidentally, drawing a deep moan from the woman above her.

'She likes that,' Erin considered silently. 'Let's see if . . . '

Once more she moved her leg, getting a similar response. The look on Carol's face told Erin she was doing all the right things. And the sounds she was making only fueled Erin's growing desire even more. With that desire came a movement of her own, reaching and searching for a similar contact from Carol. Carol was more than happy to oblige, forcing her hips downward to meet Erin's thrusts, which were starting to come more and more frequently.

But soon that wasn't enough. Both women needed more flesh to touch, more skin to kiss. In response to that gnawing need,

Carol worked the sash free on Erin's robe. She was delighted to see that Erin was naked underneath. The sight of Erin partially dressed and waiting to be taken made Carol's heart melt and her passion swell. Both had ragged breaths as Carol's eyes examined and admired Erin's body. Carefully, she slipped the garment from Erin's shoulder leaving the young woman totally naked and exposed - a state in which the hippie seemed quite comfortable. Erin's confidence excited Carol even more.

Carol's hand tentatively reached out to stroke the blonde's breasts. She'd touched Erin before but it was never this intense, never a skin upon skin contact. She was unsure of many things: would Erin allow such a pleasure and would she be able to give the young radical pleasure? Erin sensed Carol's sudden uneasiness but instead of talking or giving instructions, she took hold of Carol's wrists gently, giving permission to explore, showing her how to touch and what she liked. The gesture, the tutelage of tender fingers and burning friction put Carol at ease once more, allowing her arousal to be the leader in her movements again.

Seeing and feeling Carol's confidence gave Erin the power to seize a little bit of control. She pulled Carol close and rolled the larger woman over as their lips locked together for the hundredth time that evening. Carol whimpered a protest when Erin rose but soon smiled as she watched Erin working the snap and zipper on her fly. Moments later Carol's jeans lay in a heap on the floor at the foot of the bed. Erin took the opportunity to pull the robe from the bed, watching it puddle next to Carol's bellbottoms.

"God, you're so beautiful."

Carol wasn't sure if she'd spoken the words aloud or if they were just screaming in her head. Erin's sudden sly grin gave her the answer. Hypnotically, she watched the hippie straddle her lap and pull her into a sitting position. Once upright, Carol felt Erin's hands travel over her breasts and down her stomach, stopping at the edge of her sweatshirt. In one quick tug, the sweatshirt, and t-shirt underneath, joined the other articles of clothing on the floor. Without delay, Erin went to work on the satin white bra.

However, Erin found that kissing Carol while trying to achieve this task just wasn't working. She couldn't help it and started to giggle, not wanting to break the mood but unable to refrain from chuckling at her own ineptness.

"Having trouble?" Carol teased, relieved at the release of tension. "Here," she said, reaching behind her to unclasp the offending article and finally sending it clear across the room.

"Thank you," Erin said with a grin.

"Anytime," Carol answered in a smoky voice. The seductive tone was all Erin needed to get things back on track, rebuilding the passion that had taken a short detour to the comical side for first time blunders. Her fingers worked their way through Carol's hair, starting at the dark woman's temples. From this position, with Erin straddling her lap, Carol was eye level with Erin's breasts. The tautness of the young woman's nipples was all the invitation she needed. She reached up, pressed both orbs together and guided them into her waiting mouth.

Erin groaned at the overwhelming sensations that coursed through her veins like quicksilver. Carol seemed to delight in tasting the salty flesh, going back repeatedly for more of the young woman – her hunger still not quite satisfied no matter how much she feasted upon her. The gentle sucking was no longer enough for Erin. She wanted more. She needed more.

"Harder," the hippie pled in a tone that showed all her wanton desire. "Please."

The request wasn't lost on Carol in the slightest. She pulled the erect points deeper into her mouth with a more forceful suction. The sounds Erin made as a result of her skin being teased and pulled made Carol all the more wet. She was sure there must have been a puddle on the bedspread at this point since the throbbing at her center was so intense she could feel her beating pulse.

Erin gently pushed Carol back to the bed with her body as they kissed, her long hair tickling and exciting Carol all at once. After a few quick kisses, the blonde pulled back, placing her fallen hair behind her ear. She looked deeply into Carol's eyes.

"Do you trust me?" she asked sincerely, needing an answer before proceeding.

"Absolutely," Carol answered without hesitation, nodding for emphasis. What else could she say? Her whole body hummed with excitement.

That was all Erin needed. She could see the sincerity in the depths of the taller woman's eyes. The sparkling sapphires were diluted with passion and trust.

Erin worked her way down Carol's body with tender kisses, growing more and more firm as she went. Her hands stroked delicately across her lover's skin in the process, building the want between them. And, oh, how she wanted Carol. She could feel the azure-eyed beauty study her movements, soaking up everything around them. The sights, the sounds, the smells, the tastes – all of them were more than either woman had expected or experienced in her young life. This was heaven, Erin decided as she started to suckle Carol's breasts for the first time. This was what living was all about – not the physical sensations, although that was a wonderful factor, but the need to belong to someone, to give yourself to someone, to love and need someone as much as you were loved and needed.

Carol's hand immediately shot up to cradle Erin's head. The officer's back arched off the bed the instant Erin's lips made contact with her nipple. Carol didn't think she'd ever want the sensation to end but soon she found she had needs lower, pulsing in time to the blonde's gentle lips and tongue. Her hips began to buck and Erin read her easily, giving up the prize she'd discovered minutes before and moving farther south on the raven-haired beauty.

In one swift pull, Carol's panties met the same fate as her other clothes, revealing to Erin the glistening skin between the other woman's legs. She couldn't contain her moan at the sight and as a result Carol couldn't contain her chuckle.

She wasn't quite sure why she laughed. Perhaps it was just her fear of the unknown. She had a pretty good idea of where Erin was heading and what her intentions might be. Soon she realized that Erin had either ignored the giggle or had missed it entirely – too focused on the body before her.

Erin was enthralled. She watched as the lean, well-built body swayed in time with their desire. The tiny hairs that covered Carol's body stood at full attention. Erin licked her lips and proceeded to let her tongue trace Carol's navel, almost as a preview of what was to come. Her tongue flicked the sides before diving into the center, making the dark woman gasp in pleasure. Erin was surprised and delighted by how sensitive her lover's stomach was to her touch. Sensing that Carol was comfortable with their bodies this close, Erin worked her way lower still, planting delicate kisses as if she was paying homage to the work of art Carol's body was.

Carol felt a flush wash over her body as Erin settled herself between her long legs and placed one long, loving, single kiss on her mons. The anticipation of what the young woman had in store for her made Carol hold her breath for a few moments. It seemed like forever as Erin looked up, locking eyes with her lover. And when Erin's hair and lips brushed her inner thighs, her need for nervous laughter passed, replaced with the wanting ache for attention at her center. Carol closed her eyes at that point and simply enjoyed Erin's teasing touches. They didn't stay closed long, however, as she felt the tip of Erin's warm, moist tongue stroking her intimately.

"Oh, God!" Carol exclaimed, her legs opening reflexively.

"That's it," Erin answered, stroking her lover's inner thighs with her fingertips, moving to her center to gently part her lips.

With that, Erin's tongue began alternating between long and quick strokes across Carol. The tall woman had never had a lover before, but she wasn't exactly an angel, either. She'd spent time pleasing herself though none of those times compared to this moment. She also considered each of the bumbling attempts made by some of the boys she had dated in high school to be exactly what they were – child's play. This was nothing like she'd ever experienced before - her body begging for release.

Erin was wonderfully surprised as she felt Carol grow even wetter under her dexterous tongue. She had tasted herself over the years through her sexual experiences, but it didn't hold a candle to how Carol delighted her palate.

The dark woman's senses climbed higher and higher - her sounds becoming more urgent, almost painful, in tone. When the waves began to approach Carol fell mute for a moment. And as her orgasm ripped through her body at lightning speed, coming around and around again as her body convulsed in pleasure, she cried out her lover's name in ecstasy. When Erin heard her name on Carol's lips, a mangled sound of pain and pleasure it seemed, Erin knew she'd finally found her destiny. Her home.

Carol didn't rest. She couldn't rest. She had to give this gift to Erin. She had to make the petite woman feel the same thing. She was determined. Erin was once more surprised as she felt herself being lifted to Carol's side, her back quickly coming to rest on the bed.

Carol straddled Erin's leg, her arousal from before still evident between her thighs. The officer's time for issuing affectionate kisses had passed. She wanted this woman before her. She wanted her now.

Carol's hand shot down to Erin's center as her lips claimed her nipples; tugging and pulling them into even more erect points.

Erin loved the contact; needed it. Her body strained and bucked and thrust against her lover. Carol took her hand away to start her decent southward just as Erin had done moments before. But Erin stopped her.

"Please," the young woman begged. "Don't take your hand away. Keep stroking me, Carol. Please, just keep stroking me."

Carol would do anything for Erin and if stroking was what she needed now, that's just what she would get. When she returned her hand, Erin gave a grateful moan and resumed her movements.

Carol pushed herself to one elbow so she could watch her young lover in almost a voyeuristic sense. The erotic movements Erin was making fueled her desire all over again, once more bringing a new wetness to her center. She watched as Erin arched and groaned, striving for the same release she had felt moments ago. The young woman's body glistened from the sweat that covered her in a fine sheen. In Carol's eyes, the young woman was absolute perfection – hot, slick and insatiable.

Erin's fingernails dug into Carol's lower arm, the one whose hand was pleasuring Erin to what seemed like no end. Carol didn't mind in the slightest. In fact it was an exquisite feeling – one of both slight pain but deep passion. Erin's grip, however, soon released as the young woman's head shot back, burying itself in Carol's pillow. Erin's vibrations shook the bed and Carol felt suddenly consumed with the need to wrap herself around the quivering young woman.

Maybe it was the newness of it or their shared arousal, but it was over all too quickly. They lay afterwards, naked and sweating, each trembling, clutching tightly to the other, almost as if promising to never let go.

Erin leaned back to see her that lover's cheeks were wet with silent tears. "What is it?" she murmured, concern beginning to rise. Maybe Carol didn't think I wanted her to . . . "I wanted you to taste me, too. I just needed release, Carol. Please don't think I didn't-."

"No," Carol interrupted, pressing her lips to the blonde's sweaty forehead. "It's not that," she assured. "I'm very satisfied," the dark woman grinned rakishly. "It's just . . . like you said before . . . I'm happy," she replied, using the blonde's earlier explanation for her tears. "It was perfect. I just...I don't know what to say."

One Belief Away

"Perfect?" Erin chuckled. "Hell, I couldn't get your bra off for at least five minutes."

Carol laughed, too. "Maybe that's because you're out of practice - you burned yours years ago," the cop teased. That remark earned her an elbow to the ribcage. The officer replied with mock-pain. "And yes, despite the fact that we had . . . undergarment problems," she paused with a huge grin, "it was perfect. Not the dime store novel kinda stuff, mind you. But perfect just the same."

Carol couldn't help but grin as she thought back to the moments before, wrought with hesitant exploration and adjusting strength with tenderness that was firm enough to provide reaction. Love had guided them, however, to understanding and soon the movements had become more practiced and confident, more about pleasuring and less about doing things right.

Already, Carol found her fingers trailing across moist skin to dance along the blonde's spine to the small of her back. Erin lurched her hips in response, aroused again, her heartbeat quickening.

"Well you know what they say? Practice makes perfect," Carol murmured, nipping a pale earlobe and then sucking it in to lave with her tongue.

"Ugh," Erin moaned. "They teach you that at the firing range?"

Carol chuckled. "They most certainly did not teach me this at the firing range. This is more of a 'hands-on' learning experience. Situational training they call it. Placing you in a scenario and seeing how you react. So far I think we've both passed with flying colors."

Later that evening, they left the bed only to find some sustenance in the old, white Frigidaire. Even then they couldn't keep their hands off of each other, sharing morsels of food and kisses with equal abandon.

"Have you been to Minos' yet?" Carol murmured, kissing Erin deeply before popping the last tidbit of food into the smaller woman's mouth.

"No. Came straight here."

"Does she know you're back?" Another kiss.

"No."

"Would you like to call her?"

Erin grinned devilishly. "She can wait. Touch me again."

It was all the invitation Carol had needed. Tossing her dishes into the sink, she swept a giddy Erin off her feet and carried her back to the dark, musty bedroom. The two of them made love three more times before the night was over. Erin finally fell asleep in Carol's arms as Carol looked up at the ceiling.

Slowly, Carol realized that she wasn't the same anymore. She never would be. She was officially a lesbian now. *What ever the Hell that truly means*, Carol thought.

Suddenly she questioned everything that transpired earlier that evening. Was she ready for this kind of commitment? What would her friends like Randell say if they knew? What would this mean concerning her job? Would she ever have children? Would she ever be accepted? Or would she be forced to spend the rest of her life hiding? Would she forever be going dateless to parties and function because she couldn't bring her partner? Would she use pronouns when she spoke about Erin to others? Carol's lists of 'woulds' seemed to go on and on. And suddenly, what was once a warm embrace in Erin's arms felt like a steel trap.

Chapter 15

Erin rolled over to bring Carol back to her but her arm came up empty. She looked around the bed, finding she was alone. The thought more than the actual temperature chilled her and she pulled the covers up. That's when she noticed Carol standing in front of the closet, back turned, getting dressed in her uniform.

"Getting an earlier start today?" Erin asked casually. She gave a very feline stretch and yawn as she watched Carol.

"Yes. I have a meeting," came the short response.

"About the shooting?" Erin asked, rising up on her elbows, watching her lover.

"Yes."

Erin could sense something amiss this morning but she decided perhaps it was just Carol's nerves on edge about reporting to the department. *Can't hurt to ask,* Erin considered.

"Is that all or is there something else?" she ask tentatively, almost as if she was afraid of the answer.

"Why do you ask?"

"Oh I don't know," Erin replied, growing a bit irritated with Carol's abrupt response. "I've been speaking to you for five minutes and you haven't turned around even once to look at me."

Carol still didn't look Erin's way. She gave a sigh and took a seat at the foot of the bed. "I'm not sure, Erin," she confessed. Erin crept down to sit beside Carol and with gentle fingertips to Carol's chin, she made Carol look her way.

"What's wrong?" Erin asked softly, trying to coax the thoughts out of her officer. "Did last night upset you?"

Carol took a deep breath and turned away. She'd spent hours staring at the crack in the plastered ceiling considering how she would start this conversation the night before. Now that the moment was at hand she still wasn't sure what to say. Erin had lain so unaware in her arms last night – just happy and content to be in her embrace. Carol spent the night fidgeting wondering how she could escape the pressure that she felt blanket her. She suddenly took an intense interest in her shoes as she spoke.

"I'm not prepared for any of this," she whispered.

"Okay," Erin drawled out. She wasn't quite sure where this conversation was going. Did she really read Carol so incorrectly? Perhaps Minos was right and she was just an experiment for Carol. Erin tried her best to push those thoughts from her mind. She decided to just press on and hopefully get down to the root of Carol's aloofness. "Did you enjoy the way you felt?" Erin added, "Because if you didn't you should stop being a cop and become an actress." Erin hoped the humor in her response would relax Carol so she could find out what was going on.

"It's the 'after' part I'm having a hard time with. I realized last night - I'm a lesbian . . . and I don't know what that means," Carol said.

"Funny," Erin snorted sarcastically. "I realized I was in love with a woman, regardless of any label that someone might put on it."

Erin tossed the sheet aside that covered her and began to go in search of her clothes. She found them hanging in the bathroom on the shower rod, finally dry. She slipped the dress over her head and went back to stand in Carol's bedroom doorway.

"That's not the way things work, Erin," Carol told her, finally looking at the young woman on her own without any prompting or guidance.

"Who cares about the way things work?" Erin answered, her voice starting to rise with her temper. "Are you so regimented that you can't break free from other people's expectations? What about what you want, Carol?"

"Maybe I'm nothing more than a coward, Erin. I've fought with myself since I met you. I've denied my feelings. I wanted to take things slowly so I would be prepared for this kind of reaction. .But last night . . . I couldn't resist my desire any longer."

One Belief Away

"Why should you 'resist' Carol? Are you that wrapped up in being 'daddy's good little cop'? Why can't you just acknowledge what you feel and let it happen? This doesn't have to be as complicated as you're making it! I don't expect you to fill out a detailed report afterwards."

"Don't get upset here, okay?"

"I'm sorry, Carol, but I'm going to 'get upset here'. I feel things. I don't turn a cold shoulder to the world and I'm not afraid to say what's inside me. And right now I'm angry and frustrated...and... damn you, Carol!"

Erin darted from the bedroom but Carol wasn't about to let her go that easily. She shot from the bed and followed right behind her as Erin looked around for her shoes.

"Oh and you don't turn a cold shoulder to the world? Should I ask your parents about their thoughts on this? From where I'm standing, it doesn't look like you've made great strides with them."

Erin saw red at this point. Talking about the two of them was one thing but drawing her parents into the debate was something else and she wouldn't stand for it.

"That's a low blow, Carol. My relationship with my parents has absolutely nothing to do with what's going on between us."

"I beg to differ. You're running away just as much as you think I am. Come to think of it, you don't even want your friends to know we're dating. You've sworn Stan to secrecy about us so you can't be that goddamned open about things."

"Don't you dare throw your problems with getting close back at me. I'm willing to make this work but you're not giving us a chance."

"Erin, regardless of what you may think, I do love you. But I'm not sure if I'm willing to give up my life."

"Give up your life?" Erin chuckled in misery. "I didn't think loving me was a human sacrifice." The sarcasm dripped from Erin's voice.

"No, that's not what I meant! Will you slow down a minute?"

Erin took a seat on the sofa as she put her shoes on. "You say it's about change but I know what it's really about."

"Do you now?" Carol answered caustically.

Erin nodded. "It's not about 'giving up your life'. Oh sure, you're concerned about the closet. But it goes much deeper than that."

"Really? And just what the hell does that mean?"

"Name one person that you're so connected with you can feel it with every fiber of your being. That's what I feel with you. So come on, Carol. Let's hear it. One name, that's all I ask." Carol looked guiltily at her feet. "Thanks for proving my point," Erin sighed as she headed for the front door.

"You don't understand. This is easier for you. You-."

"Easier for me?" Erin remarked, cutting Carol short.

"Hell yeah, it's easier! You don't live in the real world. For you it's business as usual. But my life will be turned upside down. And I don't think you *get* what that means."

"I don't *get* what that means? Excuse me but where's the woman I was with last night?"

"Think about it, Erin! Your friends will be far more accepting of you being involved with a woman. But I, on the other hand, could lose my job, my friends, my identity . . . And that's not something I take lightly."

"Oh yeah. My friends will just adore me when they find out that I'm dating a pig. Why do you think I told Stan to keep his mouth shut? We've got enough pressure just dealing with our own hang-ups!"

"So now I'm a pig, huh?"

Erin closed her eyes regretting her temper. "I'm sorry . . . I'm just having a hard time with what's going on here. I figured the sheets would be cold before I got the standard, "It's been fun" . . . speech."

A brief silence fell between them and they locked eyes trying to figure out what the other was thinking. Carol was first to break it. "I know how I feel about you. It's the only thing I am sure of at the moment. Look, I don't know what I am right now. I feel like I'm trapped. Like I'm being buried alive by all this."

"I don't want to bury you. I love you and I thought you loved me."

Carol sighed. "I do love you but it's not that simple for me, Erin."

"No, Carol. It is that simple," the blonde said waving her finger. "Obviously appearances mean more to you than what's in your heart. I think you're the one who doesn't get it. Yes, you're right, my friends will chastise me - maybe even ostracize me for loving you but I'm willing to give up everything for you, Carol."

Carol felt her temper rising again and she let it shine like a beacon in her tone. "Look! Being a cop is who I am – not just something I do."

"Let me tell you who you are, Carol," Erin began, coming nose to nose with her. "You're a woman afraid of change, so much so it is to the point that it terrifies you."

"Bull shit!"

"Is it?!" Erin said waving her arms around the room. "Look at this house. It's yours but you can't bear to change the wallpaper . . . You said I made you feel alive. Maybe you should ask yourself why. Could it be because you've never let yourself feel anything before now? I see the truth, Carol."

"Whose truth?" Carol said sarcastically. "Yours or mine?" Erin seemed to totally ignore the response and kept going.

"It's not about giving up your life," Erin said, shaking her head. "I'm not asking for that. Your hang-up is that we fit. You've never felt like this with anyone else and it's scared the hell out of you. And I'll be honest, I feel the same but here's where we're different – love is something precious. It's not about candy, flowers or valentines. Love is a force. It has the power to make timid hearts strong and the biggest empires crumble. So once you find it you better hold it close to your heart and never let it go . . . That's the problem, Carol. I'm holding on to it while you're letting go."

"You're being too dramatic about this."

"No. I'm in love here. But to you it probably does seem like drama. Maybe all this is nothing more than some grand theatrical production on your part. Stupid me. I was just too blind to see it."

"Look, I know who I am. I know what I believe."

"I know you think you do . . . But this isn't about changing your identity. It's about giving up your heart."

"That's not true," Carol hissed. Erin didn't reply. She simply walked to the front door and opened it. Carol put her hand on Erin's closing it again. "So that's it? You're just gonna walk out on me?"

"What else can I do? You can't give me what I want."

"Erin, I just-."

"Got in over your head, right?" Erin remarked casually. "I've heard that before."

Carol grabbed the blonde from behind, wrapping her long arm around her thin waist. She leaned down close to Erin's ear, her voice just above a whisper. "Don't leave."

The impulse to stay was overwhelming for Erin but she knew staying wouldn't help. She was too mad to discuss this any further and she didn't want Carol to end up making empty promises. "You need to figure out what you want. You've let me in, now you have to decide if you want me to stay there. I can't make that choice for you."

"At least let me take you home," Carol offered.

Erin shook her head. *She just doesn't get it.* Slowly she opened the door. "Last night I thought I was home."

Erin walked out without waiting for Carol's response. Carol started to follow but decided to let her walk away. Carefully, she closed the door and rested her head on the back. Gently she let her forehead hit it twice, maybe to knock some sense into herself. The conversation didn't go as well as she had hoped.

Time. That's all I need is time. Is she so selfish she can't see that? Carol felt herself start to grow angry and she began to pace her living room quickly. *Who does she think she is? Damn it! She's a self-centered, egotistical...* Carol stopped her thoughts and sat down defeated on the couch. *No she's not. And now you're just fishing for a fight – even here all alone.* Carol let out a deep sigh. She had a few more minutes to spare before she had to leave for the precinct and fall under another question and answer session, which would probably be just as stressful as the one that just took place. Carol looked at her watch. *Jesus, and it's not even 7:30 yet.* Releasing yet another sigh she rose to her feet and went to her bedroom for her shoes.

Erin burst into the commune house with the speed and power of a racehorse. She was going to go straight to her room but the sight inside made her stop. Her fellow housemates were painting signs and testing a few already finished. She saw a baseball bat and a pair of brass knuckles on the coffee table.

"What's going on?" Erin asked Minos, who was rising from the kitchen table.

"Didn't you hear?" she said as she strolled over. "Your open minded cop friend gunned down Jimmy Watson."

Stan piped in. "And it's time some fucking cop heads roll."

Immediately, Erin panicked but she pulled herself together before a soul could notice. Carol didn't need this, not now, not in light of everything that transpired between them this morning. The house was angry and she knew this would end up being more than just a simple protest.

"I don't think she's public enemy number one, Stan. But since you do why don't you tell me just what you have in mind?" Erin asked sarcastically.

One Belief Away

"We're gonna teach her a lesson she won't forget," he answered before turning to the group. "And we've got someone who can get close enough to her...don't we Skylon?"

Stan took two strides closer to Erin. He towered above her, looking down at her over his nose in the most disapproving of manners. Gossiping whispers began between the large group of people gathered at the house. Erin nervously licked her drying lips.

"So what do you say, Skylon? Can you deliver her? Some place secluded?" he pressed.

Erin's eyes scanned the room knowing everyone was waiting for an answer. She looked to Minos who also anxiously wanted to know where Erin's true loyalties lay.

Confidently, yet quietly, Erin uttered, "Yeah . . . I can deliver her."

Stan smiled. "That's good to hear. Glad you know which side to take. We're working something up but by nightfall we'll figure out what we'll have in store for the trigger happy pig."

Erin simply nodded as Minos grabbed her by the arm. "We have to talk," Minos hissed in her ear so no one else would hear. "Now!" she added as she pulled Erin along. They ended up in the corner of the kitchen, away from everyone else who began to talk among themselves again.

"Go easy on me," Erin began. "I've had a rough morning."

"Have you completely lost your mind?" Minos asked. "How can you even attempt to defend that woman?"

"And just what did I say?" Erin questioned angrily.

"She's not public enemy number one? Skylon, she killed an unarmed civilian. What the hell do you think that makes her? And what the hell did she do to you that made you take such a leap away from your good senses?"

Minos watched as Erin avoided her glare, finding the crack in the countertop much more interesting. Erin ran her fingernail through it, not saying a word, and slowly Minos put it together.

"You slept with her. That's it, isn't it? She took you to bed and won you over."

"That's not exactly how it happened. And for your information it seems to be over. Morning after regret is a tough burden - especially when you're not the one who's experiencing the regret." Erin felt herself tear up but she wasn't going to cry in front of Minos and give her the satisfaction.

"I'm sorry," her friend replied softly.

"No you're not," Erin challenged. She wasn't about to let the sob she felt brewing inside pour out. "You're just dying to say 'I told you so'. Why don't you just do it and get it out of your system?"

"I'm serious, Skylon," she began. "I know I gave you hell and I am sorry. I knew it wouldn't last but I hoped that it would . . . for your sake. But now you see what she really is, right?"

Erin looked up and rolled her eyes. "Yeah, well . . . at this point she thinks she has to change her whole life for me . . . Minos, I don't want to change her life. I just wanted to be a part of it. But I guess she doesn't want me. So you were right. I was wrong. Let's just drop it, okay? Stan wants her so I'll bring her." Erin's irritation was evident in her short, snappy words.

"Skylon, put that Irish temper of yours on hold and listen to me for a minute, okay?" Erin pursed her lips and nodded to let Minos continue. "Everyone has an identity," Minos began. "It's the essence of who we are whether we choose to accept it or not. Carol has her place and you have yours, Erin."

As Minos uttered Erin's given name it took her by surprise. She hadn't called her 'Erin' in years but maybe this was some kind of sign - something that said she belonged to something more than a cause of the week. Perhaps it was something even greater than herself. And maybe in the course of the last few weeks she found an identity and Minos recognized that. But with the house now plotting against Carol and using Erin as the key it just didn't sit right with Minos. But she wasn't going to remark on it. Not here. Not now.

"Go on," Minos said with a wave of her hand. "Get outta here for a little while."

Chapter 16

Carol had spent the morning at the station doing reports and aggravating her dust allergies in the precinct filing room. Today had been especially long due to harassment from her fellow officers and chiding remarks about her that floated through the halls and to her ears. Of course, that was after the 'Spanish Inquisition' as Randell had called it. To make matters worse, she'd worried about Erin's departure that morning and wondered if she'd ever see the blonde again.

"Hey, Johnson. How you holdin' up?"

Randell's voice behind her broke her wandering, depressing thoughts. "I've been better. And yourself?" she asked conversationally.

"Just got done with another interrogation. Chief is worried we're gonna have a riot on our hands."

"And I'm sure Erin will be leading the pack."

"What?" Randell asked, confused.

"Nothing. Just thinking out loud," Carol grinned. Quickly, she changed the subject. "So what are you doing today while I keep the streets safe by making sure all the 'j's' are in their proper place?"

Randell took a moment to look at her. "I think this is a bum rap. You did everything by the book. Hell, if your old man was around, Johnson, he'd tell you the same thing."

"You think?"

"Hell yes. I mean, I've had to shoot someone myself. I know how it feels."

"Did he die?" Carol asked.

"No," Randell sighed.

"Then you don't know what it feels like," Carol said, trying to give him a brave smile. "But thanks for trying to make me feel better."

"Suppose you're right," Randell sighed as his toe dug nervously into the floor. "But consider this," he began, "when I found out my new partner was a woman . . . Well, I won't tell you my first reaction," he chuckled as he thought back to that day. "But over time I realized this gal knew what to do. She's got it together. And if it was the other way around yesterday . . . and that goddamned junkie charged you, I would have pulled the trigger, too. We did it all by the book yesterday, Carol. You've got nothing to be ashamed of, believe me."

"I'm not really ashamed, Randell. I'm just . . . I ache inside . . . Like a thousand daggers to the stomach. Thou shall not kill, right? I regret that it ended the way it did."

"Listen Carol, that kid had a choice. We gave him every option. But he didn't take it. That's his fault and the way I see it, his blood is not on your hands. It was his own doing."

"Don't let this go to your head, Randell, but you are a wonderful partner. I might not always agree with you, but . . . your trust means a lot to me. So thanks for trying to make me feel better."

"Don't mention it kid. Hey, we're on our way to lunch. Wanna come?"

"No thanks. I don't think I'm up to it."

"Fair enough," he said starting to walk out, "but Carol . . . if you need anything, don't hesitate to ask, 'k?"

"Will do."

Randell nodded and walked out. Carol let out a deep sigh and closed the cabinet. She grabbed a box and started to head out to the desk sergeant's area. She watched as a woman spoke with the sergeant and he pointed to Carol. Carol put the box down on a bench as the women came over.

"Officer Johnson?"

"Yes?"

Before Carol could stop the swing the woman's palm connected with her face. The sergeant saw the blow and raced over quickly to restrain the woman.

One Belief Away

"Why?" she yelled beginning to sob. "How could you kill my son?"

"Whoa! Easy there lady!" the sergeant said, holding her back.

"You answer me! Jimmy never hurt anyone, ever. And you killed him! You tell me why!"

Carol was stunned. "I'm sorry," she muttered.

"Sorry doesn't bring him back!" The desk sergeant tried to take the woman away but Carol stopped him as she quickly regrouped.

"Wait. Mrs. Watson . . . I can't bring your son back. I know that."

"Then why did you shoot? I don't understand. Make me understand why my son is dead!"

The woman began to cry openly. Carol swallowed hard, trying to think of a starting place for the despondent woman. She'd been caught totally off-guard but she knew this woman deserved some kind of explanation. Taking a deep breath, she began.

"I know you probably won't accept it but your son...he was out of control and dangerous . . . I tried to talk to him; to reason with him but he wouldn't listen. I thought he was gonna kill my partner. And I couldn't let him do that so I did what I had to do. And I know no matter what I say . . . it will never be enough for you. It will never be enough for me . . . I'm sorry for the pain I've caused you . . . and I wish it didn't have to be this way."

"Come on," the desk sergeant told the woman

"Let her go," Carol told him politely.

"But she hit you. She-.

"She's upset and I don't blame her. Let her go."

Reluctantly, the desk sergeant loosened his grip. He eyed the situation a moment longer then proceeded to his desk. Once he was gone Carol turned to the woman. "Mrs. Watson . . . I know what it's like to love someone and lose them to a bullet. And like I said, if I could find some way to take away your pain, I would."

The woman pulled out a hanky and blotted her eyes, taking a deep breath to regain herself. "I thought if I came here and told you what you've done . . . I'd feel better . . . But I don't feel better. I'm still empty...And he's still dead."

The woman turned and walked slowly out the station house doors. Carol waited until she was out of sight before taking careful steps back to the file room. Quietly, she closed the door and slid down it, shaking and quivering as she made her descent. By the time she was sitting she was in a pool of silent tears.

She didn't look much better when Randell got back from lunch and when he heard of the woman's arrival at the station house, he didn't ask but ordered Carol to come home with him.

Later that night Carol and Randell sat on his porch drinking a beer or two . . . or five. In all honestly, Carol lost count. The sun had almost set below the horizon and the street lamps were now on in the quiet suburb filled with ranch-style houses. Except for the occasional sigh between the partners and the chirp of the crickets, it was relatively quiet. Now and then a car would pass down the small street but for the most part, people were already tucked away in their houses, going through their nightly rituals. Carol and Randell both had to be to work the next day but they also knew they needed to unwind a bit after such a difficult week. They sat. They drank. They talked. They drank some more.

"You know...I have this theory," Carol said with a slight slur, breaking the quiet grandeur of Randell's front porch.

"Let's hear it," Randell said, raising his bottle.

"Take two people...any two people...I mean, first what're the odds of two *right* people meeting each other? It's like a zillion to one, right?"

Randell just nodded, taking another swig.

"Let's take you and Phyllis, for example. You two are right for each other, wouldn't you say?"

Again, another nod from Randell and another swig.

"Right . . . So call it dumb luck or fortuitous chance-."

"Fortuitous chance? Sounds like a pretty deep theory already," he chuckled. "You must have given this some thought . . . either that or it's the beer talking," he added.

Carol sighed. "Come on, I'm serious. Stay with me here . . . It's fate, kismet, whatever . . . You two meet, right?"

"Right."

"Instantly, there are these sparks of sexual tension but it quickly grows into something else, right?"

"Right."

"Eventually, you find a mutual ground and you hit it off like gangbusters. You connect with each other. You fill each other's thoughts throughout the boredom of what seems like never ending days. You can't wait to see each other. You can't wait to hear what the other one thinks, right?"

"Right."

"You fill each other's thoughts and you're perfect together. You can't explain it, you just fit . . . and maybe, just maybe, it doesn't need any explanation. Maybe you should just take it for what it is . . . a soul connection."

"I follow you, Johnson," he answered taking another drink.

"So you take her out for...let's say...ice cream," Carol offers.

"Phyllis can't eat ice cream. She's diabetic."

Carol proceeded, totally ignoring the comment. "You make her laugh. She makes you think on deeper levels – levels so deep that you didn't even realize they existed within yourself. Finally, the moment comes and you take her to bed and for the first time in your miserable life, you find out what it means to make love – to honestly feel someone so intensely it's like your lives are intertwined – a yin to a yang. You can't figure out where you end and she begins. And despite all your shortcomings as a human being she desperately loves you. And you, her."

Randell set his beer down and turned back to Carol. "Are we talking about me and Phyllis?"

Once more Carol seemed too deep in thought to hear his question. "So you're both supposed to live happily ever after, right?"

"Right."

"Wrong!" The tone in Carol's objection made Randell jump just a tad. She was obviously pissed about something, but what exactly he had no idea. He just thought it would be safer to 'play along'.

"She gives herself to you – heart and soul. She'd walk away from everything she's known just to make things work. And what do you do? You piss it all away because you're too afraid of change. You care more about the opinions of others than what's in your heart. And you know something else, Randell? Love really isn't about greeting cards and boxes of chocolate. Those are just petty tokens of something far greater than just about anything else in this world."

Jesus, am I really that blind? Carol thought as she downed the rest of her beer. Quietly, she set her empty bottle down on the step.

"Johnson?" Randell said in the momentary silence. "If you need to talk about something-."

Carol cut him short with a wave of her hand.

"Okay," he nodded, taking a long drink. As if a light bulb went on he quickly turned to her. "So what exactly is your theory here?" he asked sincerely.

"The point, my dear partner," Carol said with a grin and a raised finger, "is never take Phyllis for granted."

"I'll second that."

The pair turned around to see Phyllis come out from the house with a smile and two more beers. She handed one to her husband and one to Carol before taking a seat on Randell's lap. Carol started to get a bit misty eyed at the display before her.

"What's wrong, Johnson?" Randell asked.

"Look at you two," she said on the verge of sobbing.

Randell and Phyllis examined each other. "What about us, dear?" the woman asked.

"After all these years she'd rather sit on you than just next to you. Do you know what that means? Do you see how deep that is Randell? That is very, very sweet . . . I could have that too if I was brave enough." Carol put her face in her hands and started to sob.

Phyllis looked at her husband, unsure of what to make of the crying woman. Randell just brushed her off. "She's just had one too many beers," he chuckled.

"I'm not drunk," Carol proclaimed, her eyes shooting up to meet Randell's. "I'm in love...With Erin . . . totally, helplessly."

"Aaron, huh?" Randell smiled. "And have you told Aaron how you feel?"

Carol nodded, taking a long swig of her beer.

"But I did a really stupid thing," she confessed. "I told her I'm afraid of labels but deep down I'm not. I'm afraid of getting hurt. Somehow, I'm afraid of losing her like I lost my dad. Not like she'd get shot or anything," Carol slurred in explanation. "Just that . . . I'll wake up one day and she'll be gone and I'd be all alone again. And she's absolutely right. She's right about everything . . . I should go tell her." Carol stood up and tried to walk but Phyllis jumped up and grabbed her by the arm.

"Tell her tomorrow, sweetheart," the older woman said. "You're in no shape to drive . . . Or to give deep confessions. Okay?"

Carol swayed a bit as she considered it. Then she remembered. Erin had exams coming up and she didn't want to disturb the young woman - exams and the fact they didn't part company in the best of terms.

Besides, she realized that if Erin could tell she was drunk then she wouldn't believe a damn word she had to say. So Carol gave a nod and let Phyllis lead her into the house, putting together a makeshift bed on their sofa.

One Belief Away

As Phyllis pulled the afghan up, Carol captured her hand. "Randell got a great gal. You know that?"

Phyllis let her hand slip from Carol's embrace and she ruffled Carol's bangs. "He's got a pretty good partner, too," she complimented.

Carol gave a slight grin and closed her eyes, snuggling into the throw pillow for the night. Quietly, Phyllis went back out to the porch to where her husband still sat, a stunned expression on his face. Phyllis took a seat beside him and took a drink of his beer. She handed it back but he wouldn't take it. He still sat there with a blank expression from total shock. Phyllis physically had to open his hand and close it around the bottle again.

"Erin is a woman," he finally muttered. "When she said Erin I thought she meant Aaron but she really meant...Erin."

Phyllis burst out laughing and that was enough to break Randell from his surprise.

"What's so funny?" he asked.

She leaned over and kissed his cheek. "You," she answered with mirth in her voice. "Why are you so shocked?"

Randell tried to respond a few times – his mouth opening and closing. Phyllis smiled even more. He looked like a catfish on a hook. The way he sputtered along made his wife laugh out loud again.

"This is not funny," he said, finally finding his voice. "This is very serious." He quieted his tone down and whispered. "She's queer."

"She's in love, Randell," Phyllis answered sympathetically.

"Yeah, with a woman. It's an affront to God, Phyllis. How can you sit there and-."

"Remember my Aunt Patty?" Phyllis asked.

"Yeah, the one that told dirty jokes that made ME blush," he chuckled as he remembered her. She was always so full of spirits, wearing a smile everyday of her life. No party or function was complete unless Aunty Patty was there. He smiled as he remembered her but the smile started to slip away and he turned to face Phyllis.

She saw the look on his face and simply nodded.

"You're kidding?" he asked, slack jawed.

"Nope," she answered. "Not many people in the family knew. My mother did because they were tighter than tight. She wasn't the old 'spinster' that everyone thought. That's why her 'roommate' Agnes was so torn up at the funeral. She didn't just lose her evening checkers partner. She lost her better half . . . Aunt Patty wasn't disturbed or evil," Phyllis added. "She was quite loving and generous. Even gave us the money for the down payment on this place, remember?"

"Yeah I remember. But I had no idea that her and Agnes..." he trailed off, still lost in his amazement as he looked out over his well-manicured lawn.

"I know," Phyllis smirked. "And I bet if you ask people on the street if they know someone who's *that way* they'll tell you no. But I'm sure they do. They just don't know it," she chuckled at the irony of the statement before turning serious. "It's a shame really. It's love and I can't sit and think that love, no matter what package it comes in, is an affront to God."

Randell considered her words but something still just didn't sit well with him and he started to shake his head and roll his shoulders.

"What is it?" Phyllis asked, knowing the debate was far from over.

"I just don't get it," he said. "Look at Johnson. She's a beautiful woman. A very beautiful woman-."

"Watch it buddy," Phyllis warned, playfully swatting his knee. Randell smiled at the reaction of his wife.

"You know what I mean. Johnson could have any young man she wants. Just the other day she said a deliveryman asked her for coffee. Good looking kid. You know – clean cut, respectable," he told her. "They'd trip all over themselves just to get close to her so why a woman?"

"Do you think she's settling somehow?" Phyllis asked.

Randell considered the question. "Yeah, maybe."

"Perhaps," Phyllis agreed, trying to stay neutral. "But I heard that speech of hers tonight. Those weren't the words of a woman who's settling and we both know it."

Randell let out a deep sigh. "Well, if it is true love, now what?"

Phyllis chuckled at the question. "What do you mean?"

"If she really does love this girl what does that mean – between she and I?"

Phyllis could see Randell was having a real problem with this new information about Carol. She realized she had to help him work this out. And the best course was to stick to the facts. She took a deep breath before she began.

"It's simple really. When you ask her what she did this weekend you include Erin's name." Randell was going to speak but she stifled him with a lone finger across his lips. "As for your partnership, she's still the same woman who was willing to take down a psycho wielding a baseball bat. Like you told me, she did everything right out there that day. You've got a bruised arm instead of a busted skull. She did her job. She brought you home to me. And I will forever be grateful to her . . . So you better consider that when you speak to her tomorrow." Randell protested non-verbally with a slump of his shoulders and a twisting of his head. But Phyllis wouldn't let him get away that easily. "And you will speak to her - or it will be a problem between you." She paused a moment as she watched him consider it. "You know I'm right," she added, bumping shoulders with him.

"Yeah and I hate it when you're right," he said turning to her. His grin turned into a smile the longer he watched her gloat.

"Come on," she said, rising and pulling him toward the house. "Let's get some rest. You'll have to get up early tomorrow to do the sensitive chat," she teased.

He groaned in response but it was overshadowed by Phyllis' deep chuckle.

The sunlight woke Carol, along with the smell of frying bacon. For a moment she wasn't sure where she was and she shot up. *Big mistake*, she thought as her head began to pound in response to the sudden movement.

She clutched her temples as she swung her legs off the sofa, making sure both feet were firmly planted on the ground before attempting to stand. It felt like it took all her strength to push her body up but finally, after what seemed like hours, she was upright in Randell's living room. With careful steps she went to the kitchen where she could hear breakfast being prepared. Phyllis heard the shuffle behind her and turned around from the stove. As she moved she vaguely remembered talking about Erin, but what she said exactly she couldn't remember.

"Good morning, blue eyes," Phyllis teased.

Carol winced at the noise, her head continuing to throb. "Please, not so loud," she begged, holding the sides of her face.

Phyllis restrained her chuckle as much as she could. "Hungry?" she asked, a devious smile on her lips.

"Oh god, no," Carol answered, now clutching her stomach. She didn't think it was possible for this many parts of her body to hurt at once. At that moment Randell came downstairs in his uniform.

"Morning, Johnson," he called out. Again Carol had to hold her head in place from the explosion of pain.

"Why is everyone yelling today?" she asked rhetorically to the room.

Randell smiled and went to the refrigerator. He pulled out a beer and walked over to Carol. "Drink this," he ordered.

Carol shook her head as little as possible as she took a seat at the kitchen table. "I had enough last night," she said softly.

"Seriously, this will help," he told her. He went to the sink and brought over a bottle of aspirin, placing it in front of her authoritatively.

Carol looked at the full bottle of pain relievers. "I think I'll need more," she replied dryly.

Randell began to laugh but quickly quieted his tone when he watched Carol's eyes close and her nose wrinkle in discomfort from the loud sound.

"Come on, Johnson," he said motioning to his patio door. "Let's go have a talk."

Carol watched him walk out and turned a concerned eye to Phyllis. "I didn't just imagine my confession last night, did I?" Carol asked her, trying to piece together the events of the prior evening.

"No dear, you didn't," she answered. "But it will be okay," she supported. "Go on."

Carol paused a moment and took a steadying breath. *Oh god. I have to move again*, she thought as she stood up and took a few aspirins and the beer with her. As she walked outside to meet Randell she popped the pills in her mouth and took a big drink. She cringed at the taste and stopped walking, afraid she might get sick. When the beer settled she took slow steps out to Randell, who was sitting at his round picnic table.

"What is it with your generation?" Randell started in his gruff style. "The drugs, the music, the sex . . . I don't get it," he told her.

"Well," Carol began as she sat herself slowly down on the bench at the table. "I don't do drugs . . . I'd take Buddy Holly over Jimi Hendrix any day . . . and as for the sex, I've only had one lover," she confessed.

Randell took an unsteady breath. "Erin, I assume?" he asked.

Carol just nodded.

"Starts with an 'E' and not an 'A', right?" he teased.

One Belief Away

Carol snorted. She might have laughed but that might involve working muscles she knew just couldn't move at the moment.

"Yeah with an 'E'," she answered. "Are you gonna find a new partner now?" she asked. Phyllis' earlier reaction calmed her a bit but she still had fear about what he might say. She'd never admit it but she respected his opinion of her – as a cop and as a person. He wasn't saying anything and she felt the need to end the silence so she continued. "Most of the department hated the fact that I was a woman even before the shooting. Now they really have it in for me. If they knew I love Erin . . . Let's just say I'd see why you'd want a new partner."

"Hell no, I don't want a new partner," he finally answered. "It's always been tougher for you, Johnson. I know that. I'm not blind. And with this shooting business they think it proves that you can't cut it. But I know better. Besides, I spent too long breakin' you in," he teased.

Carol realized in that instant that maybe it would be okay. Maybe Randell could be more understanding than she gave him credit for.

"Look, kid," he began again. "It's like I told Phyllis. I don't understand it all but as long as you're happy and keep watching my back out there . . . I've got no complaints."

Reluctantly, Carol took another long drink of the beer. Her reluctance to consume the barley and hops was evident by the disgusted look on her face.

"Are you sure?" she asked as she wiped her mouth. "Because I think you're trying to kill me by making me drink this," she said raising her bottle.

Randell simply smiled. "If you're gonna drink with the big boys you gotta learn the tricks," he winked. "Trust me. In a few minutes you'll be as good as new . . . Well, maybe not that good . . . But the feel of the earth's rotation and the overwhelming urge to upchuck will pass. You'll be okay by roll call."

A small silence passed between them as Carol finished off the beer. "So . . . we're okay?" she asked.

Randell knew what the woman meant and he had to admit his heart went out to her. Sure, he didn't understand it but he knew Carol. He knew she was dependable, hard-working, always looking out to do right by everyone she encountered.

"Yeah, Johnson. We're okay," he smiled. He rose and motioned her to follow. "I'm gonna get some breakfast. Why don't you clean up and we'll start the day? What do you say?"

Carol looked up at him with a timid smile. "Thank you," she said softly.

Randell knew the gratitude went much deeper than the use of his washroom.

"You're welcome, Johnson."

Chapter 17

Carol sighed as the door slammed closed behind her. She knew the entire precinct was watching her every move. The desk sergeant muttered something unintelligible when she passed him, but she knew it wasn't good by the snickers from the other officers standing nearby. Being one of the few women on the force she was far from accepted by the majority. The shooting only served to compound their doubt in her abilities. Instead of making a retort to their snickers, Carol walked out the back door so she could be out of the stifling building. She tried to remember the weekend instead, which had been much more pleasant, but the events of yesterday morning dampened any luck of finding peace. Lunch would be an isolated affair.

At least she thought it would be isolated. She had no idea that handful of reporters the day before had suddenly become a press mob in front of the stationhouse. As she made her way around the building to the parking area she found the front of the precinct was littered with reporters and journalists wanting to hear more about the shooting. Carol noticed them immediately but what she didn't see was Erin and Minos parked across the street in Mino's van.

"You sure you're up to this?" Minos asked.

"I'm positive," Erin replied, although her tone didn't convey it. "Besides, there's no turning back now," she added with a sad grin.

"Well, good luck. I'll be at home tonight when you get there."

"Thanks Minos. I appreciate it."

With that, Minos just nodded and hopped out of the van as Erin made her way into the parking area. The crowd of reporters now began to follow Carol, who they spotted walking across the lot. Carol quickened her pace and so did they. Erin saw the chase and laid on the gas before coming to a squealing stop in front of Carol.

"Hurry up!" she waved. "Get in!"

Carol didn't need to be told twice. She hopped inside and Erin sped away into traffic, making a sharp turn. She looked in her rearview mirror to see if anyone was giving chase. Once it appeared they were alone she settled into the seat.

"I came by last night but you weren't home," she said as they drove down the road.

"I had a few beers last night and crashed at Randell's house."

"So when the going gets tough, the tough get drinking, eh? Sounds like my step-father."

"So now I'm your step-father too, huh?" Carol asked with a quirked eyebrow. She gave a sigh. Maybe Erin was right to make the comparison on some level. "I guess I am your step-father. I was a real shit the other morning. Would it help if I said I'm sorry? Because I really am sorry, you know?"

"It might."

"Well, regardless, let me officially say it - I am sorry. I thought about seeing you but . . . I reconsidered."

Erin swallowed hard. She could tell that Carol was hurting too over everything that transpired between them and she found herself reaching out to her in spite of the anger she still held inside.

"I'm sorry, too," Erin admitted. "About the comment, I mean. I know you're not my stepfather. Believe me, there is no comparison there at all. But...I gotta say, Carol, I'm still pissed about it all. But I'm trying really hard to be mature about everything."

They drove along in silence for a few moments until Carol spoke. "So what brought you here today?"

"The house did," Erin answered cryptically.

"The house?"

"They're after you, Carol. Despite anything between you and I, I couldn't let them do that . . . They're gonna hurt you."

"Let 'em."

"Look, you don't understand," Erin replied. "This isn't just about protesting and holding a sit in. They're out for blood. I was supposed to take you out to Benton Harbor where they're waiting."

Carol chuckled miserably and shook her head. "So you were gonna give me up to your friends? Jesus, you're madder than I thought."

"No! I played along so I could get to you first and warn you," Erin said quickly. "They just don't understand. I know you're a good person, Carol. Misguide and confused at times, yes. Someone who doesn't know when she's got something worth keeping, certainly," she jabbed. "But still...you're a good person. I've seen it, first hand."

"Good person or not, I keep replaying the same scene over and over again in my head . . . I can't help but wonder if I've made the right choices lately. With you, I screwed up, without a doubt...but I mean, about the shooting...I'm not sure if I made the right call. But I'm never gonna know, am I?"

"How could anyone know something like that? Like you said, he didn't give you a choice. But if it meant losing you then I'm glad you made the decision you did. You're an honest person Carole and the world seems to be in short supply of them nowadays."

"I don't feel very honest . . . not about anything in my life right now."

An awkward silence settled between them before Erin cleared her throat.

"I'm sorry about yesterday morning. I shouldn't have walked out but at the time I was just too angry to stay. I want you to know that if you need time to . . . adjust . . . Then I'll give it. I won't push. I promise. That's if you even want to try," Erin considered in after thought. "You said you were sorry but you didn't say for what exactly. Maybe I'm jumping to conclusions and you don't-."

Carol leaned over to reached out and caress Erin's knee affectionately.

"You're not jumping. And I do want to try to make it work. But I just have all these fears going through my head right now. And it's not just us. It's my career, too. If I'm lucky, in 10 years I might get to be a metermaid."

"Is it bad?"

Carol shrugged, "Well, I don't know if it's really that bad. It just feels that way. And the way I reacted to you...that's bothered me. In fact, I made a drunken confession to Randell about us."

"Randell knows about us?"

Carol simply nodded.

"What did you tell him?"

"That I'm in love with you. But I'm too chicken shit to do anything about it."

"How'd he take it?"

"Much better than I expected," Carol grinned. Since her lover wore a smile Erin assumed she still had her partner.

"Well don't worry about us right now. I'm not going anywhere and if you need time to sort all this out, I'll give you that."

"Then why do I feel so bad?" the officer asked, tilting her head sideways to meet the emerald eyes peering in her direction. She found in them affection and compassion. It was almost her undoing.

"Cuz you were an ass," Erin replied. She tried to look serious. A large part of her still felt angry regarding Carol's cowardliness. But saw the pain the casual remark inflected and wanted to take it back somehow. Quietly she added, "And because sometimes life stinks. There's no easy way out - - any way you look at it. You just gotta enjoy the ride while you can," Erin added with a grin, hoping to lift Carol's spirits.

It worked and Carol grinned. "No argument here."

They pulled into the donut shop and sat silently for a few minutes, soaking in the late morning sunshine. "How long did you wait for me?" Carol asked suddenly.

In truth, Erin had waited close to three hours, often questioning the stupidity of sitting by the curb and watching the morning mist break with the rising sun. During all this time the only thing she'd thought about was how much Carol would need her and how much she needed to be there for her friend. Her anger had given way to the fear she felt if her friends got to Carol first. She hadn't considered what would happen now. Without a looming threat, she felt that frustration and annoyance with the situation between them a bit uncomfortable. Finally, Erin raised green eyes to her companion, meeting dubious blue.

Erin shrugged, the corner of her mouth lifting upwards in a smirk. "A while," she answered, trying to stay neutral.

"Thank you for warning me. It means a lot to me that you came here," Carol responded softly, squeezing the fingers that were laced within hers.

"Wouldn't be anywhere else," Erin assured her friend with a warm smile. It was true. Carol wasn't the only one that believed in justice. Erin did too. And having her friends drag Carol to some deserted area to beat her wasn't right in her eyes. "Do you have some time?" Erin asked.

Carol looked at her watch. "Yeah. I'm supposed to meet with the desk sergeant at one to get some more files for my new assignment," she grimaced.

"Not good, huh?"

Carol snorted and shook her head. "Probably not. What did you have in mind?"

"A light meal and some semi-heavy conversation – nothing too overbearing. I promise," Erin grinned.

"Okay, but I pick up the bill this time. I insist."

Soon the two were sitting inside the local diner eating some tea biscuits and hot soup. Carol blew on her spoon before she spoke.

"So you diverted the angry mob, huh? Did they have pitchforks and torches?" Carol grinned.

Erin wondered silently why she couldn't stay angry with this woman. She saw the grin and felt herself smirking in response. "No. But I think Stan has a voodoo doll with your picture on it."

Carol resisted the urge to laugh out loud. She might have if not given the fact that a kid had senselessly died and she was the one to blame. The lighthearted comment did lift her soul if only for a moment. Turning serious again she faced Erin.

"Why did you do it?"

"Do what?"

"Double-cross your friends . . . especially after the way I acted yesterday morning?"

"Well, at the risk of sounding like I'm pushing, I'm in love with you." Erin paused with a slight grin before turning serious. "I knew you felt terrible about the shooting and it was tearing you up inside. You don't need the campus storming the stationhouse or beating you up. I had the chance to protect you. So I did. That's what you do for people you love. That's what you did for Randell. Someone was going to hurt him and you took the only action you could."

"I find that hard to believe. I feel pretty shitty right now."

"How would you feel if Randell had been killed because you didn't fire?"

Carol look up from her bowl. Actually, that was something that she hadn't considered in all of it. She was so wrapped up in her guilt over the shooting that she didn't take the time to look at all the angles. Erin did and Carol had to admit she admired the young woman more now than ever.

"You had a choice," Erin continued. "Either your partner or a strung out kid breaking the law. You made the right choice."

"Doesn't sound like the philosophy of an establishment rebel," Carol chided softly.

"No it doesn't," Erin agreed. "But I'm not looking at it from that perspective."

"Then how are you looking at it?"

"I'm looking at it as a woman in love . . . Yeah, I'm still mad. But I do love you, Carol."

"I love you, too."

"You don't have to feel obligated to say that," Erin said sincerely.

"It's not an obligation to say it. I feel it, too. Making sense of what to do with it is my problem."

"Why not let it be and go with it? Just something to consider," Erin added quickly. She didn't want to get into another heated debate. She wasn't ready for another one like the other morning and by the look on Carol's exhausted face, neither was she, nor would she be any time soon. The worry lines on Carol's face aged the woman in a matter of days and Erin ached for her. But she watched Carol smile and magically the woman seemed to look younger again.

"You're very wise," Carol complimented.

"Was there any doubt?" Erin laughed before quickly adding, "Don't answer that."

Carol had to chuckle, too. "What I mean is, some might say you have an old soul. You're intuitive. I like that."

"You also like the fact that I'm a free spirit. But it's what keeps you uncertain too I think. It's ironic, really. What you love most about me is the thing you fear most in yourself. Yet it's something you're searching for deep down. But you're not alone, Carol . . . We're all searching for that."

"So you're Miss Right? I'm not being flippant here. I'm asking sincerely."

One Belief Away

"Only you can answer that question . . . As long as I can be with you in the end, that's all that matters to me. I'm trying my best to understand the reluctance," the radical replied.

"I'm not sure I understand it myself, Erin. Maybe you're right. Maybe I am afraid of change. When I lose my inhibitions I'm certain of how I feel. Actually I almost came over last night to tell you."

"Why didn't you?"

"Well Phyllis...Randell's wife, she thought it best I sober up first," Carol said with a slight chuckle.

Erin smiled before growing serious again.

"Look," she paused, wanting to make sure she had Carol's full attention as well as consider her response carefully. "You make me feel whole, Carol. And it's not about whether I can see myself with you forever. It's the fact that I can't imagine my life without you in it. It sounds like the same thing but it's very different. I don't want a ball and chain. I want to share our lives. If you feel it someday, that's wonderful. If you don't . . . then that's okay, too. I want you to be happy, even if I can't be the one that makes you happy."

"I wish I could give you what you want . . . I'm just not sure and I don't want to hurt you as a result."

"I realize that - it's why I came back. And it's also why I'm leaving."

"Leaving?" Carol asked.

Erin simply nodded. "You need time to consider it all and I don't think you can do that if I'm in your life . . . I don't think you regret what happened the other night. You just don't know how to deal with it. So, let's take a step back. Okay? Maybe some time apart will help you figure out what makes you happiest."

Carol gave her a nervous grin. "I don't think you'll wait and it's wrong of me to ask you to."

"You're not asking. I'm offering. And of course I'll wait. I can't say I'll wait forever," Erin admitted with a slight chuckle. "But I'm in no hurry to get somewhere right here and now." She paused and looked up seeing the clock on the wall. "You, however, lack the time to dwell on it any longer. You need to get back to work."

"Is it that late already?" Carol looked at her Timex. "I guess it is," she said wiping her fingers with her napkin. "What are you going to do, Erin? The house is waiting."

"I'll figure out something. I'd like to say that I have Minos' support like you have Randell's but I can't. She agreed that I shouldn't turn you over to them but I think it has more to do with the prison sentence our housemates will get more than the target being the woman I love." Erin began to chuckle. "It's funny. Here're my open-minded friends who'll end up hating me for loving a cop and the only supporter we seem to have is the old-fashioned, middle-aged beat officer . . . I never thought it would come to this."

"I'm sorry," Carol said sincerely.

"You're worth any trade off, Carol. I mean that."

"Maybe I should go home with you tonight?" the officer answered.

"With the mob after you?" Erin grinned.

"I'm not worried about me," Carol replied. "I just want to be sure you're safe. I'm afraid of what they might do."

Erin smiled at the gallantry and concern of her lover. "I love the fact you want to take care of me but I'm sure Minos won't let anything happen . . . Besides, I have to study for exams again tonight. And I think you need sometime away from me. As hard as that is to say . . . I honestly think it's true."

"That's fine Erin. I understand," Carol answered trying not to sound disappointed.

"Are you sure? Because I don't want you thinking I'm shutting you out, Carol." Erin began to ramble and Carol took her gently by the shoulders with a grin firmly in place.

"It's okay," she said softly with a growing smile. "I won't fall apart because I won't see you tonight. I'll live. And we'll be okay. I'm just worried about what they'll do to you for siding with the enemy."

Erin started to chuckle, realizing how ridiculous she must have sounded. "Who knows? By the weekend this might have all blown over," she offered. "Minos is having a party and in my house recently, parties take precedence over political statements."

Carol grinned knowingly as they began to make their way out. "Will I disapprove of this party?"

"Probably," Erin smiled, knowingly. "With the semester ending I need to blow off a little steam"

Carol grinned before turning serious. "You just be sure to take care of yourself, okay? I know you said you want space but . . . Promise to call me tonight? Let me know you're okay?"

Erin gave a grin and a salute. "Yes, ma'am . . . I think I can do that."

One Belief Away

A few minutes later Erin drove Carol as close to the back door as possible. A few reporters were camped out but Carol managed to avoid them as best she could without comment until she was inside again. Once Carol was safely tucked away in the precinct Erin proceeded to the campus. She went to class but her mind was far away from the classroom. She knew that when she got home in a few hours she'd have some pointed questions to answer from some angry housemates.

With much dread, Erin walked in to find the gang from Benton Harbor waiting in the living room. Stan was the first to rise.
"Where the fuck did you go?"
"None of your goddamn business. Let's just say I saved you all from a lengthy prison sentence," Erin retorted.
"You sold us out? You fucking bitch!"
Stan raced across the living room to Erin but a mutual friend, Davy, jumped up coming between them. With as much force as possible he pushed Stan back.
"Don't touch her! We're not gonna turn on each other. That's how the establishment treats each other."
The house was divided and literally started to take up sides in the room behind Stan or Davy. As always, Minos stood in the middle and looked on.
"Fuck you, Davy! What do you know? I say we go there ourselves."
"I think you should drop this right now."
Stan ignored Davy and focused on Erin.
"Where the fuck does she live?"
"I'm warning you Stan - drop it! You're not fighting for a cause - you're just looking for a fight like the rest of your asshole friends," Erin challenged.
Stan was finished with words. He pulled out a switchblade and pointed it at Davy. The startled man raised his hands and took two steps back letting Stan pass. Helpless, he watched Stan walk over to Erin while his friends quietly cheered him on.
"Now, I'm gonna ask one more time. Where the fuck does she live?"

Carol's gun and nightstick were hidden safely in her bedroom but she was still in her uniform after getting home from work. From her living room window she watched Minos' van pull up. She thought perhaps Erin had changed her mind and decided to stop by as she went out onto her porch. Her smile, however, began to fade as she watched the passengers unload. Stan and five men got out of the car. She watched as the six of them approached and she moved to meet them. The sight of Erin with them stopped her in her tracks. Stan continued to walk Erin over with a knife to her throat.

"You think killing students is okay, huh? Let's continue in that spirit with this one."

Stan shook Erin for effect and Erin knew it was her opportunity of escape. She sent a forceful elbow to Stan's gut, making him double over and release his hold. She darted toward Carol.

"Run!" Erin screamed.

The men charged but Carol wouldn't run away, not with Erin still outside. In fact, she ran directly into their path and started to swing.

"Get in the house!" Carol yelled to Erin.

Two of Carol's attackers fell with the swings she delivered but the last three got a hold of her and began to beat her with fists and homemade nightsticks. Stan looked on with laughter. His smug appearance set Erin off. With no regard for her own safety, she jumped on the back of one of Carol's attackers but he tossed her off with ease. She landed flat, knocking the wind out of her lungs. They continued with their assault on Carol's body until they heard a gun shot ring out. They all looked over to see Randell in uniform. Quickly, they scattered back to the car. Randell looked over to Carol on the ground. Instead of giving chase, he rushed up to Erin first, who was in his path to Carol, as the van sped away.

"Are you Erin? Are you alright?"

"Help her," Erin squeaked out, still trying to get air into her lungs.

Randell gave a quick nod and made his way over to Carol, coming to rest on his knees beside her.

"Hey, kid," he called out to his partner.

Randell rolled her over to see how bad she was. She was a bloody mess and he cringed inwardly – she had a gash at her hairline. Her left eye was red and swollen shut. He knew it would be one hell of a shiner. But more importantly, he wondered what damage she took internally. He felt himself start to shake in both fear and anger. But he knew he had to hold it together. Erin, who was now on her feet, limped her way over.

"Go call for help," he ordered her. Without delay Erin hobbled inside the house to the phone.

"Hold on, Carol. Hold on, sweetie. We're gonna get you out of here," Randell coaxed taking off his tie.

"Erin? Where's Erin?" Carol asked. She could feel a warm liquid spilling into her right eye and knew it had to be blood. It didn't stop her from trying to look around, though. Randell used his tie to try to stop the bleeding.

"She's okay. She's inside getting help. Just relax, kiddo."

"What are you doing here?" Carol asked.

"Perfect timing like always, huh?" he teased as he continued to wipe the blood away. "Wish I was here five minutes earlier."

Carol was obviously confused. "But how did you know?"

"Frank cornered me, talking about his new GTO, when the desk sergeant said I had a call. I went to the phone and an anonymous caller told me to get over here fast."

"Anonymous?" Carol asked.

Randell nodded. "A woman. Didn't say who she was only that she knew me through a mutual friend. Figured it might be Erin calling so I hauled ass over here. I'm just sorry I was late."

Erin would have been with Stan at the time, Carol considered. Her mind was slightly cloudy and a bit slow from the brawl. But she knew the only other woman that might know Randell's name would be Minos. Carol figured Erin must have mentioned his name in their conversations. She had to be the one who knew about the impending attack. Slowly, Carol picked up on something else Randell had just mentioned - his guilt at not being there to stop it.

"No. No," she said quickly, making up time for her lack of response. "Don't be sorry. I'm lucky you came when you did."

"You've got a guardian angel out there someplace, kid," Randell smiled. He watched as Erin made her way back outside and he rose up after gently putting Carol on the ground.

"I'll be back," he told her. As he passed Erin he pointed to Carol. "Stay with her. I'm gonna get some towels."

Erin continued on and knelt next to Carol, holding her in her arms.

"I'm so sorry," Erin told her.

"Not your fault," Carol said, trying to grin. Her mouth hurt too much for it to last any real length of time.

"I shouldn't have brought them here."

"And gotten stabbed instead?" Carol replied, keeping her answer brief. "No. You did the right thing."

She heard the words but she still couldn't believe them. Randell brought the towels out along with some bandages and started to doctor up Carol.

Moments later a squad car and an ambulance pulled up to the house. A few of the neighbors had come from their homes to watch the exciting commotion. As a paramedic moved Carol to a gurney she protested.

"It's not bad, really. I'll be okay."

"Officer Johnson. We're here anyway. Let's just take you in to be sure, okay?"

Carol, resigned to her fate, just nodded her approval and turned to face Erin.

"I'm so sorry," Erin repeated again to what seemed like the hundredth time to Carol.

"I told you, don't be sorry. You tried to save my life."

"Guess that means I'm responsible for ya, too," she smiled.

Carol grinned but turned sober for a moment. "You gave up a lot for me today. I'm sorry you lost a home because of me and I-."

Erin put a gentle finger over Carol's lips. "We'll have lots of time to talk about it. Besides, half of the house sided with Davy and me. I'm not homeless, just living in a place with a little tension for now. But what's life with out a little conflict?" She gave a grin before patting Carol softly on the arm. "Go on and get out of here. I'm gonna talk with Randell."

Carol nodded and Erin watched as the medics loaded Carol into the back of the ambulance. Once the doors were closed and the vehicle on its way, Erin made her way over to Randell, who was speaking with the officers who arrived at the scene.

"Did you see them?" the first officer asked Randell.

"Briefly. There were five or six of them, I think."

The officer then turned to Erin who was at Randell's side. "What about you? Did you see them?"

"I live with them. They brought me here against my will."

"You know where they are now?" the officer asked.

Erin gave a grin remembering her conversation with Stan. "Oh yeah . . . I can deliver them."

Chapter 18

The week had been stressful for Erin to say the least. Not only did the visit with her mother leave her feeling drained, her dilemma with Carol wasn't much better. That wasn't exactly true, she had decided. She could reason with Carol no matter what the subject matter. Her mother on the other hand...She knew from their conversation at the hospital that things still hadn't changed in spite of the years that had passed.

But that was over and she focused on the future. She imagined she had done well studying but it had been hard for her to focus. All she could do now was just hope that she would get passing marks and, finally, after 4 long years, have a degree in her hand.

As for the melee at Carol's, after Erin had given her statement to the police they arrived at the house and rounded up all six of her housemates involved in the attack. Erin rode along with Randell, who was officially off-duty, but went along anyway to see that justice was served.

Erin had to admit she expected Randell to work in a few shoves or even a few punches to her former housemates but much to what Carol had told her before, Randell remained professional and cool headed. The glare that Erin got from Minos as they carted them away, however, chilled her soul.

Erin couldn't understand it. Minos had called the stationhouse so why was Minos upset that she had brought the police to their door? Once things had settled down Erin cornered Minos to find out. She explained that she made the call for Erin's sake, not Carol's, and as she put it, she 'sure as hell didn't rat out her other friends in the process'. From Erin's perspective, she didn't want to choose but her so-called friends didn't give her an option. Erin could still feel an underlying tension between her and Minos over the whole incident.

The next day Carol had been released. In fact, she was already back at work in the file room, protecting and serving as more of a secretary than a cop. Her review still hadn't come down but Erin was confident that Carol would be exonerated of any wrong doing in the shooting. She spoke briefly with Randell about everything that had transpired recently and felt a bit more at ease. Erin thanked him for his kind words.

She skipped down the stairs of Minos' house. She felt a bit of relief and relaxation settle over her spirit. Of course, the joint she smoked earlier helped. Aside from waiting for grades and graduation, school was finished, she'd confronted her mother, and things would improve with Carol over time.

So she convinced herself that things were indeed looking up no matter how bleak the week had begun. As she rounded the corner into the kitchen, she saw the house engaged in the usual Friday night toke-fest, which actually started more like Friday afternoon than Friday night. She caught only half of the argument between Bill and their fellow housemate Marlow – as he called himself now. His given name was Steve, she thought, but she'd heard it only once in the two years he'd lived there. She took a seat at the large kitchen table and watched Minos' light up.

"Just relax and light up, would ya?" she heard Marlow tell Bill.

"I've got that rally meeting and shit," he said looking at his watch, "I'm already gonna be late."

"Come on," Marlow insisted. "Just mellow out and hang with us awhile. It's been a wild two weeks since you've been gone, pal."

Bill had gone away for two weeks, doing interviews in his hometown. Like Erin, he was set to graduate and also like Erin, he was focused and did have goals he wanted to fulfill. He had just arrived back the night before and simply crashed. Being out of the loop in regard to recent events, he figured he'd catch up when he had the chance. For the moment, however, he went in search of his shoes.

Erin offered nothing to the conversation between the two men. She just strolled over to Minos who offered the petite blonde a hit.

Erin inhaled deeply; pausing to let the drugs work into her lungs, soothing her mind.

It was then that Minos finally spoke to her. "I still say she's a fucking pig."

"What?" Erin asked, unsure of what Minos was talking about.

"I said your cop, Carol, is a fucking pig."

Erin rolled her eyes. Now just wasn't the time for a discussion so she tried to avoid it the best she could. "Lighten up, Minos . . . You're being far too serious for someone who's stoned."

The table chuckled but Minos didn't find it humorous.

"What the fuck is her appeal? Six house mates are in lock up now because of you two!"

"YOU called Randell! What was I supposed to do? Lie about knowing them?"

"I called to stop them," Minos countered. "I didn't bring the cops into my home to take them away. That was your doing, not mine!"

Bill overheard the conversation and bent an ear to listen. "Who got locked up?" he asked.

"Stan and his boys," Minos said. Bill was aware of just who the boys were. They were a younger set of students that looked up to Stan. Bill liked Stan but he never had a deep friendship with the man. Stan was a bit too edgy for him so instead Bill often shared company with Erin and Davy instead. Bill didn't get a chance to hear the rest of the story, however. Erin slammed her hand down on the table, making everyone stop momentarily.

"No! Six house mates are locked up because they beat up someone who I happen to love."

"She's okay - they released her already," Minos added.

"Eight stitches, one black eye and three bruised ribs are *not* okay! Sure, they released her but that's not the point!"

"Hell yeah, it is! And if you love her so much why the fuck don't you go live with her!"

Bill was scratching his head at all this but soon realized he just didn't have the time to piece it all together and continued his hunt for his foot apparel. Erin didn't want to continue the debate any longer.

Instead of continuing with her angry speech, Erin just muttered, "It's not that simple." She hoped Minos was too high to hear her reply.

Unfortunately, Minos heard every word and began to give a hearty laugh. "Told you - fucking pig. She's using you and you can't even see it."

Erin got up from the table but not before leaning down to Minos' ear. "You don't know shit," she whispered in a heated voice.

"The hell I don't!" Minos yelled.

Erin simply walked to the refrigerator. "I need a drink," she sighed. She opened the door pulling out a Pepsi bottle before taking her seat again. "I can't see how this is my fault. I tried to stop them. You tried to stop them. And you know damn well if I didn't say anything they would continue to hunt Carol. Maybe even kill her."

"Eye for an eye," Minos muttered.

Erin nodded. "Well, that PIG saved my life months ago so let's just say I returned the favor. Eye for an eye, after all. And as for the shooting, if Jimmy wasn't breaking the law he never would have gotten killed in the first place."

"How 'establishment' of you to say," Minos harrumphed. "Gonna end up joining the force next?"

"No," Erin countered. "Just finally waking up to some realities in life. Everything isn't black and white, Minos. It's not always *us* verses *them*. Sometimes the establishment is wrong but here's a news flash – sometimes we are, too. Stan and his buddies certainly proved that point. And if you can't see that then I'm sorry for your blindness. But I won't apologize for doing the right thing."

Minos gave a reluctant sigh, her anger seeming to disappear as quickly as it came. Erin was sure – it had to be the effects of the pot.

"Maybe it's not you. Maybe it's everything else. It's ending, you know?"

"What?" Erin asked.

"We tried to change the world . . . and we failed. Everyone's moving on . . . Even you."

"I don't consider myself a failure," Erin replied.

Minos paused. "We helped end segregation but blacks are still second class citizens. We brought that wasteful war into the spotlight of the mainstream but we're still in it. We burned our bras, which left us nothing but role confusion. Truth is, nothing we hoped for has been achieved. And I wonder if it ever will."

Minos got up from the table, staggering a bit as she went to the refrigerator for a drink.

Erin watched Minos considering what she said. "Change doesn't happen overnight, you know?" Erin countered.

"And sometimes not at all," Minos retorted.

"It will happen. Someday . . . The war will be over. Blacks in this country will have a voice in government and it wouldn't surprise me if we see a female Supreme Court Justice in the next ten years."

Minos chuckled. "Now who's stoned?"

"I honestly believe it will happen. It will just take time, Minos. The thing is to never give up."

Minos took her seat again next to Erin as she took a drink. She set the bottle down on the table, playing with the blue and red logo on the glass, her eyes purposely diverted from Erin. "And what about you? You're gonna run off and join the establishment soon. You'll leave us."

"I might," Erin confessed. "But I'm not joining the establishment. I'd like to think I'm on my way to set a new standard within the establishment. You know, one where my ideals and beliefs are no longer the counter-culture but the culture in which we live...I'm not selling out, Minos. I'm growing. I'm trying to make a difference. I'm just doing it in a different way."

Erin grinned immediately after the words left her mouth. *At what point did I become Carol?* It was her voice but it sure did sound a lot like her lover. She remembered the first day with her at the park. Once they looked past each other's exteriors to find the people within, they found that commonality. And now that Erin was facing the real world that Carol faced everyday she began to understand her lover's perception much better.

"Well," Minos sighed. "Whatever road you take Erin, make sure you never sacrifice your ideals. Never sell out. Promise?"

Erin nodded. "I promise."

A sense of relief seemed to pass over both women. Both knew they would never see eye to eye again but perhaps that common bond they shared would always be in tact, in effect, keeping their friendship bound. Erin was more convinced now that things would certainly get better. But like everything else it would just take time.

Two joints later Erin found it harder to stay upright, her eyes were glossing over at a startling rate. She reached for her bottle of Pepsi and watched it literally melt before her eyes. Something was wrong-very wrong. She couldn't remember how long she had been sitting there. It was as if time had slipped away, without her knowledge, in a single instant. She tried her damnedest to focus on the things around her but it was of no use - everything was melting.

A sudden thud and the resulting laughter made her turn to her right. But the quick turn of her head seemed to take forever. Time was slowing down. When she was able to focus briefly, Minos had passed out over the table and the room, filled with roommates and their lovers for the night, chuckled at the sight.

Erin looked over and watched Bill start to make his way out the door. She must have called his name because he walked back to the table, obviously frustrated that he couldn't leave yet.

"What is it, Skylon?" he asked impatiently.

The words were quick and to the point but he sounded like a stretched 8-track tape to her - the tones long and deep. Erin couldn't reply. She felt herself begin to twitch and jerk. Bill's impatience began to slip from his face and concern took over.

Erin could hear the gagging noise but she didn't know it was coming from herself. Bill managed to catch her as she began to tumble out of the chair. He felt Erin lightly grab his shirt and stutter something.

"What?" he asked in panic. "What did you say, sweetheart?"

Erin struggled with the two syllables but finally she spit them out. "Ca-rol. Car-ol."

"Carol?" Bill asked and saw the slightest nod. "You want me to get your friend Carol?" Again, another slight nod. Bill remembered Carol from their meeting in the kitchen because it was seldom that Skylon brought anyone into their circle.

"Woooo! What happened to her?" Marlow asked in laughter as he saw Erin on the floor. He looked over and watched as Bill searched frantically through scraps of paper by the phone. Finally, he found the name and two numbers.

"What are you doing, man?" Marlow asked as he watched Bill.

Bill simply ignored him and dialed the first number on the slip of paper. Unable to wait, he let it ring three times before hanging up and trying the second number. This time it rang only once before a gruff voice answered, "Police Station."

Quickly, Bill hung up and looked to Marlow with bewilderment written all over his thin features.

"You got Carol's number?" Bill asked quickly, thinking the second number might have been written incorrectly.

"Yeah, it's in your hand, man," the drugged-out roomie answered, not sure he understood the worry in his friend's features.

"No," Bill retorted hotly. "This number is to the goddamn police station." He was exasperated, eyes glancing quickly from the writhing blonde on the floor and Minos passed out at the table.

"Yeah," Marlow answered without concern. "She's the cop."

Bill ran his fingers through his long hair. "The cop? What do you mean the cop?" he yelled loud enough to get the room's attention.

Marlow looked confused, which wasn't difficult given his drug-induced state. "Ohhhh yeah," he answered with realization. "You've been gone. Well, it all started when Erin left to see her folks and-."

Bill didn't have time to hear the run down of what had transpired during his brief departure from the group.

"Carol's a fuckin' cop? Just great!" Bill shouted. Of all the people, Skylon had asked for her. Bringing a cop here would be like walking right into the sheriff's office and turning himself in.

"What's the problem?" Marlow asked again, still completely confused, not sensing the urgency of the situation. "Carol's cool."

"Jesus Christ! Look at her! She's trippin' bad, man!" Bill responded, pointing to Erin. "Where the hell did you get that shit?" he accused, indicating the bag of joints on the table. Bill tore the bag open and ripped the cigarettes apart with trembling fingers. Taking a small amount of weed he sniffed and licked it. "Oh fuck," he nearly cried. "This shit is fuckin' laced, man. Oh shit! We're fucked. We are seriously fucked here, man." He ran his hands through his long hair again, tugging it lightly as if willing his brain to kick into motion.

"What are we gonna do?" Marlow asked, finally, paranoia beginning to creep inside him as he realized the extent of Bill's words. He looked back to the small blonde on the floor and could feel her agony as she trembled and moaned. "If she dies . . . "

"She's not gonna fuckin' die, okay?" Bill growled as he returned to her side. "Look, I'm gonna go down to the stationhouse and get Carol. She'll know what to do."

"You can't do that. She's a fucking cop!" Marlow argued. "You can't bring her here . . . let her see this."

"I'm not gonna stand here and fight with you! So get your stupid ass over here and help me take her to her bedroom. Skylon needs help and she asked for Carol. Carol will take care of her and figure out how to handle this. She won't turn Skylon in."

Apparently, Bill's words had little impact on Marlow, who still stood stupidly watching his friend bend over the small woman. With a grunt of dissatisfaction, Bill lifted Erin into his arms and balanced her slight weight before starting toward the steps that would take him to the bedrooms. With his head bent in tender concern, he listened to the young woman beg for Carol.

"Just relax," he coaxed as they walked along. "I'll find her, sweetie. I'll bring her to ya," he promised softly. The words seemed to calm her and she appeared less restless when he finally settled her on the mattress in her room. Bill took great care to roll her onto her stomach, tilting her head in hopes that she wouldn't choke should she vomit.

Marlow had followed them and now stood swaying in the doorway, appearing as if he was going to pass out at any second. Bill turned around and shook his head in disgust, gained his feet and pushed past his useless friend. "Keep an eye on her," he ordered. "Make sure she doesn't choke. I'll be right back." And with that, he left the house.

"Whatta ya want, kid?" the desk sergeant asked, barely even looking up from the forms in front of him. He sounded disinterested at best.

"Carol, please," Bill requested nervously, shifting his weight from foot to foot.

"What do you want with Officer Johnson?" the other man asked, looking up for a moment to scrutinize the lanky kid in front of him. *Figures Johnson would keep company like this.*

"There's an emergency. I have to speak with her." Even though he was angered by the other man's obvious disdain, Bill spoke softly and politely. He didn't want to cause any trouble at this point. He had to find his target and get her to the destination as fast as possible.

Luckily, Carol walked in from the filing room and she spotted the young man at the counter. Though he looked familiar, she couldn't remember his name, so she slowly walked over and cocked her head at him, wondering why he was at the station. He wasn't cuffed so he obviously came in of his own accord, which seemed slightly unusual.

Suddenly, inexplicable concern took hold of Carol and she picked up her pace toward the young man. Randell had just walked into the stationhouse and saw the look on Carol's face. He stopped, sizing up the situation.

Bill was getting frustrated with the desk sergeant's lack of motivation to find Carol when he spotted her out of the corner of his eye. Quickly he raced over, taking her by the elbow to a semi-secluded area.

"What's wrong?" Carol asked. She could see the worry lines deep in his young forehead and she tried to stay calm even as her body hummed with the need for action.

"It's Skylon," he said quickly. "She's . . . in trouble."

"She hurt?" Carol asked, cold with fear.

"She's really sick. We were . . . smoking and she got sick. She's calling for you," Bill explained meekly. He knew that he was doing a poor job of delivering the story; he just hoped it was enough to get the officer to come with him. "Please come back to the house. I'm not sure what else to do." *Begging might help, too*, he reasoned with himself.

"Something wrong?"

Randell's voice startled them and both Carol and Bill jumped at the sound.

"It's Erin," Carol said making her way over to the desk sergeant. Randell followed behind the two of them.

"A friend of mine needs some help. I'm taking off," she told him.

"Oh no you're not," he replied, finally showing some action and coming around the desk to confront her. "You've got reports to finish. If you want time off, ya gotta request it from the captain just like the rest of us."

"The reports can wait," Carol replied angrily as her body shook. "I have a personal emergency to attend to," she added, turning to face him and hoping to resolve this reasonably. She was already in enough trouble here but there was no way in hell she wouldn't go to Erin's aid. Before the sergeant could respond Randell piped in.

"Come on," he said hoping some levity would help. "We all know that file room isn't going anywhere soon. What's the problem with starting the weekend a little early?"

The desk sergeant wasn't amused. Carol and Randell exchanged a long look. He knew what was about to happen. Carol was going. And nothing was going to stop that. Quietly, he gave the briefest of nods, encouraging her to follow her heart, consequences be damned.

"You're on the clock till five, Johnson," the sergeant reminded her. "It's only four right now. If you wanna keep serving and protecting, I suggest you get your ass back in that cellar," the beefy man said smugly, enjoying this power game.

Ever since the shooting review began and she was assigned to desk duty, they had done everything they could to make Carol's life miserable. The force was no place for a woman and he was going to prove it any chance he got. He was pleased to have yet another opportunity to jerk her around.

It only took a moment to make the decision of a lifetime. Some choices were hard to make and were debated privately and publicly, the pros and cons weighed meticulously before an answer was reached. This was one of those choices that was made instantly and on instinct.

Carol responded by ripping the silver emblem from her uniform and tossing it at him. It slid across the wood desk before clanking to the linoleum where it stopped at his well-polished toe. "I suggest you take this badge and shove it up your ass."

Carol grabbed Bill's elbow and propelled him toward the door. The young man had to drag his chin off the floor and start jogging to keep up with Carol's pace. She stopped for a moment and looked back at her former partner. Randell stood with a smile, nodding his head. His support, however, still made Carol's heart break. She didn't want to leave Randell partnerless. The intuitive cop saw it in her eyes.

"Bring Erin over for dinner some night. I'm sure she'll love Phyllis' spaghetti as much as you do," he called out supportively.

Carol gave a grin, trying to keep her composure. She really hated good-byes. His comments, like always, helped. Besides, it wasn't truly a good-bye as much as a see you later.

"Will do," she nodded briefly before pulling Bill out with her. "Oh God, please let Erin be okay," Carol murmured under her breath as they hit the sidewalk in the mid-afternoon sun.

Chapter 19

Carol took the porch steps two at a time, not even bothering to knock at the door. She bolted inside, assessing the situation. It was eerily quiet except for the sound of David Bowie playing on the radio in the background. There was a scattering of people at different levels of drug-induced highs spread throughout the lower level of the rambling home and though they appeared relaxed, it was obvious the house was wrought with anxiety. Some of them spotted Carol's uniform and tensed immediately. Without giving the others a second thought, the tall woman looked frantically around for Erin and instead spotted Minos lying face down on the table.

Bill charged inside, having taken a few extra moments to park the car, and watched as Carol pulled Minos from her chair and laid the woman on her back on the kitchen floor. She checked for a pulse and quickly began CPR. Marlow, who had come downstairs at the bursting open of the door, looked on from behind her in shock.

"Call a goddamn ambulance!" Carol barked at him. He paused a moment, more in surprise than defiance, before rushing to the phone. Carol looked up and saw Bill watching her. "Come here!" she ordered. "Watch me."

Carol went through the steps just once. "Think you can handle that?" she asked, looking into his eyes, determining if he was sober enough to be of any help. He seemed to be keeping a level head throughout and had watched her movements intently.

"Yeah," he replied, coming to his knees next to Carol to take over, gently nudging her out of the way.

"Where's Erin?" Carol demanded.

"Upstairs. Her room," he answered quickly.

"Keep that up until she's breathing and have someone down here open a goddamn window. Some fresh air would be nice," she ordered sarcastically over her shoulder as she took the stairs two at a time, making her way through the smoke filled house.

Carol slid to a halt upon seeing Erin through the open doorway. She was a shaking mess, lying on the mattress in a fetal position. Carol shoved aside her initial reaction and raced to the edge of the bed, falling to her knees. "Erin, honey?" she whispered, hesitantly touching the girl's face. Her skin was flushed and warm, her eyes dancing beneath the thin, closed lids. Carol brushed aside damp bangs with trembling fingers.

Suddenly, Carol could feel a presence behind her and looked back to see Marlow standing in the doorway.

"Yes?" Carol asked sharply, furious at the ineptitude of the man.

"Uh . . . ambulance is coming."

Carol didn't have a chance to reply because just then Erin heaved sharply, not giving Carol enough notice to move. Vomit covered nearly everything: Erin, the bed, Carol's uniform. Quickly, the officer rolled Erin forward to ensure that her young lover wouldn't choke to death. She used deft fingers to clear Erin's mouth since the girl had little control over her own muscles at this point.

"What was she doing today?" Carol asked Marlow.

"What do you mean?" he mumbled, not sure how a recital of the blonde's day could help the situation.

"Drugs," the officer growled. "What did she take? We have to tell the doctors what they're dealing with," she lashed out angrily, her voice dripping with dark sarcasm. Her patience was worn well beyond thin with this man.

"I thought it was just pot but Bill thinks it might of had something extra. I had a few hits but Minos and Skylon had the most. I feel pretty groovy so I'm not sure why they're trippin'."

Carol didn't give a damn about how Marlow was feeling and was about to say just that when Erin groaned and began to cry.

"Shhhh," Carol coaxed, her manner suddenly becoming tender as she wiped the young woman's forehead. She turned her attention to Marlow briefly, not wanting to take her eyes from the blonde. "Get me some towels, a cold damp hand towel and some dry ones."

Without question Marlow did as asked, seemingly relieved to be away from the woman's wrath if even for a few moments. He stumbled down the hallway toward the community bathroom at the end.

Meanwhile, Carol stripped out of her soaked clothing, leaving only her T-shirt and underwear. She also stripped the bed and tugged off the blonde's paisley peasant blouse and hip huggers. As Marlow returned with the items, Carol cleaned up the young woman as best she could with the large cotton bath towels and tossed them aside. Then she placed the cool rag on Erin's forehead.

"Get these out of here and get me some more clean ones," she demanded, pointing to the stack of soiled towels. "A larger one; damp like this one. I've got to cool her body down."

Once he left to get more, Carol climbed behind Erin onto the now sheetless bed. She lifted the young woman up and placed Erin's head in her lap. Erin flailed for a moment at the change of position. She was obviously disoriented but Carol's soothing reassurances seemed to calm her a bit.

Marlow returned once more with the requested cloth and Carol used it to rub down Erin's feverish body. "What happened?" he asked.

Carol could feel her anger burning deep within. At whom, or what, she wasn't sure. Perhaps it was just the uncontrolled situation. Carol liked having a say in her destiny and as she sat there rocking a mostly nude Erin gently in her lap she realized Erin's fate, as well as her own, was now in God's hands. She very well could lose the young hippie and that hadn't been something she'd planned for.

She wondered just where the hell that ambulance was and why it was taking so damned long. Carol had never been on the other side of an emergency situation. She was always called into the scene as a professional - never had she been part of a tragedy. Never did her heart ache as it did now. Even when her father died she wasn't present for the event. She learned about it all after the fact.

Suddenly, she understood the hysteria of victims and family members. For the first time, she also understood the public's frustration with emergency personnel's reaction time. No matter how fast she could respond to a call she'd never get there quickly enough to stop this kind of pain and uncertainty. She realized in the same instant that she'd never have that problem again since she'd walked away from it to be here, now, with the woman she loved. The woman she was going to grow old with. The woman who could die at any moment. All the recent indecision she felt slipped away instantly.

Would she lose her friends if they knew of the love she shared with Erin? Perhaps. But if she did then they were never true friends to begin with. Would she ever have children? Perhaps. She realized she could try to adopt. And most importantly, would she have to live her life 'hiding'? To the outside world she could show them her true self – a compassionate, caring woman regardless of whom she loved. The only type of hiding she ever truly had to be concerned about was hiding her feelings from Erin. And she decided that would stop here, at this moment. She finally had all the answers that added up to only one conclusion.

"No," Carol whispered aloud, her steady voice reduced to a strangled plea. "You fight. We both know you're a fighter Erin, so don't you give up on me. This is the most important cause of your life right here . . . I get it now, Erin. You're everything to me and you make me whole and if you give me the chance I'll spend the rest of my life proving it. I promise . . . You were right about me, Erin. And I'm willing to take that chance so you better keep fighting here . . . Besides, you don't want to miss the chance to gloat, do you? Come on, sweetheart, please stay with me."

Marlow realized Carol had either not heard his question or had chosen to ignore it, but he sure wasn't going to ask what happened to Erin again. Instead, he decided to wait downstairs for the paramedics. Carol continued to rock Erin gently while trying to keep her body cool.

"Where the fuck are they?" Carol yelled, growing impatient. Almost as soon as she finished the sentence, Bill appeared in the doorway.

"They're here," he sighed, pushing his fingers through his sweaty hair. He was frazzled. The slump of his shoulders reflected the concrete evidence of his strained emotions.

Carol simply nodded. "Did she respond?" The man knew what she was asking and he looked at his feet, quietly shuffling without saying a word. "You did the best you could. Remember that," Carol said honestly, hoping to relieve some of his guilt in his inability to revive Minos.

She watched Bill move quickly from the doorway, taking a spot farther down the hall as the two paramedics worked their way inside. Reluctantly, Carol backed away to give them control and they placed Erin on a flat backboard stretcher to carry her downstairs.

"Both women were smoking marijuana," she told them as they strapped down her lover. "My guess is it was laced with PCP - judging by the symptoms of both of them." She was trying to remain focused on the job, wanting to tell them whatever might help them save Erin's life.

"Such as?" the paramedic said skeptically, barely affording the tall woman in her underwear a once-over.

Carol didn't quite understand his superior attitude. Then she recognized the disdainful look in his eyes. Without the uniform, he assumed she was just another member of the house. She was angered for not being taken seriously and the discussions she and Erin had had about the establishment came into real focus for her for the first time, the young woman's lilting voice echoing in her ears.

"I happen to be an officer of the law," Carol informed him, lowering her voice an octave to let him know she was displeased with his attitude. "And this woman is a dear friend of mine so cut the authority bullshit and listen to me if you want to save some lives today."

The man's eyes widened and he quickly apologized but Carol brushed it off impatiently. She didn't need his platitudes; she needed his medical expertise. "She's been convulsing, vomiting and sweating, in and out of consciousness.

"We'll check it out, ma'am," the paramedic responded, respect returning to his voice.

"You do that," she warned in a growl.

"Okay," the chagrined man turned to his partner. "On three. One, two . . . three." With that, they hoisted Erin up and out of the room. Carol followed them down the stairs and watched from the front doorway as the ambulance doors closed. She released a long sigh as it started on its way down the street.

Before, in the stationhouse when she'd first been told Erin was in trouble, she'd felt the fear of the unknown. Now, watching the red and white vehicle make its way down the street with its own symphony of sirens, her fear was based in reality. She could lose her lover today as they had lost Minos. It was no longer a fear of the unknown. It was a knowledge-based fear, which was far scarier.

"Come on," Bill said, moving forward to rest a hand on Carol's shoulder. The touch startled her and she flinched slightly under his gentle fingers. "Let's get you some clothes and I'll drive you to the hospital."

Given Carol's height and size, she fit somewhat comfortably in a pair of Bill's jeans and a bright red T-shirt with the university symbol across it. When he first handed it to her she flashed to the young man she shot who wore the same logo. She didn't have time for that though and briskly put it on.

They'd arrived at the hospital nearly ten minutes after the speeding ambulance and had spent the better part of an hour pacing the waiting room. Carol was barely able to control her temper. Was it the slow, uninformative nursing staff? Maybe it was the doddling doctors who weren't issuing any updates? Perhaps it was more personal. Maybe the fact that Erin foolishly risked her life for a 'good time' had her on edge? Or maybe, just maybe, Carol was angered most by her own actions.

She never took the time to tell Erin how much she truly meant to her. She was too wrapped up in her fears to tell her. Maybe Erin would meet Minos' fate and that chance would be lost forever.

Bill spoke calmly to nurses and doctors, allowing his dark companion the distance she needed, watching her pace with slow heel to toe steps. Finally, they were told that Erin had been admitted and they gave a room number on the second floor. Carol stopped mid-stride and spun on her heel to run up the stairs near the waiting area. She couldn't wait for the elevator or Bill as she raced along.

Carol stopped short of the door, catching her breath and not wanting to startle Erin with a sudden entry. Carefully, she opened the door, peeking her head inside. Erin was lying asleep in the hospital bed and Carol took a chair directly across from her, not wanting to disturb the exhausted woman. For several long moments, Carol merely sat and watched the small blonde. She still looked dangerously unhealthy: her skin nearly stark white and clammy. But her breathing was even and the machines continued to beep reassuringly around them.

Slowly, Bill walked in with two cups of coffee. "I didn't know how you take it. Is black okay?" he asked, handing the cup over hesitantly, not sure if the woman wanted companionship. He glanced to the prone figure in the bed, his heart lurching at the state of his gentle friend.

Carol gave him a genuine smile. "That's fine. Thank you very much."

A silence passed between them until Bill asked, "Has she woken up yet?"

Carol shook her head and examined Erin a few more moments, sipping her brew. She cringed as the liquid touched her palette. "Is it just me or does this taste like motor oil?" she teased.

"Hospital coffee is just as bad as the food it seems," he countered good-naturedly, relieved to find the woman in good spirits. A lot of the worry and tension had drained from her broad shoulders once she'd found her young lover.

They both grinned at each other and Carol offered her cup over in a toast, which Bill accepted by clinking his paper container against hers. "I'll drink to that," she replied.

This lighter moment was a much-needed relief from a day filled with so much tension.

"Well, despite the taste," Carol said with a grin, "the sentiment is appreciated."

Bill simply returned the smile and Carol watched as it slowly slipped away, his thoughts traveling to the earlier events she was sure.

"Thank you," Carol whispered sincerely.

"For what?" he asked, truly uncertain of Carol's appreciation.

"For getting me. It took a lot of guts for you to walk into that stationhouse. And you did your best back at the house by taking care of Minos." Bill was going to pose an argument but Carol silenced him with a finger. "It may not seem like it but you were a real hero today. I hope someday you see it for yourself. I think Erin has a wonderful friend in you, Bill."

He tried not to smile or blush, given the severity of the situation but he couldn't help himself. "Thank you," he replied with heartfelt gratitude. The compliment meant a lot coming from Carol. "I hope someday I'll see the positive, but right now it's hard, you know?"

Carol was going to reply but Erin uttered a light groan and slowly opened her eyes.

"Erin?" Carol called softly, returning her attention to the blonde and setting aside her coffee.

Erin recognized the voice and willed her eyes to focus, wanting very much to see the familiar face. Finally, the tall brunette's concerned features became clear. "Carol? Is it really you? Where am I? What happened? Are you real?"

Carol had expected this reaction and wouldn't have been surprised if it had been more dramatic. Time was lost for the young woman and her surroundings would be unfamiliar. All of that would pass; the bigger concern was damage to the small woman's vital organs and nervous system. Hopefully, such would be minimal, if at all.

"I'm real, sweetheart. I'm real," she whispered, taking Erin's hand. "Here. Feel. You're in the hospital." With that Carol guided Erin's hand over her cheek, letting the young woman feel her skin to see she was in fact the genuine article and not some hallucination.

For several long minutes, the blonde's cool fingers danced on Carol's skin, reassuring herself that the dark woman was real. It also gave her an opportunity to awaken more and run her green eyes around the stark white room.

"How did I get here?" the young woman asked as she began an attempt to sit up. Carol helped with her assent from the mattress by supporting her slight weight and tucking pillows behind her.

"They brought you and Minos here. Seems whatever you were smoking had PCP . . . angel dust," Carol said to clarify, watching Erin closely for her reaction.

"Angel dust?" Erin asked, surprised. Slowly, her mind remembered a conversation in the kitchen earlier that day about Joy and how this week's weed was from another seller, not their usual contact. "I feel like I've been hit by a truck," she said groggily as she rubbed her face with a trembling hand. Her whole body ached and her head throbbed as she tried to search her memory for more details. It was then that she noticed Carol was wearing Bill's University T-shirt. "Why are you wearing those clothes?"

Carol grinned, trying to keep things as comfortable as possible for Erin. "We kind of had an accident. You lost your lunch all over me," she teased as she used long fingers to smooth back Erin's unruly hair.

Erin winced at the image though she couldn't actually recall the incident. Her mind still felt fuzzy. "I'm sorry," she apologized.

One Belief Away

"Hey, what's a little vomit between friends, huh? Besides, having a flower child puke on my uniform was a fitting end to my career," Carol answered with a wry smirk, capturing Erin's chin between her thumb and her index finger. She traced the smaller woman's jaw gently, focusing on the cloudy emerald eyes.

"End?"

Carol nodded. "They wouldn't let me leave so I quit. Even threw my badge at them in some grand anti-establishment gesture. You would have been proud," she chuckled. "But Randell made me promise to bring you over for dinner."

"I don't know what to say," Erin answered. "Being a cop meant everything to you."

"YOU, Erin O'Fallon, mean everything to me. Did you hear what I said at the house?"

Erin considered it for a moment. "Yeah, bits and pieces," she decided. "But I promise not to gloat too much," she added, grinning widely.

A comfortable silence passed between them until Erin spoke again.

"How's Minos?" Erin asked next, trying to sit up a little bit more. Because of her movement, she missed the flash of regret in the blue eyes.

Carol knew the question was going to come sooner or later and she tried to figure out how to best relate the bad news. She decided the truth, without unnecessary padding, would be the best. "She's . . . she's gone, Erin. She didn't make it."

Erin didn't say anything. She had no reaction whatsoever. Carol thought for a second that perhaps Erin had blacked out again or maybe hadn't heard what Carol had said. But the activist's voice soon echoed Carol's statement.

"She's gone? What do you mean, she's gone?" The young woman's voice strained with the question, quavering slightly.

"She died before I got to the house, Erin," Carol explained gently, trying her damnedest to hold it together. She still stroked Erin's chin and cheek, moving upwards to push back long blonde tendrils at the woman's temple. "Bill and I tried CPR but the doctor thinks she had a brain hemorrhage . . . She died almost instantly. I'm so sorry, sweetheart. I know how much she means to you."

"No," Erin thought aloud. She was shaking her head, pushing away Carol's tender touches. It was all too much for her. "That can't be," she replied. "It was only weed. Weed doesn't kill you."

Erin's voice had begun to rise with the resistance that was building in her mind.

"On the street it's called 'superweed'," Carol told her patiently, dropping her hand to rest on Erin's blanket clad knee. She was glad when the young woman didn't resist that touch as well. "It was a very potent formula, honey."

"I just . . . I can't believe it . . . How can she be dead, Carol? She can't be dead."

Erin wanted to say something, but she didn't know where to begin, her mind was spinning with shock and sorrow. She was confused by the severity of the situation, since she'd been smoking weed with Minos for years. She'd heard all the stories and read the establishment's propaganda, but had never believed any of it. The reality of the situation was physically painful when the reality of it all rested in her heart.

Soon she gave up trying to speak, trying to come up with excuses or rationalizations and she simply started to cry, repeating that it couldn't be possible. She just saw her that day. She couldn't be dead - not Minos. It couldn't be so. But she had learned a long time ago that wishing something to be true didn't make it true. Her friend was gone and she was lucky to have survived.

Bill watched silently from across the room as the two women clung to each other. He was saddened by their loss yet he saw the peace they held from still having each other. He knew he had to go back to the house, which was expecting an update. Quietly he made his way from the room out into the sickly white hallway so he could spread the news, both good and bad.

"Did she suffer?" Erin asked through her tears. "Did it hurt?"

"No, sweetheart," Carol said kissing her forehead. "It happened so fast I don't think she even noticed it. So no, she didn't suffer."

The news didn't matter. Erin's tears still tumbled down her cheeks. And all Carol could do was hold her.

Chapter 20

Carol drove up to the funeral home and checked in her car. A well-dressed gentleman had come out to meet her asking if she was staying for the ceremony and the procession to the cemetery. Carol replied with a nod and he made sure to tag her car so it reflected such.

Quietly, she walked into the small parlor where she watched Erin, dressed in gray, facing the casket, her back to the room. As she entered, Carol took note of all the arrangements and wondered if she'd ever seen that many flowers in one place. Even the countless plants and vases at her father's funeral paled in comparison. It would still be several minutes before anyone else would be entering for the family's private viewing. Quietly, she stepped forward.

Erin told Carol that she needed some space the night before so she could prepare for today. At first Carol was concerned that the young woman was shutting her out but Erin assured her that was not the case. She just had to go through some of Minos' paperwork that was in a strong box and take care of other preparations, such as finding clothes for her friend. Erin also had a brief meeting with an attorney who was an old friend of Minos'. Carol stopped her journey toward Erin when a gentleman walked in from a different parlor and took a space beside Erin. She watched as Erin faced the man and responded with a brief nod to a question, spoken too quietly for her to hear. At that moment, Erin saw Carol out of the corner of her eye.

"How you holding up?" Carol asked as she resumed her journey toward her grieving lover.

"I'm numb," Erin answered honestly. "And sad . . . An odd combination, huh?" Erin looked as if she was really considering the question, wondering how valid that statement could be and if it honestly conveyed what she felt at the moment.

Carol could sense the young woman's confusion. "Not at all," Carol answered. "I felt the same way when I lost my father," she added.

It was true. Carol thought back to her father's funeral and how she watched people come and go, listening to them offering their condolences yet it meaning very little. Their words wouldn't sink through no matter what was said. No matter how many sympathies she received it didn't change the fact her father was gone. And she was numb. And she was sad. And she knew exactly how Erin felt at this moment. Minos may have been Erin's friend but she also knew the young woman saw the older one as a mentor of sorts. And to lose the one who 'raised' you was one of the worst losses you could feel.

A small silence passed between them before Carol spoke again, looking inside the casket. Minos was dressed in a floral print top, love beads around her neck. Her eyes were closed and her arms folded. The only thing that was missing was the woman's smirk that Carol had come to know.

"Did you pick that out?" Carol pointed to Minos' attire.

The young woman nodded. "It was one of her favorites and I couldn't see dressing her up since she never was one to rely on appearances too much. I found some dresses in her closet," Erin commented. "But not once in 4 years did I see her wear them so why should she wear them now?" the young woman grinned. "It just wouldn't have been her . . . you know?" she added as the grin slipped away, replaced with a sober look.

Carol just gave a nod, understanding fully what Erin meant.

"Did you know that Minos had a will?" Erin asked as they continued to keep vigil over Minos. "Here's a woman who was so anti-establishment and yet somehow she managed to make a trip to a lawyer."

"What did it say?"

"She gave it to me," Erin chuckled, a bit in disbelief. "All of it. The house, the savings accounts, all of it. I don't know why. I'm not even the oldest person in the house. And I wonder if I'm the most responsible."

"You're a good person, Erin," Carol reassured her, reaching out to run a hand smoothly over her back in support. "She knew you'd do the right thing for everyone concerned."

"I suppose so," Erin shrugged her shoulders.

"I know so," Carol answered firmly.

That brought a smile to the blonde's lips before another small stretch of silence fell between them.

"You know," Erin began. "I walk into the house and I still expect to see her there, but she's not." Erin paused to take a breath. Carol could tell the young woman was holding back a sob as she continued, "And part of me knows she never will be. It's like some kind of bizarre karmic twist. I've taken her place in the house yet I still search for her. Everyone is looking to me for support but I can barely support myself at the moment."

Erin broke down as she confessed, the tears flowing freely from her eyes. Carol wrapped her arms tightly around the young woman and let her cry herself out. Erin had spent most of her evenings prior to the funeral sporadically weeping in Carol's strong arms. Her older lover would reassure her that things were going to be okay, that Minos would want her to move on and let go of her grief.

Erin disclosed that the last conversation she had with Minos was in fact an argument over Carol. Erin said she knew that Minos was just high and looking for a fight but still, it haunted her. She wondered if Minos died not realizing how much Erin truly cared about her. And again, Carol did her best to comfort the young woman with reassurances that Minos knew how important she was to Erin. Carol figured today would be the hardest of all and so far she was correct. But even in Erin's despair the young woman still exuded a sense of dignity and reserve.

As Erin's sobs began to quiet Carol spoke to her softly. "You may find it hard to believe but there will come a time when you can remember the light she brought to your life instead of the loss. I promise . . . You'll be okay, sweetheart."

Erin pulled away and wiped her eyes.

"I better pull it together before they start coming in, huh?" Erin said with a warm chuckle. "I get to be the leader. Minos wouldn't want me to be a big puddle, would she?"

"I think Minos would let you be anything you wanted," Carol answered sincerely.

Erin gave the comment deep consideration. "I think you're right. We had our differences but I think she understood . . . In the end, she didn't give me too much grief for falling for a cop," Erin grinned, looking up at Carol.

"I'm glad you fell."

"I'm glad you're glad."

Carol and Erin exchanged a soft smile. Slowly, friends and family began to filter into the area and Carol took Erin by the hand.

"If you need support today," Carol whispered. "Lean on me."

At the service Erin kept her head high and even smiled from time to time. Lots of stories went around the room of Minos and happy memories they had with her. And it seemed everyone had a story to tell. Many wondered just what had changed in Erin since Minos' death. She looked the same, dressed the same but the way she carried herself, the way she acted, was somehow different in just three days. She suddenly seemed . . . grown up, mature, a woman in every sense of the word. The truth was, it wasn't an overnight change. Erin had been changing all along but no one took the time to stop and notice until now.

At the funeral, Carol stayed by her lover's side, surrounded by an odd mixture of people from scholars to hippies to store owners. Even Randell stopped in briefly to offer his condolences to Erin. It seemed Minos had touched countless lives and their gratitude showed in grief-stricken faces in between the happy tales. And the young radical Carol had in cuffs months before, the one in which she sensed an air of leadership and promise, oversaw the ceremony with that very same confidence but on a much grander scale.

Erin was relieved to have Carol near her and she leaned against the former officer who was clad in a simple sundress. Erin remembered how she had grinned when she'd first seen Carol walk into the parlor room, thinking her in the floral print dress possibly the most beautiful thing she had ever seen. When things had slowed down that day Erin made a point to tell Carol. She was grieving but she still wanted to stay 'connected' to life and telling her lover how gorgeous she was seemed like a fitting way.

Besides, Minos wouldn't want Erin to let simple moments, which could be so rich, pass her by. Carol had blushed and brushed off the compliments with a shake of her head and the

One Belief Away

wave of her hand. However, she did make certain that she thanked Erin for noticing in light of the young blonde's emotional turmoil at the moment. So rarely did she wear dresses that she'd actually had to go purchase this one the night before.

Erin would have gone shopping with her lover, however she had that appointment with an attorney who stopped by the house. Although Minos was anti-establishment, she wasn't stupid. She had made sure that the will was drawn up naming Erin sole heir to her estate - an estate, which Erin learned after the services, contained a savings account of roughly $5000, a checking account of $2000 and the house in which everyone lived. Erin was shocked to learn that Minos was that well off. Five grand was enough to buy two supercharged Camaros. And Erin knew if Marlow or someone else had gotten the estate that's probably where the money would have gone. One white. One blue. Well, maybe he would be more responsible and just buy one, she thought jokingly.

When the other housemates learned of Erin's position many questions began. The biggest being, did they have to move? Erin assured them that Minos had named her as her beneficiary for a reason - and that reason being Minos knew Erin had the sensibility and responsibility to oversee the house. No one would be moving. No one would be cast out onto the streets because of a greedy home sale. Erin hadn't quite decided what course her life would take but she did reassure everyone the situation would remain the same for them.

When the service was over, and all had spoken, the group of people moved to the big, run down house and had a reception in Minos' honor. There were sandwiches and salads, soda spilling from the cooler, but no drugs or smoking. In fact, it was that night while curled around each other in Carol's bed that Erin swore she would never smoke again. Carol was mildly surprised but greatly relieved. She stroked the smaller woman's bare back warmly, placing a kiss on her forehead.

"You saved my life," Erin murmured into the darkness.

Carol shook her head. "No. You saved yourself. You fought to stay here and I thank you for not giving up. I'm not sure what I would have done if you'd died in my arms."

Erin snuggled in closer. "Let's not think about it."

Problem was there was little to think about that was actually good right now. Carol had walked away from her job and was unemployed. Now she had to walk back in.

Her locker needed to be cleaned out and her service revolver and identification card turned in. *They already have the badge* she thought smugly. So she handed both her I.D. and her revolver over to the desk sergeant, resolved in the fact that she had done the right thing.

No one tried to talk her into reconsidering and she wouldn't have entertained those thoughts anyway. She had made her decision and she'd make it again. She would always put Erin ahead of herself or her career. The certainty of that had shocked her since she'd spent her life without emotional attachment. But through the façade of bravado and political opinions, Carol had seen the young woman's compassion and soul. She knew she wanted to stay with Erin at all costs and she knew that her blonde companion felt the same.

Many officers in the precinct saw it as the fact that Johnson just couldn't cut it – that she would never break free from the guilt of taking a life. Of course Carol, and even Randell, saw her sacrificing her career for something greater than the police force. She walked away because of love.

As Randell stood and watched Carol clean out her locker, unknown to her, he realized that if the situation were reversed and Phyllis had needed him, no badge or position of rank would have kept him at the stationhouse. Maybe understanding what Carol felt for Erin wasn't so hard after all, he considered. He cleared his throat to make his presence known, making Carol turn around.

"Hey there ex-partner," she smiled. "How you doing?"

He gave her a crooked grin and walked over to lean against the row of metal lockers. "Pretty good, all things considered," he replied. "How's Erin?"

"She's doing well," Carol nodded. "It's been 48 hours and she hasn't twitched so that's a good sign," she told him proudly.

"She's damn lucky," he answered in his gruff style. "Too bad that friend of hers wasn't as fortunate." Randell had heard about the incident through the department as well as a phone call that Carol made to him the night of the overdose. He saw Erin at the funeral home but the girl still looked a bit rocky.

"Yeah, but she's handling it better than I expected," Carol replied, continuing to load her belongings in a sturdy cardboard box. "It hasn't been easy but she's accepting it more each day."

"Well, that's good to hear," he conceded. A small silence passed between them as Carol continued to pull more things out of her locker. "You know, I talked to the captain," he said conversationally. Carol didn't reply. She simply waited for him to continue. "He said if you want your position back all you have to do is ask."

"You mean beg, don't you?" Carol grinned coyly.

"Ask. Beg. What's the difference?" Randell replied with a grin and a shrug of his shoulders. Carol wasn't amused. "Yeah, I know there's a difference but he assured me no begging would be necessary . . . well, not a lot of begging. And an apology for the 'shove it up your ass' might be required." He grinned rakishly. "Internal Affairs finished their review and they said we did it by the book, Carol."

Carol sighed and placed the last item in the box. Quietly, she took a seat on the wooden bench. "I don't think I can, Randell," she answered. "And it's not about the shooting . . . I think of all the time I've given this job and it comes down to one time that I need them to do something for me. And what happens? I get slapped in the face with 'you gotta stay another hour'. It's not right and I don't think I fit in here."

"Where do you fit?" Randell asked.

"With Erin," Carol answered firmly and without reservation. "As for how I'll survive, I'll worry about that later." She grinned modestly. "For now . . . I like where my feet are standing."

Randell rose and picked up her box. "Well, if you need anything you know where to turn. I swear to God, some days when I talk to Phyllis you'd think she adopted a new daughter," he said with a laugh. "But that's okay. You're a pretty good kid," he said motioning her to the door. With one arm around the box and the other around Carol, they left the locker area together.

Erin graduated with honors later that week but she felt little pride as she walked down the aisle with the degree clutched in a sweaty, pale hand. That is until she'd glanced up to meet cerulean eyes watching her from the crowd. Carol beamed with pride and it made Erin grin. The only high point of the last few days was the certainty of her relationship with Carol.

The ex-cop had sacrificed quite a bit for her and, in fact, had seen the young woman at her worst but didn't turn away. It wasn't so much the sorrow as the emotional outbursts that Erin felt at times that created a strain. The dirty cup that Carol left on the counter could set Erin off in a heartbeat but Carol took it for what it truly was. She knew a used cup or coffee ring wasn't the real problem.

Erin was on an emotional roller coaster and her anger and frustration over Minos worked its way out and onto Carol with the little things around them. Of course, Erin recognized it as well but only after the fact. That in turn sent the young woman onto a crying apology, which Carol took in stride and accepted. Erin knew she was hell to live with at the moment but she admired Carol even more for sticking it out when anyone else might have given up.

For the moment, however, they were content. She ran a hand along the dark woman's well-muscled abdomen, nuzzling into her neck as they lay in bed that evening.

"I love you."

Carol smiled. "Love you, too."

"What are you gonna do about work?" the blonde ventured softly. It was something they hadn't discussed and it seemed a much safer topic here in the darkness of the middle of the night. The tall body beside her moved slightly.

"Nothing."

"What do you mean nothing? You're the best cop they've ever had," Erin whispered.

Carol shrugged. "They asked. Well, Randell claims they asked but no one made an effort while I was there," she said with a chuckle, not caring about much more than Erin's embrace. "Besides, I don't want to go back. Maybe something else will come up. I have some savings from my dad. I'm okay for a bit."

Erin nodded solemnly, turning her head to place a kiss on warm skin. Something would come up . . . or . . . perhaps . . .

"Carol?" the petite woman questioned, burrowing deeper into her lover's shoulder. "Would you consider a move downstate . . . to New York?"

Carol wasn't sure why but she could feel a certain tension in her young lover's body as she asked the question. "Why do you ask?" Carol wondered.

Erin wasn't quite sure how to express herself and made a humming noise as she considered things. "I was offered a magazine job. Gloria Steinem is the editor. She did an exposé of Playboy clubs a couple of years ago. With my journalism background they think I might make a good reporter from the clips I sent them. Plus, they said if they have space they could feature some of my artwork."

"That's wonderful!" Carol said, quickly shifting to a sitting position. "But why didn't you tell me?"

"Well, I wasn't going to take it," Erin said honestly. "It's in the city. I'd have to move . . . and I didn't want to let you go."

"Oh, Erin," Carol sighed. "Don't give up a promising career for me."

"This from Miss Take Your Badge and Shove It," Erin mocked.

"That was different and you know it," Carol threatened, putting her forehead on Erin's, doing her best to look menacing.

"Why? Because it was you?" Erin asked defiantly with a bit of mirth in her voice.

Carol tried not to grin but failed miserably. "Well . . . yeah," she answered. "But that doesn't mean you shouldn't listen to me," she warned with a smirk, waving her finger authoritatively.

Erin simply grinned. "You're not very intimidating when you're naked," Erin remarked. "Alluring? Yes. But not intimidating. And sorry to say, it's no different. My life wouldn't feel complete without you in it."

Carol smiled. She understood just what the blonde meant and settled back down with Erin wrapped in her arms once more. A thought occurred to Carol. "Well, why are you telling me now? Do you want me to move to New York with you?"

The amazement in Carol's voice scared Erin. Perhaps she was asking too much, too soon. It had been 10 months since they met but to Erin it felt much longer. It was a big step but one she was ready to take. She thought perhaps Carol was ready too but then again . . .

"I mean, not if you don't want to," Erin quickly replied. "I'm sure I could find something locally. I'm not sure why I even brought up that silly job offer. Just forget it."

Carol found Erin's slight insecurity a bit endearing and she kissed her tenderly on the crown of the head as a result. "No," Carol said, stroking her lover's hair reassuringly. "I kinda like the idea actually. I mean there's nothing here for me now."

"You've got your family's house, Carol."

"Exactly," Carol said, "My family's house, not mine. There's very little in this place that's me, Erin. I could sell it and that would be enough to get us started."

"I couldn't ask you to do that," Erin said sincerely.

"As you once said, you're not asking. I'm offering," Carol corrected. "There's nothing here for me now. No real home. No job whatsoever," she added with a chuckle. "The only thing I have, truly have, is you . . . and I think we should start our life together."

"Are you sure?"

"Look. We've gone through more things in your school year than most couples have to deal with in a lifetime. And we're still intact . . . I think that says a lot. Now maybe I'm wrong but I think you feel the same way, too."

"Yeah, I do," Erin answered without having to consider it. "You know . . . I could go to work and you can use the money from the house sale to go to college. NYU is a pretty good school."

"Hold on a second," Carol said, putting her hands in front of her. "We didn't say anything about that. Besides, I'd be the oldest living freshman," she sighed.

"You don't care about others' perceptions anymore, remember?" Erin retorted.

"That may be true but also consider that I have to earn my keep. I won't be leeching off you. I can't work and go to school, too. As much as I'd like to be two places at once I haven't perfected that yet."

"How about this?" Erin offered. "Classes during the day and a few hours someplace in the evenings. Will that make you feel less like a freeloader?" Erin chuckled.

"Yes, it would," Carol said with a grin. "I'm not gonna be a gold digger."

"There's one job that I could hire you for," Erin said playfully as her fingertips traced Carol's areola.

Carol stole Erin's fingertips from her tautening skin and kissed them lovingly. "You forget. I used to be a cop and there are laws against that."

"I won't tell if you won't tell," Erin said quickly as she straddled Carol's waist.

Carol simply gave a light-hearted chuckle before growing silent. She reached up and began to stroke her lover's cheek with the back of her fingers. Erin closed her eyes in reaction and soaked up the feeling of Carol's delicate touch.

"I love it when you do that," Erin confessed softly.

"I love doing it," Carol admitted freely. "We could do this every night if we lived together y'know."

Erin opened her eyes to gaze down at her lover. "So . . . we have a deal then?" She grinned warmly.

"Yes. Perhaps going back to school for me isn't such a bad idea. I'm sure I could find something to study where I'd be making a difference - if not police work then some other field." The dark woman's mind wandered. She'd wanted to be a cop to honor her father and to prove herself; surely there were other occupations where she could do the same.

As if reading her lover's mind, Erin smiled warmly and traced one dark eyebrow. "I'm sure you'll still make your father proud." She'd known all along that that was the biggest disappointment for Carol in her employment fiasco and subsequent departure.

Carol gave Erin a genuine grin. This woman could see into her very soul at times - and although frightening now and then, it was the best feeling in the world.

"You know, I think you're right," Carol answered. After a brief silence, she pulled the woman closer, tucking her in once more and asked, "Now tell me all about this magazine of yours?"

"Well . . . " Erin began taking a deep breath. The young woman explained the format, the audience, and the political movements behind it. After two prior interviews she finally had an interview with Ms. Steinem herself. She was impressed with the young editor, finding her very tenacious in her ideals but friendly in nature. Erin felt like she could fit in well with the two-year-old magazine that was finally moving beyond its prior infancy.

They discussed ideas for future issues and her chances of her artwork being seen by possibly millions of people. She felt like a chatterbox by the end but Carol assured her that she was very interested. Besides, she loved to watch Erin when she got inspired and excited, totally taking off with an idea. It was obvious the blond honestly believed in the endeavor Ms. Steinem had undertaken.

"What's it called?" Carol asked.

"Ms," Erin answered. "It's aimed for all women - not married women, not single women but all women. It's an expression used to show that a woman isn't dependent on a man for her identity. Personally, I find that oh so appealing," Erin said with a laugh.

Carol joined in as they began to tumble and twist on the bed. Tumbling soon turned to caressing, caressing to kissing, and kissing to exploring. By the end of the evening Erin lay sound asleep, exhausted, in Carol's arms. The former officer sighed in contentment. Despite all the recent tragedy, grand and small, they had survived. And they were rebuilding their lives, together, as one.

About the Author

CN Winters makes her home in Southeastern Michigan with her husband, daughter and a menagerie of pets. She began writing at age 10 after listening to stories her grandmother told about her journey to America from England. With an Associates degree in psychology and journalism she now pursues a full time career writing novels, short stories and screenplays. Her first book, <u>Irrefutable Evidence</u> was published in February 2003 with Renaissance Alliance Publishing, Inc. When not writing, she enjoys an array of music, movies and painting. Her Internet homepage can be found at http://www.wintersproductions.com.

Look for these upcoming lesbian fiction titles at local and on-line booksellers or visit us on the web www.baycrestbooks.com

Inferno by Trish Shields (Fall 2003)

and

Contractor for Hire by CN Winters (Winter 2004)